NOBODY
CARED
FOR
KATE

NOBODY CARED FOR KATE

GENE THOMPSON

Random House
New York

For Florence and Frank Auingier

NOBODY CARED FOR KATE

1

For Dade Cooley, sixtyish, white-haired, vigorous, that particular Wednesday morning in San Francisco dawned full of promise. The city sparkled under a bright May sky, and stropping his razor and looking out the window across the Straits, Dade saw that there was just enough of an offshore breeze to make whitecaps on the dark blue waters of the Bay. Shaving, he thought with pleasure of the prospect before him. At day's end he and Ellen would catch a flight for San Diego, spend the night at the Coronado Hotel and then, the next morning, drive on down into Mexico for a few days' fishing off Ensenada. Of course, he had not yet told Ellen about driving the Baja 500, but there was time enough. He would tell her later, maybe after they got there.

He went downstairs. Ellen, who had been up since six working on her piece on ancient Roman cookery, got up from her desk, gave him a kiss and a radiant smile and served him breakfast. When he had finished his boiled egg and coffee, he waved good-bye, promising to be home no later than three. At seven-thirty he left the house, walked to California Street and boarded a cable car that took him up to the top of Nob Hill and then down its east slope to Montgomery Street, where he jumped off and strode a block to his office, going over in his mind what he had to do that day, sure he could get away early, there was nothing pressing, only to get a call on the stroke of eight as he walked in the door of his office, Rose gesticulating at him, her green eyeshade askew, saying that Kate Mulvaney was on the telephone with an urgent request and, no, he couldn't get back to her, she was calling from a phone booth in a town in France, Sarlat.

Rose, a gnarled hand over the mouthpiece, said to him in a stage whisper, "She says she wants you to get on the next plane to France. She has to see you."

"Bring me her file, will you do that, Rose?" Irritated, Dade went into his office, closed the door and sat down in the swivel chair behind his desk, taking a moment to collect his thoughts. Kate was demanding. Well, with an income of two million dollars a year, that was hardly surprising. She was also eccentric. Kate, who had begun life in abject poverty and had herself made every penny she had (Dade could see her now, the stringy neck, the protuberant eyes behind the oversize black-framed glasses she always wore, which she carried fastened by a heavy chain around her neck, the thin, wispy reddish hair pulled back into a little knot that sat on the back of her neck like a carbuncle, the greasy man's jacket with the narrow lapels—it had been George's, her husband's, and she had pulled it out of the skimpy bag of things for the Goodwill, saying, "Seems to me it's got plenty of wear left in it, George"), Kate would simply not take no for an answer. Two years before, she had insisted on giving him a ten-thousand-dollar retainer and when he had protested, saying, "I'm a criminal lawyer," she had answered shortly, "I want you to be there if I ever need you. That's what I'm paying for."

Rose entered, put the file on the desk in front of him, then padded out, shutting the door firmly behind her.

Dade picked up the phone. "Kate, how are you?"

"Dade, I need legal advice."

"I'll give you the name of a lawyer friend of mine over there. Best there is."

"I want *your* advice. This is a criminal matter, having to do with the Remords reliquary."

"The what?" The connection was bad. He could hear her speaking, but the words were garbled. All he could make out was the phrase "stolen from me." "I can't hear you, Kate, honey!" he bellowed into the phone.

"Well, I can hear *you*." The connection was clear now.

"Kate, I missed some of what you said and I'm not sure I know what you're talking about."

"It's worth a fortune! How much more do you need to know than that?"

"Well, then, you've got to go to the police. Maybe they'll be able to track it down."

"I don't need them to track it down! I know where it is. It's in Aigues-Mortes."

She pronounced the name of the French town as if it were Egmort, with the stress on the first syllable, and for a moment Dade had trouble understanding her. Then he realized what she meant. "You say it's in Aigues-Mortes?"

"Yes, and don't tell me to go to the police. I can't." She sounded hoarse. The impatience now verged on desperation. "It's a family matter! This is something that must be kept quiet."

"Now, just calm down and tell me what's going on."

"Dade, I can't explain it over the phone. You get over here and you'll find out soon enough."

"I can't practice in France."

"Not asking you to! I need you to handle this and I need you here and now!" She told him that she and her family had chartered a barge and were about to make a trip from Toulouse to Carcassonne, boarding late that afternoon. She had worked out the schedule, and if Dade got on the evening plane to Paris and then caught the sleeper to Toulouse, a cab would take him the short distance to the town of Narouze first thing the next morning, Friday, and he could board the barge there. He thought, Same old Kate. Well, there was nothing he could do but send back the retainer and tell her she would just have to go elsewhere. He started to decline tactfully, expressing regrets, when she interrupted him, saying harshly, "Now, you listen to me—" Then her voice broke. "Dade," she said. She sounded as if she were on the verge of tears. "Dade, I have nowhere to turn. Please help me."

"Kate?" he said. "Now, Kate, honey, you just get a grip on yourself, you hear what I'm saying?"

"Dade, I'm not one to beg. I've never begged. It's just that—" She broke off again. There was a long silence.

"Kate?" he said. Then, when there was no answer, he said, "Kate?" again, only this time more sharply.

"I'm here," she said finally. "If you can't, you can't."

"I'll come," he said. "Now, pull yourself together, you hear me, Kate? Head erect and tail over the dashboard."

"All right," she said.

Sighing, Dade put down the phone, made a note of the town, Narouze, and the name of the barge: *Péniche la Veuve*, tipped back in his maroon leather chair, looked around the mahogany-paneled office with its arched windows and glass-fronted shelves filled with law books and shook his head, thick fingers rubbing the lidded crocodile eyes. He reached over and pressed a buzzer.

Rose's voice came over the intercom. "Yes, Mr. Cooley?"

"Get my wife on the phone."

"I'm afraid she's out."

"Try her anyway."

A few moments later there was a rap at the door and Rose entered with a sheaf of letters for him to sign, the green eyeshade pulled down over the matted yellowish hair. "No answer. She's out, Mr. Cooley. I just talked to her about the Mexican reservations. She was going out the door just before you got here. She'll be back at one."

"Well, listen here, Rose. Turns out I have to go to France. Get us two tickets on the first flight and then a flight to Toulouse. First class."

"Client paying?" The cat's eyes peered out at him from under the visor.

"We'll send her a bill."

"Her? She won't even pay your wife's way. You'll go tourist."

"I want to go first class."

"You want."

"Rose, why are you so bossy?"

"You don't like it, fire me. What are you waiting for? I'll go back to the Mechanics' Library. They'll be glad to have me any time. First flight is at six P.M., British Airways."

"Just how do you know that?"

"I have a telephone in my office. I called after I canceled your reservations to Mexico." He opened his mouth and then closed it again. She handed him the letters for his signature, two of them lengthy and filled with technical terms. She stood there while he read through them carefully. There were, as usual, no errors. Signing them, he handed them back to her.

"Rose," he said, "there's a lawyer friend of mine in Paris, Maurice de Saint-Cloud. I want to talk to him. Now, the number is . . ." He pulled out his address book and began leafing through it.

"I've got his number in my Rolodex." She went out the door, clutching her sheaf of letters.

Dade sighed again, took a dog-eared brief out of a drawer, and spreading it open on the desk in front of him, picked up a stub of pencil and began going over what he had written, lipreading, nodding to himself from time to time and scribbling notes. Rose buzzed him a few minutes later. "Yes?"

"Can't reach him. He's still in court."

"You keep trying, Rose." He worked steadily all morning uninterrupted, the lights flashing on and then off on his telephone, indicating that Rose was holding his calls.

Just after one o'clock, Dade collected his papers, jammed his hat on his head and went out of his office. He picked up his telephone messages, going through them. Rose was sitting at her desk, eating lunch out of a paper bag, her nose in the *Law Review*. Putting his brief on her desk, Dade dictated replies to each of the messages. Rose made rapid notes in shorthand. She eschewed Gregg for the curlicues of Pitman, which Dade found as elegant as Arabic. Dade studied her. "You ought to go out to lunch every so often. Get you some fresh air. Do you good. Why don't you?"

"I like it here."

"Well, I'll be in touch."

"I'll call you at home about the reservations, Mr. Cooley. Meanwhile, I'll keep trying to reach Monsieur de Saint-Cloud." Then, setting aside the *Law Review*, Rose looked up at him, pulling off her glasses and pointing them at him. "You take care of yourself, Mr. Cooley. That woman is trouble."

"I'll do that, Rose."

"That woman is trouble and everybody knows it."

"You take it easy." Dade went out of the office, got into the cage elevator, rode down one floor and walked out into the hurrying crowds on Montgomery Street, made his way a couple of blocks to Podesta's on Grant and bought Ellen a bouquet of spring flowers, then hailed a cab. He arrived home just after one-thirty, let himself in with his latchkey and called out, "Honey?" There was no answer.

He went into the Victorian sitting room. "Honey?" he called out again. Hearing nothing, he walked toward the kitchen, pushing open the swinging door, and saw Ellen, her back to him, cleaning out the refrigerator. "Honey?" he said again. She did not turn around. Uneasy, he went over to her, kissed the back of her neck and thrust the bouquet in front of her. "Surprise!" he said.

She turned and stared at him, her lidded blue eyes hard. "I've already had my surprise for the day," she said.

"Whatever is the matter, my little angel?"

She folded her arms and continued to stare at him. She was seldom so angry and the expression on her face was almost unfamiliar. It occurred to him that she did not look so much like a Watteau as a Renoir. He would tell her that as soon as she was calmer.

"I found out," she said.

"Found out?" he echoed. He kept small secrets from her, and it was still possible that something other than the Baja 500 had come to light.

"Valdez called," she said. No, he thought, it had to be the 500. "To confirm the arrangements. He thought I knew."

"Honey—"

"I have two things to say to you, Dade. First, I am not going. Second, neither are you."

"Ellen—"

"You are sixty years old, you have four children—"

"They're grown up."

"I wish I could say the same for you, Dade. You amaze me. You skipped your class reunion at Harvard, saying you were just too busy to go, but this, you have time for."

"All right, all right! As it happens, we're not going. But you're overreacting."

"Oh, am I? Racing a pickup twenty miles along a beach below Ensenada, then across dry creek beds and up a mountain road to some Godforsaken place forty-five hundred feet high, where they hit a hundred and fifty along a dry lake bed—why, last year, some poor soul was killed doing just that—and I'm overreacting?" She was almost shouting.

"Refugio told you all this?"

"Not Valdez! Our sons. Our grown sons, Dade."

"Oh."

"Just what were you going to tell me, once we got in that pickup you rented? That this was a rally?"

"In the first place, it's a dune buggy, not a pickup. In the second place, it's one car at a time and you race against the record for your own vehicle. One fella does it every year in a bus and always wins because he's the only one in his class. In the third place, I had no intention of driving a hundred and fifty miles an hour in a dune buggy, particularly since its top speed is around fifty."

"Oh." She sat down on a stool, nonplussed. "I guess I just lost my head."

"Well, if that's all the good it was doing you, maybe you're just as well off without it."

"Is that so? Well, maybe if you'd let me know your plans at the beginning—"

"I guess I should have. Anyway, the point is moot. We're not going. Something's come up and we're going to France instead."

"Where, to Le Mans?" Then, seeing he was serious, she said, "What's come up?" He told her. She stared at him. "Kate Mulvaney?"

"Yes."

"We're going to be stuck for three days on a barge with that woman and her relatives? Those . . . those people?"

"You've got to remember they're a theatrical family."

"That is a masterpiece of understatement."

"It's business, honey."

"I take back what I said about the Baja."

The phone rang then. Dade went into the study and answered it. It was Rose. She said, "I've got you on that flight at six this evening."

"You get hold of Saint-Cloud?"

"I've left word. Now, you'll get to Paris at four-thirty their time tomorrow afternoon. Then, I've got you reservations on a sleeper at eleven tomorrow night—"

"Can't we fly to Toulouse?"

"Domestic airline strike over there."

"Hell."

"You'll arrive in Toulouse seven-ten the next morning, Friday. Are you writing this down?"

"Just a minute." He searched for a pencil and, finding one, began scribbling down what she had said.

"Take my advice and get a room for a few hours. Weather's bad. That way you can rest up and then have dinner at the hotel."

Ellen entered and began putting guidebooks in a satchel.

"All right, get us reservations at the Crillon."

Ellen took the phone away from him and said into it, "Rose?

There's a place . . . just a minute"—she moved papers around on the desk, found an envelope, took a letter out of it and, finding what she wanted, said into the phone—"it's called the Relais Poulenc on the Left Bank, just off the rue de Lille."

"I'll see what I can do." She hung up.

"I don't want to stay at some damn hole-in-the-wall!" Dade said.

"It's a sixteenth-century private house, recently converted, and the rooms have the original furniture."

"Including the beds?"

Ellen began pulling off her apron. "You call the children while I start packing."

"We're already packed."

"You want to go on a barge trip in France with hip boots and fishing gear? Of course, with a woman like Kate, you'd look right at home." She started out of the room. "We'd better move fast."

"Fast!" He snapped his fingers. Then, pulling a little notebook and a gold pencil out of his pocket, he wrote down the word. "One away, nine to go!"

"Again?"

"Fella bet me—"

"That fella hasn't paid you for the last time."

"Offered me ten times what he owes me. For ten new words that mean their own opposite."

"Fast?" she echoed, not sure.

"As in, 'Make it fast.' Think about it."

2

They took off at six that evening and arrived in Paris around four-thirty in the afternoon in a driving rainstorm, Dade complaining about having to spend the next five or six hours "in some damn fleabag," meanwhile scowling at Ellen. The airport was freezing because the gas workers were on strike to show their sympathy for the domestic airline workers, and arriving passengers were being told that most of the hotels were without heat.

By the time they got to the relais the skies had cleared but it was still cold. The concierge handed Dade a telephone message. Saint-Cloud would be expecting them in his office at the Palais de Justice just after six-thirty.

Their room, as Ellen had promised, was sixteenth century. The parquet floor slanted and the doorway into the bathroom was so low that Dade had to duck his head to go in there. The relais had no central heating but their room had a fireplace with a crackling fire in it, and the fourposter was a feather bed. Ellen looked at Dade triumphantly. "What do you think?"

"Well, as fleabags go—"

"If you'd rather we went to the Crillon, dear . . . of course, it's without heat—"

"For a few hours, this is fine. What say we go downstairs and I'll buy you a drink?"

"If you think a fleabag like this has a decent bar."

They went downstairs and were shown into the sixteenth-century salon, where a fire blazed in a huge stone fireplace. The headwaiter seated them in velvet armchairs at a little table and, at Dade's request, handed them the wine list.

Ellen leaned toward him and said, "Are you warm enough, darling?"

He eyed her. "This table can't be more than six feet from the fire."

"I was just asking. A man your age takes chill so easily."

"That's one! Now, I'm warning you . . . !"

She looked at him steadily. To avoid her eyes, he examined the crowded salon with its low, beamed ceiling and tapestried walls, the air full of the soft, musical sounds of French voices. The lights went out.

"It was expected," the headwaiter said to them. "The electrical workers are striking to show their sympathy for those at the gas works. It is only a manifestation of support and is not expected to last more than two hours." He bowed, moving away.

Dade tried not to look in her direction. Finally, he said, "Will you stop it, please?"

"Stop what?"

"Staring at me."

"I'm not staring at you. Anyway, why would I be staring at you in the dark? How could I see you? How could I make out that wonderful, great head, those noble features, that mane of white hair—?"

"That's two!"

Waiters were now going around the room lighting candles. Ellen said, "Would you like me to read the wine list aloud to you, dear?"

"That's three!"

"'Some damn fleabag' indeed!"

"All right, I'm sorry!"

"Truce?"

"Truce." Hearing that the specialty of the house was chicken roasted on the hearth of the dining-room fireplace, Dade asked to have a bottle of Château Latour 1970, corked in time for dinner at eight o'clock. He ordered a bourbon. Ellen had a kir.

Raising her glass, she said to him, "If you're really sorry, I have a present for you." He looked at her. "Corked," she said. Eyes lighting up, he pulled out his notebook and his gold pencil and wrote down the word.

Half an hour later, they set out to meet Saint-Cloud, walked to the Seine, crossed Pont-Neuf to Île de la Cité and, after a short distance, came to the gilded spikes of the gates guarding the forecourt of the Palais de Justice. They went into the darkened marble lobby, then climbed the broad stairway to the third floor. Lawyers in black robes and triangular black hats hurried by them. Dade took Ellen's arm and escorted her around the crowded gallery to a far corner, where he opened a door and ushered her into a small unlit reception room.

A young law clerk in a black robe trimmed with velvet got up to greet them. "Monsieur and Madame Cooley?" When Dade nodded, the clerk went into another room to announce them and then, returning, escorted them into Saint-Cloud's private office.

The light was dim. The floor was covered with an Aubusson carpet and the furniture was Boulle. Seated behind a large desk with a green-shaded oil lamp on it was a hunched figure, the hands crippled with arthritis: Saint-Cloud. He looked up at them. The dark eyes were cold, the iron-gray hair brushed smooth and flat over the large skull. Struggling to his feet, he reached for a pair of crutches and made his way around the desk toward them, one deformed hand outstretched. Dade shook hands with him.

"My dear Cooley," Saint-Cloud said. He took Ellen's hand and kissed it, then waved at the oil lamp burning on his desk and cried out triumphantly, "You see, I am prepared! I am always prepared!" He gestured toward a pair of armchairs drawn up in front of the desk. Dade and Ellen seated themselves and Saint-Cloud made his way back to his chair and sat down once again behind his desk, asking, "How may I be of help?"

Dade said, "I think I may have to ask you to give me a job."

Saint-Cloud said, opening his hands, "I wish you were serious."

"I am. Listen. A client of mine, an American woman, sent for me." Saint-Cloud nodded. Dade said, "I want to be able to tell her that if she retains you, you can hire me, and, as your assistant, I can help represent her in this country."

Saint-Cloud inclined his head, took his card case from his pocket and, extracting a card from it with difficulty, took out a fountain pen and, forming the letters slowly with his crippled hand, wrote something on the back of the card, then handed it to Dade.

Dade looked at it. Printed on the card was the name and address of Saint-Cloud's law firm. On the other side, Saint-Cloud had written in French, "To introduce our representative, Mr. Dade Cooley," and signed his name. Dade pocketed the card, thanking him. "The name of your prospective client is Mrs. Mulvaney. Kate Penrose Mulvaney."

Saint-Cloud gave him a look of surprise. "I know the name," he said.

"You know much about her?" Dade asked him.

"Only that when she learns what our firm customarily asks as a fee, she will probably seek other representation."

"That's the lady."

"Has she told you why she wants your help?"

"It concerns something called the Remords reliquary."

Saint-Cloud looked at him sharply. "Concerns it in what way?"

"Well, she seems to be trying to get her hands on it—"

"My dear Cooley, if she has any idea of trying to acquire it, then I cannot be involved in any way, nor, I think, can you." He put his deformed hands together on the desk in front of him. "It is a national treasure, stolen some years ago."

Dade rubbed the tip of his nose. "Kate just wouldn't involve herself in anything crooked. She may be eccentric, but Kate, she's as honest as the day is long."

"You will keep me posted?"

Dade nodded. He and Ellen got up. Saint-Cloud struggled to his feet and shook hands with them. Holding onto his hand, Ellen looked into his eyes and said, "Maurice, how are you, really?"

Kissing her hand, he hesitated, then shrugged and said, "Since you ask, my doctors tell me that in six months' time I must expect to be confined to a wheelchair."

"Oh, my dear," she said quietly.

"Before, there was doubt. Uncertainty is a burden. Now, we know. Now I am prepared. My dear Ellen, it is very reassuring to be able to predict anything, even a calamity." She leaned across the desk, kissing his cheek. Saint-Cloud reached for his crutches, made his way slowly around the desk and saw them to the door.

At seven-ten the next morning, just as they were finishing breakfast, their train pulled into the station in Toulouse. When they got to the street, the traffic was already heavy. There was a line waiting at the cab stand. The pavement was wet from a light rain the night before and the skies were gray. It took them almost fifteen minutes to get a cab. Then, to avoid fighting his way through the crowded streets of Toulouse, the driver took them north to the autoroute and then southeast through a forest, finally branching off on a country road running parallel to the Canal du Midi.

Just outside the little town of Narouze, the driver slowed down, pointing. Below the embankment they could see a barge moored to the bank where it had been tied up for the night, *Péniche la Veuve* painted on its stern. The little yellow bus that followed it, to take passengers on excursions, was parked beside it. A narrow, rutted road sloped down from the highway to the canal, which was bordered on either side by a towpath. The road was muddy. Afraid of getting stuck, the driver was unwilling to take them further. Paying him, Dade helped Ellen out of the cab, picked up their one suitcase and the two of them made their way down the slope to the towpath, then started toward the barge, tied up some distance away.

The sky was overcast. No birds sang. The canal, which narrowed as it reached the lock, was still and green, lined with centuries-old plane and sycamore trees planted to hold the banks. Red and yellow poppies and golden buttercups were hidden in the thick grasses bordering the path. The barge was moored to the bank with a couple of thick ropes, one pulled around the trunk of an ancient tree, the other thrown over a carved stone pillar sunk in the earth. Beyond the barge and just to the left of the towpath was the stone house of the lock keeper, just opposite the next lock. A sign on the front of the house read ÉCLUSE DE LA MÉDITERRANÉE. From here, on the man-made green river that da Vinci had first conceived as a way of connecting what he called "the two seas," the barge would begin its descent from its highest point, would be lowered lock by lock, meanwhile traveling mile after slow mile back into the past, beyond the medieval battlements of Carcassonne to journey's end, the Mediterranean. They quickened their pace.

Ahead of them a husky, baby-faced boy in a black turtleneck sweater and a black knitted cap jumped from the barge's port gunwale onto the towpath and cast off the first rope. The barge's engine started up at the same time, and the still waters of the pound were suddenly churned by the barge's propeller. The boy in the cap now unhooked the second rope, tossing it aboard.

Dade hailed him, waving. The boy, not hearing him, jumped back on board as the barge eased away from the tree-lined bank and nosed toward the open iron gates of the lock ahead. Dade slammed down the suitcase and swore under his breath.

"My land," said Ellen, "we come seven thousand miles to see her and she doesn't even bother waiting for us!"

Dade looked at his watch. "Eight o'clock. The locks are just opening. They can't tie up traffic. My guess is, they'll be waiting for us on the other side of the lock, down where it's wider. Come on." Grunting, he picked up the suitcase and the two of them walked along the graveled towpath to a point just opposite the lock.

Now, abreast of them, the barge glided into the oval stone basin of the lock, only inches to spare from the gates on either side. The barge, a long craft with sloping gunwales rising at either end, had a big saloon amidships, and, in front of it, a large deck with umbrella tables and chairs. The passengers were gathered there, leaning on the rail, all of them looking out at the canal ahead of them, winding away through the woods of Narouze, but now the canal was about twelve feet below them, while they floated on their lock-bound barge, like passengers on a toy in a bathtub.

The young sailor now put down the rope he had been coiling and jumped off the stern of the barge onto the catwalk from which the open gates of the lock were suspended, as an elderly lock keeper in a blue smock came out of his house and crossed toward him on the catwalk, pulling a pair of cranks out of a big pocket in his smock. The old man and the young sailor shook hands, then walked away from each other and took up stations at a pair of tripods on opposite towpaths. They began cranking shut the huge gates at the barge's stern. After that they hurried along their separate towpaths toward the lock gates in front of the barge's prow and crossed to the center of the narrow railed catwalk on top of the forward gates.

They began cranking. Vanes in the gates, like guillotines, were now ratcheted up, and Dade and Ellen could see the water begin to rush out of the downstream end of the lock through these sluices, foaming into the canal ahead. As the water flowed out of the lock the barge slowly sank, the slimy stone walls of the lock seeming to rise and imprison the barge and its passengers as if in a dungeon. When the water in the stone basin had dropped to the level of the canal ahead, the sailor and the lock keeper took up new stations on the banks and got ready to open the huge gates, so the lowered barge could sail out into the canal. Suddenly, a woman started screaming.

She screamed without stopping. Dade caught sight of heads turning on the barge far below them. Then, wheeling around, he saw that the screams were coming from an old woman at the upstream end of the lock through which the barge had just passed. Surrounded by the chickens she was feeding, she let go of her full apron, scattering grain everywhere, and, two sticklike arms outstretched, she pointed with both forefingers at something down below her in the lock.

At the same time, far below, they could see the pilot on the barge reacting. Instantly shutting off the barge's engines, he slid out from his seat behind the big wheel and clambered quickly down a ladder to the aft deck and looked over the stern, then started to climb over the side. From up on the bank, the sailor yelled down at him in English, "Don't! Oh, Christ, *don't!*"

Ellen's fingers dug into Dade's arm. They both saw it now. Below them on the stone sill of the lock just inside the closed gates at the stern of the barge, sprawled there and clearly visible through the few inches of water that covered it was the body of a woman. It lay face up, the man's double-breasted jacket with the narrow lapels unmistakable, one floating hand upturned and moving back and forth in the roiling water as if waving to them.

"Oh, no!" cried Ellen. "It's Kate! It's Kate!"

3

Ellen covered her face with her hands. Dade put an arm around her. He peered down into the depths of the lock, his attention caught by something odd in Kate's appearance. Then he realized what it was. The ever-present glasses were missing. He strained to see whether they had come off and lay in the murky water lapping on the sill. He couldn't be sure. Grunting, he looked around. Far below them, strung out along the narrow gunwale, Dade could see the other passengers, seven of them, trying to get past the pilot to see what was wrong, while he blocked their way. A girl Dade did not recognize ran to the other side and made her way along that gunwale to the stern. They heard her cry out, "Oh, no! Oh, no!"

A voice called out, "Oh, my God, is it *Kate*? It isn't Kate, is it?" It was George, her husband. Suddenly he broke past the pilot and scrambled back to the stern. He saw her body then and they heard him say desperately, "Oh, Christ, Christ, somebody *do* something!" George tried to climb over the stern.

The pilot yelled up to the sailor on the towpath above, "Mike! Help me! If the barge moves, he'll be crushed! Open those gates! Then we'll push this thing out of here!"—meanwhile grappling with George, trying to restrain him.

Mike ran to the tripod on the towpath, yelling out to the lock keeper in French, "The gates! Open the gates and get them out of there!"

The lock keeper shook his head, signaling to the sailor not to touch the crank. He called back down to the pilot, "The police! It is necessary to call the police! You must wait until they come!"

The old woman, shooing chickens out of her way, ran toward the cottage. Through the open door they could see her on the phone, gesticulating, the passengers on the barge now truly prisoners in their stone dungeon. Ellen was trembling. Dade led her over to a bench and made her sit down. Taking a silver flask out of his pocket, he unscrewed the top and made her take several swallows.

Minutes later they heard the sound of a klaxon rising, coming nearer. A police car lumbered down the narrow road sloping from the highway down to the towpath. Two constables jumped out. One of them looked over the side of the lock, waved at the lock keeper and yelled out to him to open the gates and get the barge out of there, then calling out to the sailor to get the little bus out of the way. The other went to the squad car and, leaning into the open window, grabbed a radio microphone and began speaking into it rapidly, summoning help.

The downstream gates of the lock now open, the barge glided out into the canal. As the sailor ran for the bus, drove it up and parked it on the shoulder of the highway, the passengers began clambering off the barge and coming toward them. The first constable charged in their direction, waving his white baton and ordering them all back on the barge.

Not long afterward they saw a fireboat from Ponts et Chaussées coming along the canal toward them rapidly from the direction of Toulouse, a warning horn shattering the air, men in wet suits on deck, poised to jump ashore. Once on the bank, they ran toward the lock and began scrambling down a metal ladder set into the stones. An ambulance came bumping down the slope. As it came to a stop, men jumped out and pulled a metal stretcher with ropes attached to it out of the back, then, playing out their ropes, lowered it into the waiting arms of the divers in the lock.

As constables were cordoning off the towpath and the edge of the road above them at the top of the bank, another police vehicle arrived and a man in a business suit got out of it and walked briskly over to the rim of the lock. The constables touched their caps as they saw him. One of them spoke to him. The man in the business suit nodded. He was a short, thickset man in his forties. His hair was full and dark and his eyes were brown. The left one was glass. It was ill-fitting and gave him a squint, which made him look both attentive and skeptical. He turned toward Dade and Ellen, who were still sitting on the bench.

Touching the brim of his hat, he said in French, "I am Inspector Marbeau. From Castelnaudary." He gestured. "Just over there. And who are you, may I ask, monsieur?"

Rising, Dade went up to him, taking a card from his case and presenting it. The inspector studied the card. Then he looked at Dade and asked, "Do you speak French?"

"Yes, Inspector."

"You are an American?" Dade nodded. "An attorney?" he asked, studying Dade's card. Dade nodded again. The inspector glanced toward the body now being hoisted up out of the lock on the metal stretcher, water streaming from it, then back again at Dade. The look was inquiring. Ellen got up and joined them. The inspector asked, "Are you passengers on the barge?"

Dade said, indicating the stretcher, "She sent for me. My wife and I arrived here just as the barge started toward the lock"—he took out his watch and glanced at it, then looked back at the disconcerting squint of the brown eye—"less than half an hour ago."

"She sent for you?" the inspector repeated. Dade told him about Kate's phone call. "A reliquary?" the inspector echoed, surprised. Dade repeated what Kate had told him. "Excuse me, but on the strength of that, you and your wife got on a plane and came over here at once? You must have been very close friends."

"I represented her."

"Yes, yes, but excuse me, how could you do so in France?" By way of answer, Dade took Saint-Cloud's card out of his wallet and showed it to the inspector. The inspector squinted at it, then reacted with astonishment. "You are associated with the Comte de Saint-Cloud?"

"I would have been, if circumstances had warranted it."

Returning Saint-Cloud's card, Marbeau looked again at Dade's. "Cooley," he said, putting the stress on the second syllable. "Dad Cooley."

"Dade," Dade said, "Dade Cooley."

"Dead," the inspector said, struggling for the diphthong, which eluded him. "Mr. Dead Cooley. And you speak French perfectly!"

"Not at all."

"Of course! It is the nose! You have a nose like a Frenchman! It takes a nose!" The inspector pulled out his wallet and put Dade's card into it carefully. Then he shook hands with Dade, a quick, short pump, as if they had just made a bet. He bowed to Ellen, then to both of them he said, "Everything shall be done for you. Have no fear. Is she well known to you, the poor, drowned woman?"

"Yes."

"And to the others on board?"

"Yes, indeed."

"The family!" the inspector said suddenly, as if having thought of this minutes ago would have made a difference. "They tell me that from the look of her, the poor woman must have been in the water all night! Quickly, we must notify the family!"

"They're all on board."

"Ooooo, la la!" The inspector clapped his hands together. Then, as if he feared someone would accuse him of negligence, he began a speech, saying this was indeed a terrible accident, such a thing had never happened before in his memory, he could not understand it; certainly, they would investigate the cause, would Monsieur Cooley offer the bereaved relatives the profound sympathies of all Castelnaudary and he, the inspector, would pray for the poor woman's soul. Meanwhile, what could he do to accommodate them? The body would be taken to the *mairie*, he would summon the coroner immediately, even though it was Friday and the beginning of the Ascension Day weekend as well, and whatever arrangements the poor bereaved family might care to make for the disposition of the body, let them make them forthwith, he, Marbeau, was truly at their disposal.

They all shook hands again. Marbeau said, "Good-bye, Mr. and Mrs. Cooley. And, as you continue on your mournful way, know that we here will do everything possible to see that the rest of your visit to the Canal du Midi, however brief, is without incident. We will, of course, want a statement from you at the inquest about the poor woman's strange telephone call which summoned you."

"I'll let you know where you can reach us," Dade said.

Marbeau looked surprised. "You will not be joining the others?"

Ellen said quickly, "Oh, I don't think we want to intrude on the family at a time like this!"

They were interrupted then. The pilot was running toward them. He was a man in his thirties with a full beard, a nautical cap and a jacket. Breathless, he introduced himself, telling Marbeau his name was Ned Rowan and speaking passable French but with a marked British accent, which made him sound slightly contemptuous. Dade introduced himself and Ellen, explaining that he had come there at the request of Mrs. Mulvaney, who had been his client. When Ned looked surprised, Dade asked, "She didn't tell you to expect me?"

"Didn't say a word."

"I see." Dade looked away, frowning.

Ned said to him in English, "Jesus, what a bloody awful mess."

Marbeau turned to him. "Are you able to identify the deceased as your passenger?"

"That's her," Ned answered.

Dade said, "She wore glasses." Marbeau threw Dade an inquiring look. Dade explained about Kate's glasses and the chain around her neck to which they were fastened.

Ned nodded. "That's what she was wearing on board," he said in English to Dade.

Marbeau said, "Perhaps the lady wasn't wearing them last night."

Dade said, frowning, "But she always wore them."

Excusing himself, the inspector walked quickly to the edge of the lock, speaking to one of the divers who was just climbing up the ladder, slimy water dripping from him. Saluting, the diver descended the ladder again, waving and gesturing at the diver below him. The two of them began to search the shallow waters of the lock.

Ned hitched up his trousers, and ducking his head in the direction of Marbeau, who stood at the edge of the lock looking down at the divers, he said to Dade, "Can you talk to him? The passengers back there are going batty. There's a couple of constables stationed there with orders not to let anyone off the barge—I guess I'm an exception because I'm the skipper—and all of them are making a frightful row. They want to know what the hell happened. Mostly, they all seem to want to telephone. I don't know what the Christ it is about Americans, but the minute anything goes wrong, the first thing they do is rush for a phone. Who the hell are they always ringing up? I guess one another." Catching himself, he looked at Dade, a flush mounting under his ragged beard, and said, "Sorry."

"Right now I don't think he knows any more than they do," Dade said. Then, pointing at the constables who were roping off the towpath and carefully examining the ground, Dade added, "And for now, I think they're going to have to stay put."

"Maybe you can talk to them."

Marbeau came up to them and said, "The lady's eyeglasses. They can't find them. They must surely be in her cabin." Turning to Ned, he said, "Will you take us there?"

Ned leading the way, Ellen, Dade and Marbeau climbed down a short steep stretch of the towpath that led to the downstream end of the lock, some twelve feet lower. Two constables were there, one stationed on the towpath, the other on the deck of the barge. Marbeau hung back, speaking to the constable on shore. Dade helped Ellen up onto the gunwale. They waited on deck for Marbeau.

Ned spoke to the constable on deck, then came over to Dade and Ellen and said in an undertone, "Poor husband's evidently in a state of collapse. They've got him down in his cabin with his wife's—I guess I should say, his late wife's—brother and his wife." Dade nodded. Ned walked away from them, irresolute, hands thrust deep in his trouser pockets.

Some distance away, the young woman who had been the first of them to see Kate's body was sitting at an umbrella table with a young man. Dade did not recognize either of them. They sat in silence, looking out at the placid green waters of the canal curving along ahead of them. The young man was lean, with thick, dark, bristly hair and a face scarred from acne. He wore rimless, tinted glasses. His strong hands gripped a large cup on the table in front of him. He sat motionless, staring straight ahead, seeming to pay no attention to them at all. Bare-chested, he wore only shorts and sandals.

The girl was slender. She had the face of a Botticelli, almost a child's face. She wore no make-up and her red-gold hair hung down in ringlets. She sat quite still, like an obedient schoolgirl, her fine-boned hands clasped in her lap.

As if having only just become aware of their presence, the man's eyes moved in the direction of Dade and Ellen and then toward the girl, his brows lifted in inquiry. She turned briefly, glancing at Dade and Ellen. Looking back at the man sitting with her, she answered with an almost imperceptible shrug.

Dade took Ellen's arm, indicating the saloon with a nod. "Ready?" he asked her.

"No."

"Come on."

They went up onto the little foredeck, through the hatch doors and down several steps into the saloon. At the bar, they saw Kate's sister, Maggie, standing and having coffee with her husband, Dan. Their backs were turned. Suddenly, Maggie caught sight of them in the mirror over the bar and choked on her coffee. Putting down her cup, Maggie whirled around, cried out, "Dade! Ellen!" and then started toward them, arms outstretched. Dan, lean, athletic and at least ten years her junior, his gray hair trimmed close to his head, stared in their direction with his mouth open.

Maggie, unlike her late sister, had dressed for the barge trip as she dressed for everything. She wore a yachting suit and a white boater. The trousers were white and the jacket was violet and matched her eyes. It was double-breasted with big brass buttons; a matching chiffon scarf was tied over her hat and wound around her aging neck like a wimple. Under the flapping bell bottoms of her trousers, they could see the thick ankles. She took tiny steps toward them, meanwhile glancing around the saloon with a dazzling smile, as if she imagined that it was thronged with fans. Her jeweled fingers clutched a raffia purse. She made a feint of embracing each of them briefly, kissing the air. "Where did you come from?" she gasped.

"We just arrived," Dade said. "Kate sent for me."

"Sent for you?" asked Dan. "She sent for you?"

"But don't you know what's happened?" Maggie asked. Her eyes moved. She looked out fearfully at the constables on shore, then back at Dade. "You must know." Dade nodded. Suddenly she seized one of his hands in both of hers and, gripping it, her wide violet eyes searching their faces, she said hoarsely, "She's dead! Isn't that incredible? She must have fallen into the lock and drowned!" Turning to her husband, she said in a papery voice, "Dan, I have to sit down."

Her husband put an arm around her, supporting her. He wore trim dark slacks and an open-necked dark polo shirt. "Look," he said to Dade, "we've got to get out of here. If you can just arrange to get me to a phone, the studio has an office in Paris—"

"As soon as they complete their preliminary investigation I'm sure you'll be free to make any calls you like," Dade said.

"I suppose we'll just have to be patient," Dan said to Maggie. He tried to steer her toward a chair. Her ringed fingers dug into his deeply tanned muscular arms.

Getting her to a chair, he tried to make her sit down but she only leaned on the chair-back, waving him away and saying in an unsteady voice, "No, I don't want to sit. We weren't close," she said to them. "Everybody knows we weren't close. Now, it's too late." She gripped Dan's arm. "We're leaving the barge immediately!" she said.

"Where are we going?"

"I don't know! How can you ask me such things at a time like this?"

"Do you want them to turn around and take us all back to Toulouse?"

"What is the point of that?" Maggie snapped at him. "We've just come from Toulouse! Do you think I want to spend two days looking at all the same scenery backwards?" She snatched a scrap of handkerchief out of her purse, held it to her mouth and, suddenly, the wide violet eyes filled with tears. Quickly she took a mirror out of her purse, examined her face briefly and let out a little cry of dismay. "This is a nightmare! I look a hundred years old!"

"You're as lovely as ever, Maggie," Dade said.

She turned her large eyes on him and said, "At a distance. You know, they used to shoot women of a certain age through gauze, and as dear Tallulah once said, They ought to shoot me through a screen door." She put her fingers to her forehead and cried out, "Why am I making jokes at a time like this? Poor Kate! She must have gone out for a stroll before breakfast—you know, I've always said that's a bad idea. On an empty tummy one can grow faint. Yes! That's what must have happened! I feel it! She was walking along the edge of the towpath where the stones are slippery from the moss"—she began to illustrate this, walking unsteadily across the saloon floor—"she grew faint, there was no time to cry out and she simply toppled into the lock and drowned, like Ophelia! Oh, my poor Kate!"

Dade said quietly, "From the look of things, she's been dead for quite some time."

"What?"

Dade nodded. "This must have happened last night."

"Last *night*? But last night—let me see—last night we were all together. We took the bus into Narouze for cassoulet. You know, that's that marvelous dish that originated here. It's what they fed the people who built the canal. It's made with goose, sausage, lamb, pork, beans and then the spices!" Realization flooded her face. "My God, that's the reason! She ate too much! It's a very heavy meal. That's why all of us came back on foot, to walk off dinner. She must just have collapsed and fallen into the water in the dark. You know, she had her own stateroom, so no one would have noticed that she wasn't on board. Oh, how horrible!"

"Last night at dinner," Dade asked, "was she wearing her glasses?"

"Well, of course she was. Without them the poor woman couldn't see her hand in front of her face. Why do you ask?"

"They're missing."

"They're what?"

"They weren't on the body. The police can't seem to find them anywhere."

Maggie's hands flew to her face as she let out a little scream. "Oh, my *God, that's* what happened! She must have lost them in the dark, and without them she couldn't possibly see where she was going. No wonder she fell into the lock. Oh, Kate, Kate!" She fought back tears. Then, remembering something, she turned to Dade and said, puzzled, "Why did she send for you?"

"It was something about a reliquary." Dade looked at her steadily.

"A reliquary?" She gave him a blank stare.

"The Remords reliquary."

"The what?"

"You don't know what it is?"

She shook her head, then turned to Dan, asking, "Do you?" Dan shook his head. They both looked at Dade. "What about it?" she asked.

"That's what I was hoping you could tell *me*."

"I have no idea. I know who Remords was, of course, but as for a reliquary—" She took Ellen's arm. "I think I have to sit down. I really do." Ellen led her away to a couch.

Dan said to Dade, taking his elbow and leading him toward the bar, "Christ, what a shock. We don't even know what the hell's going on and can't find out because none of us speaks French and they don't speak English. Come to think of it, our skipper does, but either they haven't told him or he won't tell us. Afraid of a lawsuit, I guess. You know something? I need a drink." Reaching for a bottle, he poured himself a Scotch. Then, turning to Dade, he said in a low voice, looking around to make sure they weren't being overheard, "I'm not going to be a hypocrite about it. I didn't like her and I made no secret of it and it was God-awful to have to introduce her as a relation, but Jesus, Dade, this is terrible." He took a swallow of his drink and then asked, "What is all this about a reliquary?"

Dade looked him up and down. Then he said, "I'll tell you something, Dan. I wish I knew."

"Come off it, Dade. A man like you doesn't travel all this way at the drop of a hat to meet a client on a barge in the south of France without a damn good reason. Why all the secrecy?" The hard gray eyes bored into Dade's.

"The reason I came, Dan, is that she sent for me."

"Well, if that's the way you're going to play it . . ." The muscles in his cheeks rippled as the lean jaw tightened. Turning away, he took another swallow of his drink. Then, suddenly annoyed, he slammed his glass down on the bar, turned back to Dade and said,

"By God, here's a woman dead in a freak accident, her whole damn family all on a barge together in a state of shock and who shows up but a criminal lawyer the minute her body is found—just like a god-damned ambulance chaser!—saying she sent for him, and when you try to find out why the hell she did that, he plays cute."

Dade said very softly, helping himself to a glass of water, "I'm sure you know that all communications between client and attorney are privileged."

Dan looked at him long and hard for a moment or two, then abruptly he muttered an excuse, left the saloon and went running down the companionway stairs. Maggie got up and hurried after him, calling out, "Dan? Dan? What's gotten into you?"

Ellen came over to Dade and said in a low voice, "God, he's rude. He must be successful again."

Dan ran back up the stairs, a pair of binoculars in his hand. Maggie went back and sat down where she had been sitting. Ellen joined her. Dan brandished the binoculars and said, "I want to see if I can find out what's going on." Then, going over to Dade, he said, "I'm sorry as hell."

"It's all right."

"I guess we're all upset."

"'Course you are." Dade turned away from him, looking up and catching sight of the young girl and her escort through the window. Still sitting at the umbrella table, they were watching him.

Seeing this, Dan turned to Dade and said, "My sister, Cissy Schuyler. I don't think you've ever met. She's out there with her in-tended. You know him?" Dade shook his head. "Kate's nephew, Billy Penrose. Maggie's and Leo's, too, for that matter, but they don't want any part of him. None of us does."

"He'd be John's boy?"

Dan nodded. "He's a Christ-awful little prick. Parents died when he was a kid, and I don't blame them." Dan frowned. "How come you didn't board with us in Toulouse?"

"Didn't get here in time, you might say."

"You mean Kate called you at the last minute?" Not answering, Dade took his pipe out of his pocket and tapped the side of it against a Cinzano ashtray. With a quick, knowing smile, Dan said, holding up a hand, "All right! All right! I won't be nosy. Bad habit. Comes of writing thrillers, I guess." He ran a brown hand over his close-cropped gray hair and said, "Not that you missed much. In Toulouse, I mean. Henry James said he had never seen a city at once so animated and so dull, and writer that I am, since we weren't scheduled to leave until five-thirty, I walked around looking at things, trying to top him. I couldn't. They do have the head of Saint Thomas Aquinas wrapped up in a napkin on exhibit in a glass case in the cathedral, if that sort of thing interests you. It would sure interest George." Dan took a packet of Stimudents out of his pocket, opened the matchbooklike folder, broke off a stiff, flat softwood toothpick and stuck it in his mouth, holding it between his teeth like an unlit cigarette. Touching Dade's arm, he said, "Excuse me, but I've got to get some air." He walked away unsteadily, climbing up the stairs and going out onto the deck.

At the same time, Billy Penrose got to his feet, pulled on a long multicolored terry-cloth robe, said something to Dan's sister and then came inside and hurried down below.

Ned came into the saloon, Marbeau following him. Marbeau stopped in his tracks, a look of astonishment in his eyes as he caught sight of Maggie sitting across the saloon on a couch with Ellen, the two of them talking together in an undertone. Marbeau whispered to Dade, "Is it—?"

"Yes," Dade answered.

"A film star! Good heavens!"

Dade said, "She was the sister of the late Mrs. Mulvaney."

Marbeau gripped Dade's arm. "Paris will ask questions. Many questions. It is always the case when the prominent are involved."

Ned preceded them down the companionway stairs to the lower deck, and along a corridor past a row of closed doors. Stopping at the last door on the port side, he said, "Mrs. Mulvaney's cabin," and then retreated.

5

Marbeau opened the door. The cabin was small, containing nothing but a double bunk placed under the sloping ceiling, a porthole beside it. Below the bunk were drawers and next to the door there was a little hanging space behind a curtain.

He began to search the cabin, going very carefully through all Kate's possessions. He examined her clothes—slacks, blouses and a raincoat, as well as a flannel robe and a cotton nightgown. He went through the pockets, finding nothing but some balled-up Kleenex and a handkerchief.

Her suitcase was locked. Forcing it open, Marbeau found her big leather shoulder bag in it. He emptied it on the bunk, then gave a cry of triumph, pouncing on a black leather case, snapping it open and producing a pair of thick-lensed steel-rimmed glasses. "Here they are!" he cried.

Dade shook his head. "Must be a spare pair. Hers—that is, the ones she always wore—were in heavy black frames and she always had them on a metal chain around her neck."

"Perhaps the lady wore these on her trip."

"The skipper, he told me she was wearing the other ones. And her sister says she was wearing them last night at dinner in a restaurant."

"Then they must be here. She came back, she left them in her cabin and went out without them for some reason. In fact, that may explain why the accident happened. Let us keep searching." He continued rummaging through Kate's bag. In it he found a number of packets of receipts for purchases she had made, even when those purchases were the equivalent of less than fifty cents. Each packet of receipts was fastened with a paper clip and all of them were held together with a rubber band. In a heap on the bed were a pair of shabby black leather gloves, a thin sweater, a handkerchief and some bottles of aspirin, Dramamine and antacid tablets. There were several picture postcards addressed to friends, with succinct notes about the places she had visited. On each one was written in block letters the word SAVE. "Well, there's no point in buying two," Dade remembered her saying when he had once asked her about it, returning a card with SAVE on it she had sent him.

In the shoulder bag, Marbeau found Kate's wallet. It contained the usual assortment of credit cards, her return ticket home and something under two hundred dollars in traveler's checks. Marbeau picked up the sweater. It was threadbare and there were holes in the elbows. He said, "I had the impression she was a woman of means." Dade nodded. "But these possessions—and the way the poor woman was dressed—"

"She was worth somewhere in the neighborhood of twenty million dollars."

Marbeau put his head on one side, studying Dade. Then he said, "From what you told me about her strange telephone call and a reliquary, you suspect foul play?"

"It is always possible."

"These people—her family—will they inherit?"

Dade shook his head. "In her will she left everything to her husband and they all knew it. I should explain something. They're all in show business. She wasn't, but she bankrolled all of them. Alive, she was worth everything to them. Dead, nothing."

"Hardly a motive!" The glass eye sparkled in the watery light coming through the porthole. Then, sticking out his lips and giving a shrug, Marbeau said, "I think we will find this is only an accident."

Dade frowned, glancing once more around the cabin. "Those glasses," he said, "they don't appear to be here."

Marbeau waved this away. "My men will find them somewhere, perhaps in the bushes. Do not distress yourself." He started toward the door.

Stopping him, Dade said, "Since we're here, mind if we have a look through the rest of her things?"

"Aha! You are thorough. Just what one would expect of an associate of the distinguished Comte de Saint-Cloud! By all means, let us look!"

In the shallow closet Dade found a large piece of paper rolled up and held together with a rubber band. He and Marbeau removed the band, unrolling it. It was a rubbing from an ancient brass, showing the head of a young man wearing a bishop's miter. Then he caught sight of something at the bottom of the rubbing and looked at it closely. In medieval Latin, he made out the words, "Pray for Bishop Remords." He tapped the rubbing with a forefinger, a faraway look in his eyes. He showed the words to Marbeau. They looked at each other. Marbeau said nothing.

Dade looked at the things on the bed. The only object that they had not yet examined was a pocket calculator. Dade picked it up, inspecting it. It had not only a digital clock with an alarm but it could also be programmed to remind its owner of his schedule. Thus, at a touch, it would display on three lines whatever appointments one had made, not just for a given day but for the entire month.

Dade tested it, touching the key for May. Kate evidently had kept a careful account, for every appointment, beginning with her departure for Paris from Los Angeles, had been meticulously recorded. There was nothing more. With Marbeau watching him, Dade frowned, tapping the calculator lightly with a thoughtful forefinger and whistling softly to himself through his teeth.

The versatile little calculator had another function: it recorded memos. This memory worked the same way as the schedule, except that it was not organized by dates. Reading a given memo required only that one touch a number and the memo key. Dade experimented, touching number one and then the memo key. A memo appeared under the crystal of the display panel. It read: "Find out how much cheaper to fly home on stand-by." A second memo gave the name of a restaurant in Paris and the name of a dish for which she wanted to get the recipe. The next three entries were the names and addresses of businesses in Paris where one could buy shoes at near-wholesale prices. After that came a memo about the driving time from Paris to Toulouse via Cahors and Sarlat. The next memo consisted only of a telephone number. After that there were no further entries. Dade translated the memos for Marbeau's benefit.

"Nothing out of the ordinary," said Marbeau. Nodding, Dade took out his notebook and his pencil and wrote down the telephone number, put the notebook away, picked up her empty shoulder bag and held it for a moment. Watching him, Marbeau said, "She was someone you cared about, Mrs. Mulvaney?"

"I respected her," Dade said, putting the bag back down on the bed. He stared out the porthole at the line of plane trees, all carefully pruned, at the wood sawed up from branches that had been cut away, all neatly stacked to dry in piles by the towpath.

"And the others?"

Dade did not answer.

They left the cabin together, Dade gesturing for Marbeau to precede him up the companionway stairs. Just then a door on Dade's left opened and a tall, stooped man, balding, with an aquiline nose and piercing eyes like an eagle's, stepped backwards into the corridor, colliding with Dade. It was Kate's older brother, Leo Penrose.

"Hello, Leo," said Dade.

The man turned and looked at him. "Dade, how are you?" The resonant voice was matter-of-fact. Then Leo reacted, delayed surprise suffusing his bony face with blotches of color. The dark eyes fixed themselves on Dade's, darkening as the pupils dilated. Dade started to say something but Leo forestalled him, stepping aside in the narrow corridor and gesturing for Dade to go ahead of him. Dade started up the stairs. Behind him, he heard a door open. He turned in time to catch sight of Leo going back into his cabin, the door closing behind him.

6

At the top of the stairs Dade entered the saloon and saw Marbeau standing motionless, staring at something. Dade followed his glance. Leo's wife, Olivia, was seated alone on a couch, smoking a cigarette. Marbeau stared at her, incredulous. Turning to Dade, he asked, "Is it . . . is it truly—?"

"Yes," Dade said.

"Another sister?"

"No, a sister-in-law."

"I have not seen a picture of hers in many years but that, my friend, is a face no man could forget." Dade looked toward Olivia, saw again the cloud of flaxen hair, the curve of the magnificent throat, untouched by age, the luminous eyes, and, when she turned, showing them her profile, the perfect nose. "Ravishing," the inspector breathed. Then, excusing himself, Marbeau left the saloon. Through the window, Dade could see him climbing off the barge and giving orders to his constables, who were keeping back a large crowd of curious onlookers, now gathered behind the police cordon at the top of the bank, all of them staring down at the barge, gesturing and pointing.

Going over to Olivia, Dade greeted her. He began to express his condolences. Interrupting him, she said coldly, "You've come about the play, haven't you? Well, you're too late. She could withdraw but the estate can't."

He looked at her sharply. "You mean Leo's play?"

She stubbed out her cigarette impatiently, saying, "Oh, don't pretend you don't know what I'm talking about!"

"I'm not pretending."

She looked at him open-mouthed. "You mean . . . ? Oh, my God, I am so sorry." She turned her compelling eyes on him with an imploring look. "Dade, please forgive me. This . . . this whole thing has upset all of us so much that I'm afraid we don't even know how we sound."

At that moment Leo came up the companionway stairs. Olivia cried out to him, "It's not about the play!"

Leo's bald head turned in Dade's direction, then abruptly he averted his face, covertly blotting at his eyes with a handkerchief. He blew his nose. Then, sighing, he turned again toward Dade and said with a half gesture, "Sometimes, you cry for what might have been."

Olivia asked Dade, "Do you know anything at all about what's going on? I mean, how long they're going to keep us here?"

"Just until they arrange to get all your statements."

"Poor Kate!" sighed Leo.

Dade said to them, "On the phone she mentioned something called the Remords reliquary." They both looked at him blankly.

Dade went on: "I was wondering if you knew anything about it. Either of you."

Leo looked at his wife. Olivia shook her head slowly. "I don't know what you're talking about." She turned toward Leo.

"I think I once heard her mention it but I'm not sure. What is it?" he said.

Maggie entered with Ellen from the deck. Ellen threw Dade a quick, questioning glance. He answered her with a slight shake of the head.

"Where's George?" Maggie asked, going to the bar and helping herself to a glass of orange juice.

"In his cabin, I think," Olivia said. "He wanted to be alone."

"Well, he got his wish," Leo murmured.

"Stop it!" said Olivia sharply.

Expressing her condolences to Leo, Ellen held out a hand to Olivia. Greeting her, Olivia pulled Ellen down on the couch beside her. Olivia held onto her hand, eyes on Ellen's face, saying nothing but only shaking her head.

Leo beckoned to a buxom, dark-haired girl standing behind the bar, saying to her, "Kitty, I would like"—and he pantomimed a big cup—"café au lait."

"Right you are, luv," she called out with a cheerful British accent. She smiled, showing a gap between her upper two front teeth.

Leo turned to Dade and said, "Crosby used to do that. He would say to you, 'Want to play a little'"—he pantomimed a slight swing of a club—"'golf?' or 'Why don't you give me'"—he pantomimed dialing—"'a ring?'." The eagle's head moved slightly to one side. "Only man I ever knew who was more relaxed in front of a camera than in real life. When he read my lines it always sounded as if he were just making them up."

The husky young sailor came through the saloon just then. Seizing his wrist, Maggie said, "He's like that! Aren't you, Mike?"

"Ma'am?" The English boy turned toward her, blushing. He pulled off his cap, showing a mop of curly red hair. In one ear, he wore a sailor's gold earring.

Still holding onto his wrist, Maggie said, "Mike here wants to be an actor, and so yesterday I was going over my lines and I said, 'Come on, I'll give you some practice.' I gave him the script, he made some remark to me and I said, 'What did you say?' and it turned out he wasn't saying anything to me at all, he was reading my cue!" She looked up at Mike. "Do you know how rare a gift that is?"

He blushed harder than ever and stammered the beginning of a reply; then, excusing himself, he ducked behind the bar and disappeared down the steps to the galley.

As Kitty carried Leo's coffee over to him, Ellen went over to get herself a cup. Dade joined her, whispering in her ear, "So far, so good."

She whispered back, "Wait till the curtain goes up." She carried her coffee back to the couch, sitting down again with Olivia.

Under a notice posted on a corkboard announcing that the day's excursion to the Montagne Noir had been canceled, a Polaroid group picture had been thumbtacked. Dade went over to it and took it down, looking at it. It showed the group of eight gathered together on the forward deck, Kate in the center, a smile on her face. Seeing Dade examining the photograph, Olivia said, "That was yesterday." She took the picture from Dade and studied it. "The last day of her life and there she is, smiling!" She shivered and handed the picture back to Dade.

"She was happy yesterday?" Dade asked.

"Oh, yes, indeed."

"How was her state of mind in Sarlat?"

Olivia shrugged. "I don't know. I wasn't there."

"You didn't go with her?"

"No, I stayed in Paris Tuesday night, and the next day took the train straight down to Toulouse, and got in just in time to board the barge."

"Who went with Kate?"

"Nobody. She went there alone. We all spent Wednesday shopping in Paris."

"Billy went," Maggie said.

"That's right," Olivia agreed. "Billy drove her down to"—she hesitated, then asking, "is it Montalban?"

"Perhaps you mean Montauban?" Ellen said.

"No," Olivia answered decisively. "I remember now. Montauban is a town; Montalban is the château that belonged to Bishop Remords. That's where they stayed. Where the hell George was, I have no idea. Ducking her as usual, I suppose."

"Now don't start on poor George," Maggie said.

"Women are always rushing to his defense," Leo said.

Maggie looked at her brother. "Women like him."

"He does have one big thing in his favor," Leo said.

"How did you find out about it?" Maggie asked.

The bald head turned in her direction. "You mustn't ask."

"Well," Olivia said, "the long and the short of it is—"

"Don't you think you should keep some things to yourself?" Leo asked. With an upward glance, Maggie left the saloon.

Reddening, Olivia said, "I was only going to say, Kate simply adored him." As she mentioned Kate's name, Olivia's expression changed. The wide gray eyes filled with tears. "My God, she's dead! She really is!" She caught her breath with a half sob and then said, her throbbing voice ringing like a bronze bell, "I'm not going to let myself go to pieces. We learn that in yoga. People used to upset me all the time—I wasted so much energy—but now, when somebody behaves badly to me, as George did downstairs when I tried to console him, I just say, *it's his problem.*"

"And remember that," Leo said with a brief smile at Dade, "if you ever find yourself pregnant by a rapist."

Olivia flung down Ellen's hand and looked up at her husband with blazing eyes, a vein throbbing in her neck. "Listen," she said in the voice she had used on the stage in *Saint Joan*, "I've had to put up with that brother-in-law of yours for twenty years and I can only do it by not making his problems mine!"

7

Just then, George, drunk, lurched into the room, almost stumbling over the top step of the companionway. He was as big as a bear, with a large red Irish face, short gray hair, a thick gray pelt showing through the open top buttons of his shirt and covering his thick arms. He glared at Olivia with reddened eyes and then said with a quick smile, "Auditioning again? I've got to hand it to you. For an actress who hasn't worked in fifteen years—"

Olivia replied in ringing tones, a smile on her lips, "For a man who once tried to save money on photographing a sunrise over the ocean by shooting a sunset over Malibu and then cleverly running the film backwards—"

"Oh, shut up!" George bellowed.

Ellen put a hand to her forehead, covering her eyes.

"It was gorgeous footage, George," Olivia said, her voice throbbing, "and what rotten luck to have all the sea gulls flying backwards as the waves rolled slowly out to sea!"

"Why, you old has-been—" George said to her, grinning.

"I'd rather be a has-been than a never-was!" she said in a measured tone, hands clasped in her lap. The smile remained on George's face but the eyes hardened. Abruptly Olivia got up and, excusing herself, left the saloon, hurrying down the stairway. Leo went out on deck.

George turned toward Dade. "They told me you were here." Dade shook hands with him, expressing his sympathy. George nodded repeatedly, then shook hands with Ellen. George said, "You've talked to them. What in the hell is going on?"

"Police routine." Then, Dade said, "You know, she sent for me."

"No, I didn't know." George looked at him without expression. "Mind telling me why?"

"It had to do with the Remords reliquary."

"Oh?"

"Perhaps you can tell me something about it."

"I don't even know what the Christ it is." He looked suddenly pasty. "Excuse me," he said. He lurched out onto the forward deck.

Dade picked up the photograph, tapped it against the nail of a thumb and then pocketed it. He and Ellen were alone in the saloon now, the reflections of sunlight from the canal dancing on the varnished wood of the ceiling. The warm air was full of the wet, mossy odor of the canal. Dade stared out a window at the growing mob of sightseers behind the police barricade up on the bluff.

Taking out her knitting, Ellen said with a shade of impatience, "It almost sounds like a prank. I mean, taking her glasses."

"Who said someone took them?"

"Well, if she doesn't have them on and the police can't find them, what other explanation is possible? She couldn't have disposed of them after she was dead!"

"Ellen, sometimes you confound me with common sense."

Maggie came up from the deck below, a stuffed toy poodle in her arms. "Do you like my Alfie?" she asked. The little dog was on a violet leash. "Watch," she said. She wound the dog up with a key and then put it down on the floor, where it hobbled around in a circle, wagging its tail and emitting sharp little barks. Then, when the dog stopped jiggling and barking, it lifted one leg and urinated. "Isn't that heaven?" Maggie cried, snatching it up and showing it to Ellen, then adding, "At a time like this, we can all use a little cheering up."

Dade said to her, rubbing the tip of his nose with his forefinger, "Dan said something to me about your all leaving Toulouse at five-thirty on Wednesday."

"That's right."

"Well, since Kate telephoned me Wednesday from Sarlat at five o'clock her time, and that's a good couple of hours north, I don't quite see how that's possible."

"Oh, we left at five-thirty, all right. We left by bus, rode for ten minutes down to the canal, got on the barge and then waited for Kate for three solid hours, waited dinner, which was by then ruined, all of us meanwhile worried sick about her, and then she shows up with no explanation at all, marching down the towpath in overalls and that hideous old jacket of George's, a shopping bag over one arm and those huge glasses that, with everything else, gave her the appearance of a battered owl."

Dade pursed his lips. Then he asked, "This trip her idea?"

"Oh, no. Olivia's and mine. We were going just with our husbands on a barge, and then suddenly she decided she would come along because it was cheap (we're all splitting expenses on the barge—good old Kate!) and she could stop off on the way down to Toulouse and make a pilgrimage to the tomb of her ancestor, Bishop Remords, at Sarlat and do a rubbing of the brass with his profile on it. *Our* ancestor, I should say, but in this case I'd like her to have all the credit." She turned to Ellen, a malicious smile on her lips. "There's an old family tradition that all of us are descended from Saint Louis' great and good friend, Bishop Remords, and so, one day, Kate took it into her head to write to Debrett's and paid them for a genealogy and when, in the fullness of time, Debrett's sent her pages and pages confirming this, Bishop Remords became a complete obsession."

She paused, looking from one to the other, sure now that she had their attention. "A handsome young man, I must say, with eleven bastards. Kate says he was martyred. Ridiculous. What happened is that a rope hoisting an enormous bell up to the tower suddenly snapped and the bell, crashing to earth, landed on Remords like an upended egg cup, ending at the tender age of twenty-six a career Kate was sure would have spread his name all over the globe. I said, 'God, yes!' then nicknaming the fallen bishop 'Ding-Dong-Daddy,' and when Kate looked startled, I told her Remords means 'prick' in French, adding that they may have named him that with some other aspect of our forebear's character in mind, that it was hard to tell after seven hundred years. You know what my dear sister did? She slapped my face! Well, that was enough for me. She was hoping we would all make the pilgrimage together, but after that, I wasn't having any, so I just let her go to Sarlat by herself."

The crocodile eyes narrowed in thought. Then Dade said to her, "You say she offered no explanation about why she was three hours late? That's odd. Was she upset when she arrived?"

"Oh, yes! We knew that as soon as we saw her trudging down the path toward us. George jumped ashore and ran toward her and she didn't even look at him and she said"—Maggie now imitated her late sister perfectly—"'The cab is up on the road. Go pay the man and get my valise.' Well, George ran off and she climbed aboard. Ned came up just then and got a look at her for the first time, and, I must say, when he saw her in that get-up of hers, he blanched. Here was this lantern-jawed woman with leathery brown skin and hard blue eyes and that incredible outfit, looking around at all of us. She said, 'What are you all staring at?' and I said, 'I was just admiring your overalls. They go so perfectly with that jacket.' Everybody chimed in, I suppose to cover for me, saying that she looked so comfortable, so right for a barge trip, and so forth, and Kate just eyed us and then said to Ned, 'They humor me because I bankroll them.' Can you imagine? Then she pulled off that greasy jacket and, I suppose because he was wearing a nautical cap, shoved the jacket into his arms and said, 'Here. Make yourself useful. Go hang that up in my stateroom.'"

Maggie, remembering, suddenly let out a peal of silvery laughter, covering her face for a moment with her hands. Then, recovering herself, she went on. "She sat down at one of the tables, which were set for dinner, saying she was thirsty. Ned asked what she'd like to drink. She said, in her usual way, 'Drinks included?' and when he said, 'Just wine with meals,' she picked up a pitcher of cream from the table, said, 'This'll do,' and drank the whole thing off. He just stared at her. She stared back and said, 'In my stateroom, I said. What's the matter, you forget already? I hope you're a better navigator than footman.' Yes, I think it's only fair to say that she was not in a good mood when she arrived."

"Anybody go anywhere that night?"

"No. We had already tied up for the night. We had a late dinner, then she sat up in the saloon with George, going over the below-the-line costs on the new picture and the two of them were still at it when we all went downstairs to bed."

"And the next day? How would you describe her mood?"

"Yesterday? Completely different. Gay, full of laughter and jokes. You know, Kate could be charming when she wanted." She looked at him sharply. "I hope you're not suggesting that she took her own life?"

"Just curious about the state of affairs before it happened, is all. Yesterday, she go anywhere, get any messages?"

"No."

"Yet her mood changed."

"Absolutely. The rest of us took walks or bike rides, getting off at one lock and getting back on at the next, that sort of thing, but Kate, all she did was sit in the saloon and play acey-deucy with George, happy as a clam, saying she just couldn't have enough of good old acey-deucy, and meanwhile, I was lying on the berth in my cabin, going over my lines with Mike—I suppose you know that the new picture is *Jericho*, based on Dan's book, of course, which Kate bought and George is producing—and I tell you, that endless rolling of dice and that cackling laugh and that grating voice crowing out over and over, 'Acey-deucy! *Acey-deucy!*' almost drove me bananas. It went on *all day long.*"

The beefy constable ran into the saloon then and said to Dade,

"The inspector asks if you will come to the towpath. He has something to show you."

As Dade and Ellen went out on deck, two constables boarded. Dade heard Cissy ask Ned, "What's going on?"

"They're looking for something," Ned answered. "Just routine."

"And what are they routinely looking for?" Cissy asked.

"Search me," Ned answered.

Leo's voice replied, "They'll get around to that."

8

Together, Dade and Ellen followed the constable back up the slope to the lock where Kate's body had been found. Since the lock was closed temporarily, traffic on the canal was backed up in both directions. Waiting barges were strung out like freight cars, and bargemen were calling out to each other and to the men on the boat from Ponts et Chaussées blocking the way, for some explanation.

Marbeau was standing there waiting for Dade, a dripping pair of glasses suspended from a heavy metal chain he held in his fingers. It twisted slightly in his grasp, the sunlight catching the lenses and making them flash. Marbeau said triumphantly, "My men just found them. Here." He pointed into the waters at the downstream end of the lock.

Frowning, Dade stared into the opaque depths of the now-filled lock. Then, looking up, he pointed to the far end. "But the body was found *there*, a hundred feet away," he said.

"When the lock is emptied, the water rushes out *here*—" Marbeau pointed to the end where they were standing. "The force of the water carried them away, from that end to this."

Dade said, "You mind if I try something? I think it's important."

"Whatever you like."

Walking to the far end of the lock where Kate's body had been found, Dade tossed the glasses, still fastened to their chain, back into the waters and then asked the inspector to have the lock emptied again. Marbeau called out orders. The lock keeper quickly opened the vanes. When the water was once more drained out, Marbeau looked inquiringly at Dade, who gestured at the yellow-suited diver standing a short distance away and said to Marbeau, "Would you ask him to look for them now?" Marbeau called out orders again, the diver ran forward, scrambled down the mossy ladder and into the shallow, murky waters, now on his knees, his hands searching the place where Dade had thrown the glasses. Moments later, he straightened up, holding the glasses and chain.

Dade said, nodding his thanks to the diver and then turning slowly to Marbeau, "I guess we were both forgetting that the lock can't be completely emptied or the barge would end up stuck in the mud. See, those vanes are about eighteen inches above the bottom and so when they're opened and the water rushes out, there's still about eighteen inches of it left in there and as a result, when the lock is emptied, the water in the bottom *doesn't move.*"

Marbeau looked at him with surprise. "Of course, you are right! But then—" He broke off, turning away and staring down into the oval stone basin. The diver came toward their end of the lock and handed the dripping glasses back to him. The slimy waters had made the chain slippery and it almost slid out of Marbeau's hand. He clutched at it. Then his face lit up, and turning back to Dade, he said, "Ah! It is quite conceivable the lady dropped her glasses—here! And then, since she couldn't see without them, she went *that* way"—he pointed toward the upstream end of the lock—"toward where the barge was moored, to get help, tripped in the dark and fell into the lock at that far end. Is that not possible?"

By way of answer, Dade took the glasses from him again and stretched out the heavy metal chain. "It isn't broken," he said. Marbeau shook his head, a troubled look on his face. Dade asked, "Then how did she drop them?"

"Perhaps she had taken the chain off her neck for some reason—why, I have no idea—and then dropped them. Would you not grant me that?"

"First, I think I'd have to hear why she took the chain off."

"Of course. Of course," said Marbeau. He walked up and down a few steps, deep in thought. Then, he turned to Dade and, squinting at him, said, "A catastrophe, most assuredly, a disaster for all those concerned, but the cause of death, that is for the coroner to decide."

"When will you hear from him?"

"A preliminary report should be ready within the hour."

"I'll wait for that."

Marbeau gave both of them a slight bow. Would they wait, then, on the barge? Trying to answer, Ellen swallowed the wrong way and choked. Marbeau eyed her. Dade patted her on the back.

It was arranged instead that a constable would put their suitcase on board for the time being and that they would ride into Castelnaudary with Marbeau and spend the next hour walking around the town. It was just after nine-fifteen in the morning.

Once in Castelnaudary, they got out in the center of town, arranging to meet Marbeau in front of the cathedral at ten-thirty.

Dade said to Ellen, "I think the first order of business is to find out what she was talking about. I'd like the story on that reliquary." They walked to the post office. Dade placed a call to Saint-Cloud only to learn he had gone to the country for the Ascension Day weekend. He could be reached at his house in Dinard, but not until the following day. Disappointed, Dade made a note of the telephone number.

Tugging on an earlobe, Dade consulted his notebook, copied out the telephone number he had found in Kate's pocket calculator, tacked on the Los Angeles area code and asked the clerk to place a call to it. Peering over his shoulder, Ellen said, "How do you know it's Los Angeles?"

"When somebody makes a note of a telephone number and leaves off the area code, it almost always means it's in his hometown." Going to a booth, Dade waited. When the clerk nodded to him, Dade picked up the phone and heard the number ringing. It rang for a long time. Ellen came over to the booth. Opening the glass door, the receiver still held to his ear, Dade said, "No answer."

"It's almost one o'clock in the morning there. Maybe whoever it is is out of town."

"Or maybe it's an office number. I'll try during business hours." He put down the phone; then, taking Ellen's arm, Dade said, "This way."

"What's this way?"

"The train station."

"Are we running away?"

"Don't get your hopes up."

Once at the station, Dade consulted a schedule. A train left Sarlat at two-thirty, arriving at five in Toulouse. Another train left at five-thirty, reaching Toulouse at eight. Dade jabbed a finger at the schedule and said, "That's the problem, right there. Why didn't she take the earlier train and arrive on time?"

Ellen reflected. Then she said, "Well, she'd come all that way to visit his tomb. Maybe she just couldn't tear herself away."

He shook his head. "She didn't call me from Paris. She called me from Sarlat. She said it was urgent. Well, on the face of it, it sounds as if she just found out whatever she found out right there in Sarlat. But why not take the earlier train? That would have gotten her to Toulouse at five and she could just as well have called me from there, reached me at the same time and gotten to the barge by five-thirty. Now, Kate, she was a punctual woman. Well, what changed her mind? That's what I want to know." He handed her a timetable he had picked up and she put it in her bag.

They spent the remaining time walking around the town. Shortly after ten-thirty, as they emerged from the cathedral of St. Michel, the inspector's car drew up alongside them and Marbeau clambered out of the back seat and hurried up to them, grasping Dade firmly by the arm, as if about to take him into custody. Dade turned and stared at him. The inspector was having trouble controlling himself. His face glistened with perspiration and the squint of his brown glass eye was more pronounced. "Let us walk," he said. "I need air, a breath of fresh air."

Ellen said, concerned, "Perhaps you should sit down."

"No, no! At times of stress, I find it good to walk." Together, the three of them walked down the street. The inspector said, "A problem has arisen."

"I see," Dade said.

"I have spoken to Paris about the matter, and as the representative of the Comte de Saint-Cloud, I am authorized to discuss the problem with you."

Dade said, "I have already explained—"

Marbeau waved this away, answering, "Paris understands." He

peered up at Dade. "Excuse me, but do the people on board speak French?"

Remembering Dan's complaint, Dade said, "Not to my knowledge."

"I feared as much. But fortunately, you can assist me. They must be told immediately."

"Told what?"

"As I've said to you, such an accident hereabouts is almost unheard-of. Oh, of course, there was that case of the nun—someone found her beads on the towpath and then the rest of her came to the surface at a later time, but she was stout and had been running in her long habit and then tripped—however, that is neither here nor there. The poor husband must be very brave."

"Oh, my land!" Ellen said, her eyes wide.

"It was no accident. The woman was murdered."

9

Inspector Marbeau slapped his thick arms against his sides like a seal. "A blow." He pointed at his right temple. "Here. The skull was crushed. There was extensive subdural bleeding. The body was not put in the lock until after death occurred. We know that because there was no water in the lungs."

Dade drew in a long breath, nodding.

Marbeau continued: "The time of death was between nine and eleven last night. No later. I asked the coroner if he were sure. He was quite definite." He cleared his throat, avoiding Dade's eyes. "One would like, of course, to believe that this was the work of some itinerant who happened along the path at that late hour, encountered the lady and assaulted her with a view to robbing her.

"But the whole notion of an itinerant is ruled out by what I am about to tell you now. It rained lightly around eight-thirty last night, not much more than a drizzle but enough so that the ground shows footprints clearly. My men were most careful. Immediately after the finding of the body, they examined the towpath. Members of the party walked up and down on it, of course, for perhaps two hundred yards in either direction, but beyond that point there are no footprints whatsoever and the wet grasses are all untrodden beyond that narrow strip of some four hundred yards on either side of where the barge was moored. There are footprints identified as belonging to members of the party coming down to the towpath from the road. They all took the barge bus into Narouze for dinner and walked back, so that there are only footprints *arriving* at the towpath, do you see what I mean? None leaving it. It would have been physically impossible for a stranger to have killed her and left the spot without leaving a trace, unless, of course, he simply flew away."

Dade started to interrupt. Marbeau held up a hand. "I know what you are going to say. He could have swum. My men thought of that as well. They also checked the other side of the canal, and the towpath there has no footprints at all. Someone swimming upstream could only have swum to the next lock. The closed gates are twelve feet high. He could not have gotten beyond that lock without first climbing onto the bank, which would have left traces. There are none.

"Well, you will say, our murderer could have swum in the opposite direction but, as it happens, water in the lock where the murder occurred was at the high point, so our murderer would therefore have found his way blocked by a twelve-foot drop from the top of the closed gates into three feet of water in pitch dark, and there are no footprints on the towpath on either side beyond that point."

He inhaled deeply through his nose, put his hands into the pockets of his jacket, hooking the thumbs over the sides, paused, turned, squinted up at the Gothic towers of the cathedral behind them and said, "I am mortified to tell you that it appears one of the party must have murdered the lady. Please forgive me if I give you pain." Dade looked away, not answering, tugging at his earlobe, a frown furrowing his brow. "Someone from the office of the Prosecutor General—a distinguished man, fluent in your language—will be sent down from Paris to interview everyone, Monsieur Gilles

Sartie. And now, if you will accompany me back to the barge and tell the others—" Marbeau signaled for his driver, the police car drove up, they got in and rode back in silence to the barge.

The sun had come out. The sky was suddenly blue. The water sparkled. The air was filled with the prolonged, shrill note of the cuckoo. Cissy, Dan's sister, had put on shorts and a halter and lay with her fair-skinned legs stretched out on a deck chair, a bandanna over her eyes. Billy Penrose sat cross-legged in a chair beside her and thumbed through a magazine.

As Marbeau's car bumped along the towpath, Maggie, standing at the deck railing, caught sight of them and clasped her hands together as if in gratitude, and the others began coming out of the saloon and up onto the deck, gathering in a knot around the gunwale, Cissy sitting up as Billy got to his feet.

At the barge Marbeau stepped aside, gesturing for Dade, as the spokesman, to go first. Dade looked up at the semicircle of waiting faces, climbed up onto the gunwale and then onto the deck. He stepped into their midst, glancing around for George. They made room for Dade. Then he saw George coming up the steps from the saloon to the foredeck, a drink sloshing in his hand. He missed the last step and Dade had to grab his arm to keep him from falling.

George saw all of them gathered together, Ellen now coming aboard, followed by Marbeau and the beefy constable, Joliet. George said to Dade, "What's going on?"

Still holding onto his arm, Dade said, "Let's sit down, George, okay?"

George shook him off. "What's going on?"

"It wasn't an accident," Dade told him. A murmur of disbelief ran through the group.

"Who says?" George demanded.

"The coroner." Dade told him what Marbeau had said.

George listened, staring into space, his expression unchanged. He turned very pale. Dade again tried to get him to sit down. George pushed him roughly away. "I'm all right," he said. "Christ," he said, "I've been drinking all morning—you know, I don't drink much as a rule—and I'm cold sober. I know I look drunk but I'm not." Frowning, he said, "She was mugged. That's what you're telling me."

"No," Dade answered.

"She was mugged," George insisted. "Oh, Jesus *God—!*" His voice broke.

"No," Dade said again. He told them the authorities believed that one of them had killed Kate. They all looked at him with the same incredulous expression, then at one another. George sat down suddenly in a chair, slamming his drink down on a table, too close to the edge so that it fell off, smashing on the deck. Ignoring it, George buried his face in his hands, elbows between his legs.

"What gave him an idea like that?" Dan said angrily, the eyes as hard as rocks in the deeply tanned face. He took a step toward Dade. "Or should I say, who?" Turning to the others, Dan said, "What did I tell you?"

Turning away as if he had not heard Dan, Dade started toward the gangplank. Olivia stopped him. As if she had only just then understood what Dade had told them, she said, "You mean, they think one of *us* killed her?"

George took his hands away from his face, and lifting his head and staring straight at her, said hoarsely, "One of *you!*" He looked around at all of them, then abruptly jumping to his feet, he stumbled back down the stairs into the saloon and out of sight.

Leading Ellen back down onto the towpath, Dade took out his watch and consulted it. "Where's that timetable?" he asked.

Ellen fished it out of the big bag she carried. "What do you want to know?"

"What time's the next train for Sarlat?"

She turned pages, then consulted a table. "There's one leaving Toulouse at eleven-ten."

"Come on," he said. He took her arm. They walked away, watched avidly by the spectators behind the police cordons on the road above.

Marbeau hurried after them. "Where are you going?" he asked.

"To find a cab. There's a train to Sarlat in fifteen minutes and I want to be on it."

"Sarlat? Ah!" said Marbeau. Then, taking Dade's arm and giving him a brown, glinting look, he said, "But Sarlat, that is a long way by train. One must change. It is faster by car. Constable Joliet will take you." Marbeau looked pointedly at Dade. "And bring you back." Marbeau then took out one of his official cards, uncapped a pen and wrote Dade's name on the back of the card and a few words to the effect that any assistance he was shown would be a favor to the Sûreté. Handing it to Dade, he glanced toward Ellen, asking, "And your lovely wife? Will she be going with you?"

"Yes," said Ellen.

"No," said Dade. She looked at him, taken aback. "Mrs. Cooley is going to the university library in Toulouse. With your kind permission, we will leave her off there and pick her up on our way back."

"Certainly," said Marbeau. "Whatever you want, Mr. Dead Cooley."

When Dade and Ellen were speeding along the road to Toulouse, Joliet at the wheel, Ellen asked, "Why am I going to the library, Daddy?"

"To find out about that Remords reliquary."

"That could take weeks."

"All you've got is one afternoon. But for you, that's enough."

"You take too much for granted."

"Honey, when a man's got a wife as full of information as a mail order catalogue—"

Her face lit up and she interrupted him, a hand on his arm. "Collin de Plancy!"

"I don't like your swearing, not even in French."

She punched his arm. "Collin de Plancy wrote a dictionary of relics. We'll start there!"

"That's my girl!"

When they got to Toulouse the traffic was far worse than it had been early that morning. Joliet, with a quick glance at Dade, eyebrows raised, switched on the siren and the turret lights and then went weaving through the stopped cars at breakneck speed, past St. Sernin's, slamming at last to a halt in front of a large stone building. Passers-by stopped in their tracks, staring, as Joliet helped Ellen out of the back. Just off the square was a narrow alley lined with little sidewalk tables in front of coffee shops and bakeries with Arabic signs. Seeing the police car, students got to their feet, craning their necks.

Ellen lifted her chin and marched up the long flight of broad, shallow stairs, her bag over one arm, meanwhile pulling out a pair of glasses and putting them on, then searching in her bag and getting out a pencil and a pad of paper.

Back in the police car, Dade, watching her progress, said under his breath, "Aplomb. That's what the lady has. I call it aplomb."

"Pardon?" Joliet asked, turning in his seat.

"Sarlat," Dade said. "As fast as you can."

Saluting, Joliet turned on the siren and the turret light and left the town the way they had entered it, then headed north on the twisting highway, climbing up into the gorges of the Dordogne, siren screaming as they raced past cars that had pulled over for them.

Once, Dade leaned forward to get a quick look at the speedometer. It read well over a hundred and fifty kilometers an hour. Rapidly multiplying by six and dropping the last digit, Dade confirmed his hunch: they were going ninety miles an hour.

Dade sat back, gripping the seat with both hands. "I could drive the Baja," he said to himself. "By God, I could!"

10

They arrived in the ancient town of Sarlat, driving past tall narrow houses built of yellow ochre stone, with mullioned windows and steep gabled roofs faced with limestone tiles, just as the deep-toned, reverberant bells of St.-Sacerdos were striking twelve.

Dade had Joliet take him first to the post office from which Kate would have had to place an overseas call. It was closed until two. Sighing, Dade asked to be driven to the cathedral. When Joliet drew up in front of it, Dade pointed at a café across the square, pulled out a hundred franc note, and handing it to him, said, "You go have yourself lunch, a good lunch, understand? Don't wait for me. I'll join you there when I'm ready."

Joliet's red face broke into a smile. He touched his cap and started across the square. Dade headed toward the cathedral steps, then in the cemetery to his right he caught sight of an old groundskeeper in a blue cap shuffling very slowly past a row of flying buttresses and muttering to himself. Dade went through the lich gate and walked toward him. Redolent with cheap wine, the old man carried a stick with a nail in the end of it and was spearing bits of crumpled paper and putting them into a gunnysack that he dragged along behind him. Dade greeted him, taking out the card Marbeau had given him. The old man ignored him. When Dade tried to press the card on him, the old man pushed him aside, then looked at him with hostility, brandishing his stick.

Dade, hearing footsteps ring out on the cobblestones, looked up to see Joliet running toward them across the square. Seeing him, the old man shrank back against the building, protesting and gesturing. Dade stepped tactfully away as Joliet spoke rapidly and heatedly to the groundskeeper. The old man mumbled a reply. There were a few more such exchanges. Then, Joliet nodded, turned away, and coming over to Dade, said, "This old man does not like Americans. He says they killed his son. When he recognized your accent he did not want to talk to you. He asks forgiveness."

The old man began talking to himself loudly, giving an account of how his son had been killed during the Invasion by a bomb dropped on Aunay-sur-Odon, meanwhile shuffling toward Dade, as if to let him overhear all this. Joliet cut him off, saying the American wanted to ask him a question on behalf of the police.

"I'm sorry," Dade said to the old man, putting a hand on his thin shoulder. The old man looked at him with rheumy eyes. Dade took out the photograph and showed it to him, pointing at Kate's picture. "This woman was here for some time the day before yesterday. An American woman. Did you happen to see her?"

The old man studied the photograph, then handed it back and said to Joliet, as if he did not really think Dade understood French, "I can't see. It's too small."

Dade pulled out his own glasses and offered them to him. The old man looked at Joliet, as if for permission, then put on Dade's glasses and took the picture from him, holding it in the light and moving his head from side to side. Then he exclaimed, looked up at Dade, nodding repeatedly and with such emphasis that Dade's glasses fell forward to the tip of his nose, meanwhile stabbing at the picture with a dirt-encrusted forefinger. "That is why Americans kill people!" he said in a loud, shaking voice. "They have no self-control! I saw that woman raving in the churchyard, no one around, raving like a maniac, shaking her fist at the air, and all this, mind you, on consecrated ground! Shall the dead have no peace?"

"When was this?" asked Dade, his eyes intent.

"It was not today." The old man thought for a moment, brow furrowed. Then, his face cleared. "She stepped on the flowers of the graves! On the fresh flowers! She did not even look where she was going!"

"When?" Joliet asked impatiently.

"Do you not understand?" said the old man. "Fresh flowers are put on my graves on Wednesday. It was Wednesday."

Bringing his face close to the old man's, Dade said, "I mean, what time?"

"It was as I came back from lunch, sometime after two o'clock, I think."

"Thank you," Dade said, taking out his wallet. He took out a large bill and said, "Do me a favor. Have a drink for both of us in memory of your son."

The old man took the money from Dade and nodded, thanking him. Gently, Dade took back his glasses that rested, forgotten, on the long French nose. The old man reached out and took Dade's elbow in a bony grip, looking to one side and saying, "I drink to his memory every day, monsieur, to the life that is no more." The rheumy eyes found Dade's. "But what have I done with mine?" he said in an undertone. "That is the question that I ask myself."

"I understand," Dade said.

"No." The old man drew himself erect and looked at him. "Only those who have to ask such a question understand." He shuffled away. Joliet looked at Dade, touched his cap again and, turning, started back across the square.

Dade walked slowly back toward the steps of the cathedral and mounted them. At the portico he went to the right, pushed open a heavy, leather-covered side door and entered the dim, cool building.

The cathedral seemed almost empty. A few worshipers sat apart in pews in the huge nave. Dade walked down a side aisle, past bays where votive candles flickered in front of the carved figures of saints. Saint Amadour was represented with his right hand outstretched. Over the centuries the lips of the faithful had worn it as thin as a leper's.

Dust motes danced in long shafts of light from the high, clear windows. To his right a shapeless old woman in a knitted dress and black stockings brandished a long-handled dust mop, brushing at the faces and the vestments of the plaster saints in an alcove. Dragging a stepstool up onto a dais where a statue of Saint Anthony stood on a pedestal, she climbed up on it, put a firm arm around the saint's shoulders and began scrubbing at the face with a dustcloth, muttering to herself. Dade went toward her, greeting her. Turning and looking down at him, the old woman said good day to him, then adding, "This one gets himself so dirty, Monsieur. He is the worst."

"It's all that poking about in dusty corners looking for lost objects that causes the trouble," Dade said.

She gave him a look of astonishment and pleasure, shook her rag at him and said, "You are right, sir! And it never occurred to me!"

"I myself am searching for something," Dade said. Climbing back down and taking the stepstool away, she gestured at the statue, as if to indicate that Dade was now free to consult the saint at his leisure. "I'm searching for the answer to a question," Dade said to her, pulling the group photograph out of his pocket and pointing at the picture of Kate. "This woman was here the day before yesterday. I'm looking for someone who might have seen her, madame."

She peered at the picture blankly, then said, "Wednesday?"

"Yes, madame."

"That is my day off, monsieur."

Dade glanced around. "I wonder if I might have a word with the priest?"

"Father Pierre?"

"Is that his name?"

With a quick sigh, she brushed a lock of gray hair out of her eyes, tucked it back under the scarf she wore around her head, then touched Dade's arm and said, "He takes chill so easily. I said to him on Sunday, when he served Mass, coughing and coughing, his head so stuffed up he could hardly speak, 'What do you want to do, give God a cold? Go home to bed.' Well, he would not and, of course, the church is not heated"—she gestured at the huge nave—

"think what it would cost to heat a church!—and two days later his cold had turned into pneumonia, and now the poor man is in the hospital!"

"And there is no other priest in attendance?"

"Father Honoré is to arrive day after tomorrow, for Sunday Mass."

"Then, when my friend—this lady—visited the church on Wednesday, there was no priest here?"

"No, monsieur."

"What about the sacristan?"

"He unlocks the church in the morning and locks it at night but he is never here during the day, since he works as caretaker at the house of Monsieur de la Boëtie," speaking of it as if it were the house of a neighbor, not a man dead for four hundred years.

"Then, when the lady came to this church on Wednesday she would have found herself alone?"

"We are never alone," she said, pointing up at the ceiling, where a painted eye looked down at them.

"Of course, you are right."

"Good day, monsieur."

"Good day, madame."

Bowing to her, Dade walked along the side aisle to a place almost as far back as the main altar, where the earliest burials had occurred. Worn brass plaques embossed with the recumbent figures of knights and their ladies and princes of the church were set in the stone floor on which he walked. Ahead, behind the bishop's throne in the apse were a number of others. He walked toward them. Then he saw it, at the end of a semicircular wall in the rear of the church, the plaque from which Kate had done her rubbing.

Going up to it, Dade could make out the dates of the birth and death of the youthful bishop, 1244 and 1270. He studied the brass profile of the bishop in his miter, the prominent nose, the full, sensual lips. The image had a glow on its cheeks, a fresh-faced look, owing undoubtedly to Kate's industrious rubbing and polishing.

At that moment there was a piercing cry that was suddenly fractured, like light through a prism, into a rainbow of sound. A choir was singing Palestrina's "Lamentations."

He turned then and saw half a dozen college students in jeans and T-shirts, some of them with CORPUS CHRISTI lettered on them.

Their lank hair was bleached by the Texas sun, their young faces were tanned, their teeth white from the minerals in the branch water of Texas towns, two of them were girls with hair halfway down their backs, they all held sheet music open and their leader, not much older than they, gestured more like a conjurer than a conductor, leading them. When they had finished singing, Dade crossed toward them, introducing himself.

"I'm Joey-Boy Sims," the leader said. "Mr. Cooley, these are my students."

"Very beautiful, that was," Dade said.

"Thank you, sir," Joey-Boy answered.

Nodding to the others, Dade asked Joey-Boy, "Traveling together, are you?"

"That's right."

"Concerts, I take it?"

"No, sir. I'm doing a paper."

"A paper?"

Joey-Boy gestured at the cathedral. "On the effects of Gothic architecture on the music of early church composers."

"Is that a fact?"

"Yes, sir."

"And you just try out different places, that the idea?"

"Well, I scout them first."

"And you scouted this?"

"Well, I checked out half a dozen around here, but I just chose this one."

The crocodile eyes narrowed. "When was that, son?"

Joey-Boy knitted his brows, then said, "That would have been Wednesday."

"About what time?" Dade asked quietly.

Joey-Boy looked puzzled. "Early afternoon. Why?"

Showing him Marbeau's card, Dade said, "I wonder if I could just have a word with you?" To the others, he said, "I won't keep him a minute. Now, if you'll all excuse me . . ." Taking Joey-Boy by the elbow, Dade steered him toward the side aisle up which he had first walked. There, Dade gestured at an empty pew, they sat down together and Dade took the photograph out of his pocket and handed it to him. He pointed at Kate's face. "You see her here?"

"Something wrong?"

"Appears to be." Dade caught the flicker of recognition on the face. "Then you did see her?"

"Yes, sir, I saw the lady."

"Remember what she was doing?"

"Taking a rubbing. Right over where you were standing."

"You here long?"

"Say fifteen or twenty minutes. In different parts of the place. Checking out the acoustics. I just happened to notice the lady, is all."

"She alone?"

"Appeared to be."

"Anybody come up and speak to her?"

"Not as I saw."

"But you did see something."

"Sir, I didn't see anything." A lean brown hand brushed back the long, sun-bleached hair. "You mind telling me what this is all about?"

"Lady was killed last night."

The boy closed his eyes for a moment, then looked at Dade and said, "I'm very sorry. Accident?"

"She was murdered." The boy gave him a shocked look. Dade rested an elbow on the back of the pew, laced his thick fingers together and leaned closer to him. "Something happened here Wednesday. I saw it in your face when I showed you that picture. You don't remember what it was?"

"I never saw anything. Honest, mister."

"Tell me where you went."

Joey-Boy began a slow, careful recital of the stations of his progress: nave, transepts, aisles, choir, chapels, plumbery, presbytery, triforium, reredos. At a mention of the reredos, he hesitated.

Dade looked at him closely. "What about the reredos?"

"I had trouble there, sir. The wall at the rear of the choir here is curved and you get lots of junk."

"Junk?"

"That curved wall bends sound and sets up an echo—" He broke off, a surprised look on his face. Then he turned to Dade and said, "I just remembered! I heard the lady talking to herself! I was maybe seventy-five feet away, on the other side. But that curve's got a kind of pocket—it's a trick—sometimes they used to do it on purpose. Wren did it with the Whispering Wall in St. Paul's. Anyways, she happened to be at one end with me at the other. I don't think I'd've heard her anywhere else. But where I stood, when I sang a few notes, I could hear this echo right in the middle of a phrase and it was no good, so I quit and I stood there balancing it out, asking myself was the rest of the space and the resonance worth that one glitch?—and right then, I heard this voice, a soft voice, right like it was somebody standing there next to me—in fact, at first, I thought it was. I turned around, but there was no one there and then I spotted her way over to the other side and I realized it had to be one of those freak things I was talking about and that it was her, way across the church, talking to herself under her breath."

Dade said softly, "And what did she say?"

"I didn't listen. Wasn't any of my business. I just walked away."

"You must have heard something," Dade insisted. "Enough to know that you were hearing her. Now, what did you hear? I want you to think. Take your time, son."

Joey-Boy thought for a long time, his expression clouded. Then his face cleared and he said, "Manitoba."

"Manitoba?"

Joey-Boy nodded emphatically. "That's what she said. Took me awhile to remember because it just didn't make any sense at all."

"You hear anything else?"

Joey-Boy shook his head. "Just the one word. Reason I know it was that is that she kept saying it to herself over and over: 'Manitoba, Manitoba, Manitoba.'"

"Saying it how?"

"Like it was some kind of private joke. Manitoba, Manitoba, Manitoba! and then sort of laughing."

"Laughing?" Dade's eyes shot him a quick surprised look.

"That's right, sir. Laughing under her breath."

Dade got to his feet and Joey-Boy did the same. "You've been very helpful," Dade said to him, "and I'm grateful to you."

"I can't say as I think it'll be much use."

Dade shook hands with him, thanked him, started to turn away and then said, "You never got the impression the lady was angry?"

"No, sir, no way." Joey-Boy swallowed. "She was really murdered? Honest?"

"Yes."

"Poor lady!"

"You a Christian, son?"

"Yes, sir, and born again."

"Then you can remember her in your prayers."

"I'll do that, sir." Dade started away. Joey-Boy called out in a loud stage whisper, "Mr. Cooley, sir!" Dade turned. The young man came toward him. "I'll need the name," he said. "The name. For my prayers." Dade told him Kate's name. The boy repeated it. They shook hands.

Dade went out a side door into the churchyard, sunlight coming through leaves and dappling on the ancient headstones. He paused, looking around at the moss-covered inscriptions, with names and dates chiseled on the stone in the Latin of the Middle Ages. He looked up, squinting across the little cemetery at the twelfth-century Chapel of the Blue Penitents, then around at the tombstones.

Nodding, he said to himself, "A man, he's entitled to a good death. Something like this, it just has to be put right or the dead can't rest." He looked around at the graves. "That's true, isn't it?" he said. He nodded to himself, saying, "It's true, all right."

He trudged toward the lich gate on his way back out to the square. Then he stopped, hearing his name called, turned and saw Joey-Boy loping toward him across the cemetery.

"It's probably nothing," he said to Dade when he came up to him, "but Wednesday they were working here repairing some loose stones"—he gestured at a scaffolding of metal rods still in place around the side door through which he had just come—"and I had to go through that rear door at the end of the side aisle, the one that leads into that old place with the terraces behind the cathedral, when I wanted to have a look at the cemetery afterward. Well, the lady you asked me about could have done the same thing. I mean, folks who visit churches visit the graveyards, often as not. It's just a thought."

"I see. Yes, she might very well have done that."

"Well, if she did, the kids back there might have seen her."

"What kids are those?"

"Americans. They're sitting back there up on the slope playing Dungeons and Dragons. They were playing it Wednesday. I saw them. Then, when we got here today, we went out there to lie in

the sun before we started and I saw them again and I said, 'Hey, how long you guys been playing?' and it turns out they been playing the same game for a week now, hours at a time and still at it today. Of course, kids who play like that are pretty much out of it— they might as well be sitting there smoking dope—but it's worth a shot. I mean, asking them if they happened to see her back there."

"I'm grateful to you."

"Yes, sir." Joey-Boy ran back toward the side door, and Dade turned around in his tracks, and instead of walking back into the square, made his way through the churchyard toward the far end of St.-Sacerdos.

11

That part of the grounds was unexpectedly still. Yew trees shaded it, and behind the cathedral's semicircular back wall, a corresponding semicircle of terraces had been built in early times, tombs on every level. Dade, standing on the flagstones behind the cathedral, felt as if he stood on the apron of what was very much like a Roman stage, above him, a kind of amphitheater filled with the august dead of ancient Sarlat.

Then, high up on one of the terraces to the left, he saw several college-age boys and girls sprawled on the grass in the sunlight, oblivious of him, a circle of bent heads. He climbed a flight of narrow steep stairs and then edged slowly toward the boys and girls as if afraid that, startled, they would scatter like birds. He drew close enough to hear their voices and sat himself down on the broad stone threshold of a vault carved in the style of a door, not to a tomb but to Paradise and flanked by stone angels who gestured toward passers-by as if to urge in whoever came there. Above the lintel, a motto in Latin admonished the stranger: LIVE TO DIE.

Dade listened to the group. The Dungeon Master, in his mid-twenties, Dade guessed, with a beard and a belly, munched on bread and hunks of cheese, which he pulled from a paper bag in his lap, helping himself to mouthfuls between throws of the twenty-sided dice on the playing board, while one of the players mapped the adventure by making marks from time to time on a sheet of graph paper, as the others moved the miniature figurines that represented each of their characters, as they descended to deeper and deeper levels of the dungeon in search of treasure, beset on all sides by monsters such as gargoyles, troglodytes, trolls and the undead. Nobody noticed Dade. The eyes in the young faces were the eyes of sleepwalkers who move through a dream invisible to others, excepting that here they dreamed collectively.

The caller, a fat girl with blotchy skin and the thick eyelashes of the nearsighted, said, "We're now going down the stairs of the secret passage."

The Dungeon Master replied, "The staircase ends in an oubliette filled with Green Slime and infested with Giant Rats. Each tread of the staircase is one foot wide. Sixty feet down the stairway is a door."

The caller said, "The Elf will listen at the door."

The Dungeon Master rolled dice and then answered, "He hears nothing."

The caller said, "The Halfling will break in."

The Dungeon Master rolled dice and then said, "The door has been broken in. The room contains undetermined treasure, guarded by a Minotaur. The Minotaur seems to be sleeping. Do you wish to advance?"

The caller said, "I, Ortrude, a magic-user who wears the Helm of Telepathy, will now read the thoughts of the Minotaur."

The Dungeon Master rolled dice again and then said, "Very good. The Minotaur is only feigning sleep, waiting to leap on you when you enter the room."

"We will retreat," said the caller.

The Dungeon Master threw his dice again. "A Berserker has entered the passageway above you, cutting off your escape. He is advancing toward the stairway. What will you do?" Then, when Ortrude hesitated, looking away through her thick glasses, frowning in thought, the Dungeon Master said to all of them, "For ten minutes, you will huddle together on the landing outside the door, rest and take counsel."

They sat back, sighing, rubbing stiff necks and arms, getting up to stretch. Dade took a step toward them. "Pardon me," he said. At first, nobody seemed to be aware of his presence. "Pardon me," Dade said again.

The Dungeon Master turned toward him, blinking, his face blank. Dade took the group picture out of his pocket and held it up for the Dungeon Master to see, pointing at Kate. "This lady came out of that cathedral sometime in the early afternoon the day before yesterday, while you were all playing. Anybody see her?" They all looked at the picture incuriously, then gave him a collective shake of their heads. Dade thought for a few moments, not saying anything. Their attention drifted away from him. Then he leaned toward the Dungeon Master and said, tapping the picture, "The lady was murdered. Last night." They all now turned to look at him. Dade held up the picture again, moving it slowly around the circle of faces. There was no reaction.

Dade persisted. "The lady was seen in the churchyard afterward. That means she had to have left by the rear door, right down there. She was alone—but here, in this place, she may have met someone. Someone who made her very angry. If one of you saw that meeting —even briefly . . ." He looked from face to face. They looked back at him, expressionless. Dade narrowed his eyes and then said, looking at the fat girl who was the caller, "But I think *you* did."

She looked puzzled. The Dungeon Master turned toward her, saying to Dade, "Becky?"

"Not Becky," Dade said. "Ortrude." She looked at him, startled. He said in a low voice, looking steadily at her, "Ortrude can tell me."

She stared at him sullenly, as if he were making fun of her, a resentful setting to the mouth, a glint in the swimming, long-lashed eyes. Then, when he continued to look at her in the same way and she saw that he was being serious, her expression changed. The thick lashes fluttered in front of the protuberant eyes, as if she were just awakening. Two or three of the others murmured, "Ortrude?" and, at that moment, they seemed, all of them, to step back over the line into the realm of the game, into the role-playing world in which they all lived.

"Why should Ortrude know?" the fat girl asked.

"Because Ortrude wears the Helm of Telepathy. If the woman who came out of the church met someone here and that someone made her angry, Ortrude would have known. She could not have helped but be aware of it. At the time she took no notice of it. It was not important. But it is important now." Dade held her eyes. "Ortrude?" he asked.

Suddenly the girl said, "Yes, I saw her. She came out of that door"—she pointed down toward the door at the rear of the cathedral—"and then met someone, she was surprised and they started to quarrel."

"Was the someone a man or a woman?"

"It was a woman."

Dade held up the photograph. "Was it one of them?" he asked.

She looked at the picture carefully, holding it close to her face. Then, she pointed to one of the people in the photograph: Olivia. "It was her."

"Did you hear anything that was said?"

"No, I couldn't. Only that they were quarreling. And the woman who came out of the church got very angry."

"Thank you," Dade said.

"Time," said the Dungeon Master. The group gathered in a circle, as before, heads bent, the sunlight bright on their hair. They began to play again, oblivious of Dade, the only sound in the silence of that amphitheater of the dead, the clicking of dice. The players watched, enthralled, as if fate had been caught and reduced to a series of mechanical alternatives. Dade moved away, pocketing his photograph.

Climbing back down the steps to the stone apron at the rear of the cathedral, Dade made his way through the cemetery at the side of the church and back into the square. Finding Joliet in the restaurant, Dade joined him at a table and, ordering himself a plate of truffled goose liver pâté from Perigord, cornichons and a split of St. Emilion, sat back, sunk in thought. When his food was brought, Dade had his luncheon in silence, the red-faced Joliet deferential, Dade preoccupied.

Afterward, Joliet drove him to the post office and waited while Dade went inside. He walked past a row of telephone booths opposite the counter and went up and spoke to an official at the far end, a wizened man in a shiny blue serge suit with gold buttons, showing him Marbeau's card. The man went to look for someone.

In a few minutes, a middle-aged woman in a black smock came up to speak to Dade, a Madame Doré. She wore gold earrings in the shape of crosses and her hair was dyed jet black, giving her strong features a hard look. Placing her hands on the dark oak counter, she looked at him with raised eyebrows, asking what he wanted. He showed her the photograph. She put on a pair of gold-rimmed glasses and studied Kate's picture. Yes, she remembered the American woman very well. Transoceanic calls were not often placed from Sarlat, so one would remember. She took out a ledger, consulted it, and showing Dade an entry containing his own office number, said that the lady had come in just at five and the call was placed then, "at the time the manifestation ended." When Dade, surprised, echoed the word "manifestation," the woman explained that there had been a demonstration of support for the airline workers on the part of the international telephone operators and that, although the post office had remained open, it had not been possible to telephone out of the country on Wednesday until after five.

"Would you say the American woman was upset?" Dade asked.

"Yes," she said, then adding, "Myself, I do not know what was in her mind. Now, if monsieur has no further questions . . ."

"I am grateful to you for your help."

"It is nothing, monsieur." She turned away.

Dade started away from the counter, then stopped, turning back and calling out Madame Doré's name. She returned, once again facing him across the counter. "Yes, monsieur?" she said.

"It strikes me that it was quite a coincidence for the American lady to come in here and place a transoceanic call just at the moment when the strike had ended."

"Monsieur, it was not a coincidence at all. She knew the strike was to end at five o'clock."

"How do you know that?"

"Because she first came in just after two and tried to place the call then, and at that time I told her about the manifestation and that calls could only be placed after five."

"And what did she say?"

"That her train left at two-thirty and she would then make the call from Toulouse."

"But she came back here instead." Dade rested his fingertips on the counter between them, Madame Doré meanwhile eyeing him across it as if it were a playing board. Then he said, "I have often noticed that those who serve the public in so vital a part of the government as this have an eye for detail, they are people who overlook nothing, is that not the case?" She inclined her head toward him, unbending a little. He asked, "How would you describe the lady's demeanor? I don't mean what was in her mind, I mean only how she conducted herself."

"Madame was businesslike. She was concerned about the time, mentioning that she had to catch the train at two-thirty. She was in a hurry. And . . ." She trailed off.

"And?" he prompted her.

"It is not my custom to gossip about those I serve."

"The lady was killed yesterday. She was murdered." Madame Doré let out an involuntary gasp of surprise and crossed herself. "The circumstances surrounding her death are mysterious. Anything you can tell me about how she seemed might prove important. Now, you were going to say . . . ?"

Madame Doré took a deep, resolute breath, then said, "A friend of mine was in here about two o'clock and was herself taking the same train to Toulouse. She speaks some English and offered to show the American woman the way to the train station. It is just a few streets away. They left together. My friend returned in the early evening, and when I met her in the street, she told me a strange thing: the two of them got to the train station early and the American woman sat on a bench waiting for the train while my friend, who had had no lunch, went to buy a sausage in a roll. When she returned, the train was just arriving. They were calling it, but the American woman did not seem to hear. She went on sitting where she was as if turned to stone. My friend took her by the arm and tried to tell her that this was her train, but the American woman at first acted as if she did not hear and then suddenly broke down and began weeping uncontrollably. My friend was very upset. She could not get the woman to board the train and did not like leaving her alone, but she had a doctor's appointment and she had to get on the train, so she took the paper with the sausage she had bought for herself and put it in the American woman's lap, thinking perhaps eating something would make her feel better, and then left her. She was, as I say, quite distressed and greatly relieved when I told her the American woman seemed quite recovered when I saw her again at five."

Seeing Dade's sudden look of understanding, she nodded in confirmation of what she had told him, Dade thanked her, she nodded again, withdrawing, and Dade walked toward the door of the post office, hands deep in his trouser pockets, eyes narrowed in thought. Then, making his way toward the car, he got in, told Joliet to drive back to the library in Toulouse and rode the whole way in silence, staring out unseeing at the dark landscape of the Dordogne as it raced by, lost in his thoughts.

12

At the library in Toulouse, Dade got out of the car to go in and get Ellen. He had just started up the broad staircase when he heard Joliet calling his name. Turning, Dade saw Joliet leaning out of the passenger door, gesturing and pointing down the alley. Dade turned and saw Ellen waving at him from in front of one of the little Arabic sidewalk cafés across the square at the end of the alley. Dade walked quickly toward her as she lifted her big bag from the table and, holding it with both arms, staggered toward him. Going up to her, he took it from her. She kissed his cheek, saying, "It's a quarter to four, I didn't have any lunch and I was just starving."

Peering into the bag, which was filled for the most part with old, leather-bound books, he asked, "You find out?"

"I'm finding out."

Joliet helped them into the police car and they started out of town through the heavy traffic, Joliet on the radio calling Castelnaudary to report that they were on their way back. Ellen had pulled a big volume out of the bag with a marker in it and now began reading to herself avidly, making little exclamations of surprise under her breath. "Forevermore!" she said finally.

"Would you mind sharing what you found out?"

"I haven't found out anything yet. I only had time to collect what books they had with Remords' name in the index. You don't know what I went through. The librarian had to get all these out of Special Collections for me."

"What have you got there?"

She began reading. "Remords began life as an Albigensian! Imagine! Of course, the Albigensian heresy was pretty much ended by then, but it had been powerful—my goodness, almost all the troubadours were Albigensians. You've heard about the Albigensians, haven't you, dear?"

"Like everybody, only from their detractors."

"If you were an Albigensian, you could pretty much do anything you wanted. There were no moral prohibitions and no religious obligations at all—but once you fell ill and were thought to be dying, they gave you a sort of Last Sacrament, and after that, if you had the bad luck to recover, they couldn't ever give you the last rites again, and since that meant you risked going to Hell, the Albigensian priests talked a lot of recuperating patients into permitting the priests to suffocate them to death so they'd go to Heaven."

She read on and then said, "*That's* why Remords was so important to Saint Louis! Even though the heresy was by then pretty much suppressed, there were still a lot of Albigensians around and Remords had been one of their leaders, so that when he became a Catholic, many of his people followed him." She turned a few more pages, scanning them, and then exclaimed, "The reliquary!"

"Finally!"

"Saint Louis gave it to Remords in Aigues-Mortes in 1270, when Remords went there to see Louis off on his last Crusade."

"Go on."

"Let's see." She ran a finger down the page, saying, "Here he is—Saint Louis, that is—sailing off to the Crusades with his wife and three sons." She began reading under her breath: "'All the men with a loud voice singing the hymn 'Veni, Creator.''" She looked up. "This is an account by Sieur de Joinville, Louis' friend. They went to school together at St. Denis—you know that abbey in Paris where all the French kings were buried." She turned more pages, rapidly running her eyes down each one, and then sighed. "No, that's all for that book." She closed it, disappointed.

"It doesn't say anything else about the reliquary?"

"Just that Saint Louis gave it to him." Reaching into her bag for another, she said, "Let's have a look here." She began reading to herself again, then exclaimed, "Here it is!"

Suddenly the car leaped ahead, the siren on, the turret light flashing. Dade leaned forward, starting to protest, but Joliet, half turning in his seat, said, "The inspector asks that I bring you back to Castelnaudary as fast as possible. He says there is a new problem. Excuse me, monsieur, madame." The car raced forward, weaving its way through the stopped traffic.

Dade frowned. Ellen bent over her book, trying to read it in the speeding car, the two of them lurching from side to side as Joliet swerved, racing through traffic. "Ellen, what's taking you so long?"

She flung the book at him and said, "Here! Why don't you try your hand at medieval French?"

"I'm sorry, honey."

She took back the thick volume and said to him heatedly, "All I had time to do was get out the books—and at that I was held up, waiting for them to call Marbeau and get his authority for me to check these out. I don't know whether anything so trifling has crossed your mind, but I don't happen to have a library card good in Toulouse!"

"Ellen, I'm sorry."

"Don't talk to me." The police car suddenly whipped around a corner with such speed that Dade was flung out of his seat, landing in her lap. She looked down at him and said, "If you're trying to throw yourself on my mercy, would you mind being less violent about it?" She began reading the book again, then caught her breath. "Here we go!"

"What?"

"The reliquary! It says it first disappeared right after Remords died—that was in 1270, the same year Louis gave it to him and sailed away—and was thought stolen!"

"Stolen?"

She consulted the book, holding her place with her forefinger. "Hm." As she read on, she began paraphrasing under her breath:

"Relics stolen all the time. People wanted them for their magical powers. Seems odd to us that anybody would steal the body of a dead saint, for instance, and think it would go on working miracles for them as it had for the people to whom it had belonged, but in the Middle Ages they just felt that it would have been impossible to steal a relic without the permission of the saint himself—that the saint somehow wanted to be stolen, if you see what I mean." She saw something and pounced on it. "My land! It was a reliquary of the *Thorn!*" Pulling another book out of her bag and opening it, she said, "Let's see what Collin de Plancy says about *that.*"

She leafed through the index and then, finding what she wanted, said, "Oh, boy! I'd forgotten about this! Baudouin the Second of Constantinople was broke. He'd hocked everything, so he offered to sell King Louis the Crown of Thorns . . ." She laughed. "Collin de Plancy says he can't help wondering what Louis thought about the Crown of Thorns they already had on exhibit at St. Denis, where he went to school! Good question!

"Well, Louis bought the Crown and then had Sainte-Chapelle built in the form of a magnificent reliquary to house it." She read on. Then her face lit up. "Here we go! It says Louis then took some of the Thorns from the Crown and had reliquaries made to hold them—it mentions one in the British Museum, a pendant set with two bean-shaped amethysts, enameled inside with scenes of the Crucifixion and the Passion—with a slot in one stone cut to hold the Thorn, and he gave these to members of his family and to friends. Remords!" She pounced on the word. "It says here that the one he gave Remords, which disappeared, turned up again in the 1416 inventory of the jewels and treasures of the Duc de Berry, Saint Louis' fourth great-grandson. But there's no other information about it." She closed the book, disappointed, and opened another volume. Then she exclaimed, "A description! Finally! Listen: the reliquary Saint Louis gave Remords was set with an enormous ruby of about thirty-five carats, placed in an ivory cross. It was considered a magical gem, said to be able to foretell death for someone close to the wearer by changing color. The ruby was hinged so that when it opened, it revealed the Thorn set in beaten gold. In those days rubies were almost unknown in Europe. Thirty-five carats! A ruby of that size is unheard-of, even today."

She ran her finger down the page, adding: "It says here—this is printed in 1978—that a ruby is the most valuable gem in the world, its value estimated at, good heavens! *one hundred thousand dollars a carat!* But when a stone is as big as Remords', the value increases astronomically.

"And here's a foolproof way to tell right off the bat if your Father's Day ruby stickpin is real or fake." She thrust the book at him, pointing at a paragraph. He studied it. Taking out his notebook and pencil, he copied out a brief excerpt. She took out another book. "Now, let's see. We're looking for—"

"A picture of it."

"They didn't take pictures back in the Middle Ages." He gave her a look. She gave him one of her own, then began leafing through a large contemporary book when suddenly her eye fell on something and she grabbed his arm. "Here it is! My God!" She pushed the book in front of him, pointing to a color plate. It showed the reliquary cross in all its magnificence, held in the mailed left hand of a statue of Saint Louis. He whistled. She read the text under the photograph, describing the reliquary, then turned the page, read on and gasped.

"What?"

"The photograph was taken in 1970 in Aigues-Mortes, where the reliquary cross lent by Sarlat Cathedral was exhibited as part of the celebration of the seven-hundred-year anniversary of Louis' sailing away on his last Crusade. During the exhibit, it was stolen from the church in Aigues-Mortes and has not been seen since. It was valued then at—good heavens—ten million dollars!" She closed the book.

His eyes narrowed and he stared off into space. Then, taking the book from her, he turned back to the color plate, studying it. Suddenly, he caught sight of something. He held open the book and showed it to Ellen. Almost inconspicuous between the open pages of the thick volume was a bookmark: a Stimudent. "I'll be a son of a bitch," he said. He put the Stimudent carefully into his jacket pocket.

She said, "But don't lots of people use those things?"

"They don't sell them in France."

At that moment the racing car lurched violently to the left, this time flinging Ellen into Dade's arms. Joliet called out an apology, saying they were almost there, gesturing at the outskirts of Castelnaudary.

Dade helped her to sit up. Ellen said, "Thank goodness. This
swaying back and forth is making me carsick." Galvanized, he
pulled out his notebook and pencil and scribbled something. She
said, "What is it?"

"Sway!"

"Sway?"

"Dominate or yield! Gotcha!"

She straightened her jacket as Joliet pulled to a stop in front of
the préfecture.

13

Joliet ushered them into a reception room, then through a frosted
glass door and down a hall to a door with Marbeau's name on it,
knocking smartly and, when Marbeau's voice called out "Come
in!," showed them into the office and withdrawing, closed the door
softly behind him.

Marbeau, hurrying around his desk toward them, gestured at a
pair of golden oak chairs, meanwhile whipping the handkerchief
out of his breast pocket and dusting the seats. As they took their
places, he said, "A further problem has arisen," whereupon he
walked back around his desk, plumped down in his chair, swiveled
toward the wall and stared at it blankly, mouth half open, clearly at
a loss. Then, turning and putting his elbows on the table, his hands
clasped, his chin resting on them, he said, "First, let me tell you
that my men have searched every inch of the barge. There is nothing even remotely resembling a reliquary on board. Second, my
men have found the murder weapon, a stick of firewood from the
pile beside the towpath. It had blood on it but, as one might have
expected, no fingerprints. There was also a trace of blood on the
ground, which enabled us to establish the place where the murder
was committed—in a clearing perhaps ten feet from the towpath, at

the upstream end of the lock. My men also found something else, next to where the body must have lain—more of that in a moment. But first, let me tell you that Paris has called me, asking for your help."

Marbeau slapped both hands on his desk, got to his feet and said, "The Public Prosecutor—that is, Monsieur Gilles Sartie—is on holiday on the Mont Blanc. He is at present scaling the south face, quite out of communication, and so will not be able to place himself at the party's disposal until Sunday, at which time he will meet them in Carcassonne. I have suggested to Paris that under the circumstances someone else might be chosen, but Paris feels this is a matter requiring the utmost delicacy, since we are dealing with people of international reputations. Even Ponts et Chaussées, which would normally be involved, has been told hands off—so the two days' delay seems advisable for all concerned."

"I understand."

"Now, for the problem." Marbeau cleared his throat. "It has to do with accommodations. This is the Ascension Day weekend. Every hotel room within miles is taken. We simply have nothing to offer the bereaved family."

"Well, there is the barge."

"Exactly! And if they will all continue with their journey, they will then arrive in Carcassonne just in time for Monsieur Sartie's interrogations, on Sunday. Since that is the day when people depart for home, we were able to arrange rooms for all of the party at the Hôtel de la Cité in Carcassonne, so they can be questioned there in comfort and privacy. Meanwhile, I will, of course, station an armed constable on the barge and"—he cleared his throat again—"I myself will also be on board to get everyone's deposition."

A ray of late sun came through the window at that moment and glinted gold in the brown glass eye as he looked at Dade. "And now, for the favor I mentioned: Paris asks if Monsieur Dead Cooley would be so kind as to assist me in this, not only because of the language barrier but because Paris feels that our esteemed guests may feel more comfortable, more protected, if their statements about their whereabouts—and, of course, anything else which may strike you as relevant—are to be made to one of their own distinguished countrymen. Will you and your charming wife therefore consent to make the little journey with us and obtain depositions from the family members?"

Dade wrinkled his brow, pushing out his lips, then turned to Ellen, a questioning look on his face. She said, "Well, she called you for help. You came. Really, I don't think you have any choice."

Dade turned back to Marbeau. "All right," he said.

Marbeau nodded with satisfaction. "Now, as to what else my men found . . ." Opening the top drawer of his desk, he took out something wrapped in tissue paper, unwrapped it and showed them an antique gold hunting watch. "Do you recognize this?" he asked. Dade shook his head and glanced at Ellen.

"No," she said. "I've never seen it before."

"One of my men found it in the bushes by the clearing, right next to where the poor lady was killed. When we take the depositions I would like you to ask each of the people whether he or she can identify it." He handed the watch to Dade, adding, "Do not be concerned about handling it. We have already had it checked for fingerprints. Establishing the identity of the owner will be very easy. What we want to know, naturally, is why no one has come forward to report the loss of something so valuable."

Dade put the watch in his coat pocket. Then, taking out his notebook and opening it, he indicated the telephone number he had found stored in the memo section of Kate's calculator and said, "I tried to call this number earlier but got no answer. That could mean it's a business. If that's the case, I might have more luck calling after seven o'clock this evening, which will be after eleven in the morning, their time."

Marbeau consulted a map on his desk. "We will tie up at Bram for the night. I'll have a car standing by to take us to the préfecture. You can place the call from there. I will make the necessary arrangements." They all got to their feet and shook hands. Marbeau said, "Your luggage is already in your cabin, number five. Joliet will take you back to the barge while I go home and pack for our excursion. I will see you on board."

Once again, they shook hands, all three of them, and then Dade and Ellen were driven back down to the canal to the waiting barge.

When they reached the place on the road where a fork led down the slope to the towpath, the crowd behind the freestanding metal fences the police had erected was even larger. Now there were mobile television units, reporters with microphones and photographers carrying quartz lights. The crowd behind the barricade surged in their direction as a constable swung a metal gate open so they could drive down the slope. Below, alongside the barge, they could see a fireboat from Ponts et Chaussées, clearly intended to keep the waterborne curious away. At the same time, floodlights were turned on them by the press, they could hear the whirring and clicking of television and still cameras and countless voices shouting out questions at them, the voices loud, demanding, making them sound hostile, like the cries of demonstrators at a protest.

They drove down the rutted slope to the barge. Maggie, lit by floodlights, and the focus of cameras on the slope above, was standing there, her back to them, calling out and waving at a bicycle disappearing down the towpath. They got quickly out of the car. Hearing them, Maggie turned and said, "It's Olivia! I told her we weren't supposed to leave the barge but she said she didn't care, that she just couldn't stand any more! It's this endless waiting! How much longer is this going to go on?"

Joliet had started toward the barge, calling out angrily to the constable on duty who was stationed aboard. Dade grabbed his arm and said, "I'll go after her." Climbing onto the barge, Dade made his way along the gunwale to the stern, and getting a bike from the rack, lifted it down to the ground, climbed on it and rode off after her.

Ahead, he could see her lifting her bike onto the catwalk of the next lock and walking it across to the other side. He pumped harder, struggling to keep his balance on the rickety bike, reaching the lock as she climbed down on the other side and pedaled away. He wheeled his bike over the walkway quickly, then mounted it again, followed her and caught up with her as she turned onto a paved road leading to a village not far away.

Coming abreast of her, he said, "If the reporters catch you, they'll be all over you."

"They're behind the barricade. They can't cross the canal at that point. Mike told me. Oh, they can go on back a few miles and cross there, but by that time I'll be on my way back, so I'm not worried. I'm sorry. I just had to get away."

She pumped faster. He kept pace with her. In another two minutes they had reached the village and Olivia dismounted, exhausted, leaning her bike against the stucco wall of a little shop. Putting his bicycle next to hers, Dade said, "Let me buy you a drink."

"I'm not really in the mood for a drink, if you'll forgive me."

"Well, you can keep me company."

"All right. On the barge."

"No, not on the barge." He took hold of her elbow.

"Dade, honestly, if you don't mind—" She tried to pull free.

"I do mind, and since we're already here, it's to your advantage. If we have our tête-à-tête on the barge, the inspector may take it into his head to join us and you don't want that."

She stopped struggling, staring up at him. "What on earth are you talking about?"

"I'm serious." He took hold of her elbow more firmly, steering her up the street toward a café. The sky was gray now and the lights were on in the shops on either side of the cobblestone street. Dade hurried her along.

Struggling to keep up with him, she said, resentment splintering through her patrician cadence, "I want to know what this is all about."

"I have something to say to you, and for your sake, I want to be able to say it privately." Still grasping her elbow, he escorted her toward the lights of the café.

14

Light came from the doorway. The tables outside were deserted. The air was chill. Dade led Olivia through the beaded doorway into a room full of soldiers, from the look of them, recruits on maneuvers, their faces young, some of them only beginning to shave, some disguising their youth with wispy mustaches. They wore badly fitted olive drab uniforms made of coarse wool. They lined the zinc bar, clustered around the few women who were standing there. Another half dozen stood around a kind of pool table where two of the youngest soldiers were playing soccer with mechanical figures fastened to long rods that they twisted quickly, the figures kicking a ball back and forth from one side to the other. Under the lights hanging over the game the air was thick with harsh, cheap French tobacco. American country-and-western music sung in French came from a juke box in the corner.

Dade and Olivia crossed the sawdust-covered floor to a little round table with two wire chairs and sat down there. Heads turned toward them, turning away as soon as they looked back. The bartender, a big man with a shaved head and a tattoo showing through his open shirt at the base of his neck, came up to them, wiping his hands on his apron.

"'sieur, 'dame?"

Dade looked at Olivia inquiringly. She said, "I don't want anything."

Dade ordered two coffees. The bartender repeated this under his breath, then went away. Olivia folded her arms and fixed her eyes on the door, as if leaving there were the only thing on her mind. She said, looking around, the sound of music and voices even louder now, "This is your idea of privacy?"

"There's a great deal of privacy in noise."

When the bartender returned with two small white cups of café filtre, Dade paid him, put money down for a tip, pocketed the rest of his change and began slowly to unwrap the cubes of sugar on his saucer and then to stir them into the tiny cup.

Finally, Olivia said, her face pale with anger, "You are being perfectly maddening, do you know that?"

Dade looked up at her, not saying anything. He sipped his coffee and blotted his lips with a scrap of paper napkin. Then, after taking a long, slow breath, Dade said to her, "As you may or may not know, the laws in this country are different. They don't, for instance, have to warn you of your rights."

"What is that supposed to mean?"

"Furthermore, if you ever find yourself in a French court, the examining magistrate can seize upon any inconsistency in any statements you have made to the authorities at any time and shake you like a terrier shaking a rat, and no defense attorney can say one word to stop him."

"Will you get to the point?"

"Depositions are about to be taken on board and if you lie to the inspector as you lied to me, I will have to make him aware of it; otherwise, I become in a sense an accessory after the fact."

She jumped to her feet, her face webbed with lines of anger around the mouth and the eyes. "What is this? How dare you try to frighten me with talk about the French courts and call me a liar?"

There was a sudden drop in the noise level in the room. They could feel the weight of covert glances. Dade got to his feet. "Sit down, please," he said. "I'm trying to help you."

Abruptly Olivia collapsed into her chair. She began tearing the paper from the cubes of sugar, her hands trembling. Stirring the sugar into the coffee, she drank it greedily, then looked away, studying her face in the dark mirror on the wall next to their table. After a moment, she said carefully, "I *lied* to you? About what?"

"I'm sorry you said that."

"I beg your pardon?"

"If there were only one lie, then you'd know I'd found out. To a lawyer, that sounds like an attempted finesse."

She caught her breath, then seemed to draw into herself. She said in a low, unemotional tone, "I don't care what you know or think you know. Tell the inspector what you like."

"You told me that on Wednesday you took the train from Paris straight to Toulouse."

"Well, what of it?"

"You didn't tell me that you followed Kate to Sarlat."

"Oh, for heaven's sake—!"

"And that you had a quarrel with her there, a bitter quarrel." His large eyes rested on her. She looked back at him, surprised, a disbelieving smile beginning at the corners of her mouth. Suddenly she burst out laughing. "I'm so relieved!"

"Are you?"

"Well, for a moment, I thought I'd done something dreadful—I mean, something that might be misinterpreted—and I couldn't for the life of me think what it was! Dade, really, how could you?" She smoothed away the reproach with a gentle smile. "I don't know how in the world you found that out, but honestly—!"

"A woman was murdered last night, your own sister-in-law. On the day before she was killed, you had a bitter quarrel with her. You concealed that fact. You're going to be asked why. I brought you here because I didn't want you caught off-guard. If you have a good reason for what you did, I'd like to hear it."

"Oh, don't be silly! Nobody wants to volunteer something like that! It didn't mean anything and if nobody knew, why on earth should I bother to bring it up?"

"I guess I'm not making myself clear. You're going to be asked what you were quarreling about."

"It's a personal matter, Dade—"

"Olivia—"

"—having nothing whatever to do with what happened to her."

"You don't need me to tell you that that answer won't satisfy the inspector."

"It's none of his business!"

"You'll have to answer. They can lock you up until you do. This is France. In a capital case you do not have the right to remain silent."

She looked at him, aghast. "But I was just trying to protect her! You know, that old thing about not speaking ill of the dead!" She took a breath. "I'd like what I say to be kept between us. You must understand, I get told all sorts of things. Some people are like that. They attract confidences. And I don't want my friends to think I can't be trusted."

"I'm listening."

She sighed. "Kate took things. Did you know that?"

"How do you mean, took things?"

"Well, you know how some shoplifters are, not the thieves who simply steal for profit but the ones who take things under compulsion and then just hide them in closets or whatever. Well, Kate did that . . . only she didn't take things from stores. She took them from her friends."

"I see."

"Very few people were aware of it. I'm not even sure George knew. We never discussed it."

"How did you find out?"

"Well, I gave a party once—this is years ago—and I happened to catch her at it. Let me back up a minute. You know those antique nails? The ones with the ornamental glass heads that unscrew so you can drive the nail into the wall, hang the picture over it and then screw the head back on? Well, I got one for an old picture in my bedroom and I didn't know about unscrewing the head, so I just took a hammer to the whole thing and only succeeded in smashing the glass head and making a big hole in the plaster. That was the day of the party, so I just had to leave it as it was, since there wasn't any time to spackle it. Well, during the party, when I went to the bathroom, I saw we were running low on guest towels, so I opened my linen closet to get out more. The closet was dark and I could see right through the hole into the bedroom. There was Kate, going through Maggie's purse, a big brocade purse I could recognize right away. I was just fascinated." She broke off, rubbing her cheeks lightly with the tips of her fingers.

"Go on," said Dade.

"Maggie had something she was just crazy about, a kind of—well, it looked like a gold monocle on a stem, which she wore on a chain. It had a button on the stem and when you touched it, the frame sprang open and the monocle became a lorgnette. Maggie is very nearsighted and she always carried it when she went shopping or to a restaurant or the theater and made a big thing of snapping it open to read the menu. I suppose it was valuable. It was gold and it was an antique and the lenses were ground to her prescription, but it isn't as if it were worth all that much. Well, as a good hostess, I should have gone into the bedroom right then and there, reacted with surprise and said, 'Are you looking for something?' but instead, I just stayed there in the closet and spied on her. I watched her take the collapsible little lorgnette from the gold chain and leave the chain clasp open, as if she wanted Maggie to think the lorgnette had fallen off, put the chain back in Maggie's purse and put the lorgnette down the front of her dress, into what I can only assume was her bra—you know, I have never seen anybody do that except in the movies?—and then leave the room. I didn't say anything. Afterward, when Maggie found it was gone, she was just beside herself. She attached some extraordinary value to it, almost as if it were a kind of amulet, but I couldn't tell her without letting her know about Kate, and that was something I wanted to keep to myself."

"The way Kate wanted Maggie's lorgnette?"

Her face hardened. "That isn't funny." She looked away. "I have—or had—an eighteenth-century hunting watch with a painted face showing Diana with her bow and her dogs in the forest. It's a sweet little thing, quite valuable, really, although the works are new. I always wear it on a chain around my neck. Well, when we got to Paris—"

"That would be Tuesday?"

"Yes. I took it off and put it in my purse and then went in to take a shower. Afterward, when I was dressed, I opened my purse to put it on again and found only the chain. With the clasp open." She looked at him, her head on one side. "Kate and George stayed at the same hotel, in the room next door. I went in to see her. George told me she had just left. I spent the whole day just beside myself, and in the morning I couldn't bear it any longer, so I got on the early train, the TEE, and went down to Sarlat, knowing she was going to be there that afternoon. I almost missed her. She had finished doing her rubbing and was on her way out of the cathedral when I arrived." She took a long breath. "Now you know why I followed her to Sarlat."

"Did Leo go with you?"

"Oh, heavens no! I didn't even tell him where I was going. If I had, he would have tried to stop me. He still thought he could get her to change her mind about the play. I just left a note saying I'd taken the early train and would meet him at the barge in Toulouse that afternoon."

"And when you spoke to Kate, did she admit she had taken your watch?"

"Oh, no. Not even when I confronted her with the fact that I had seen her steal that lorgnette from Maggie. I threatened to tell Maggie if she didn't give my watch back to me. I had her there. I was sure I'd get it back. Instead, she denied taking anything from Maggie and called me a liar. She was absolutely livid, raving like a maniac. As a matter of fact, I'm not sure Maggie hadn't found out and accused her. They did have a fight and Kate was going to have Maggie replaced in Dan's picture, or did you know that?" Dade shook his head.

"Well, when we boarded the barge, I wanted to search Kate's cabin but I had no chance. She spent the whole evening and the whole next day in the saloon, where she could have seen me if I'd gone in there, and that night, when we left the barge, we all left together. Well, now you know."

"Why didn't you say something to the inspector? You could have asked him to look for it."

"Oh, Dade, really! What would I have said? Now that she's dead, may I please have back the watch she stole?"

"You could have said that you'd lent it to her. Or that you think you might have left it in there."

"All her things now belong to George. He knows it's mine. He'll find it and give it back to me."

Dade reached into his pocket, pulled something out, and opening his hand, showed it to her. "Is this the watch?"

"Oh, you did find it! Thank you!"

"This is your watch?"

"Yes." She took it from him eagerly, opening the case and examining the face. Then, she sat motionless, as if an invisible hand had been placed on her wrist. She looked at him warily. "But how is it you had it in your pocket? If you found it in her cabin, why wouldn't you just assume it was hers?"

"I didn't find it in her cabin, Olivia. It was found in the bushes at the edge of the clearing where she was killed."

Olivia put the watch down quickly on the table, as if it had given her a little shock. Her eyes widened as she stared at it. "My God, you mean she was wearing it when"—she moistened her lips—"when it happened?"

"That is possible." He rested his eyes on her.

They remained where they were for a moment, sitting in silence. The juke box had stopped playing, there was a temporary lull in the conversation of the soldiers and the only sound was the ratcheting of wood and the monotonous clicking of the little soccer ball.

After a moment or two of silence, she said, picking up the watch and putting it in her purse, "Shall we go now?"

"Yes. I think we should." He took out his own watch, opening the case and looking at the time. It was a quarter after five.

They got to their feet and left the bar. Walking across the street to get their bicycles, they rode out of town and down the lane toward the canal. Ahead of them the steeple of a little church and the backs of low stone buildings clustered around it were dark against the pale gray sky. An occasional cyclist rode past them homeward-bound, a loaf of bread under one arm, groceries in a string bag on the handlebars. A flock of birds scattered before them, then settling quickly into the trees of an orchard. Olivia pedaled faster, riding ahead of him. Dade let her go on, eyes on her retreating back.

15

When Dade climbed up the gangplank he saw Dan standing alone on deck. He was leaning on the railing, smoking a cigarette, looking out over the motionless waters. Olivia, who was already on board, crossed the deck and went into the saloon, banging the door behind her. Dade said good evening to Dan. Turning, Dan's eyes followed Olivia's retreating back. "What's the matter with *her*?" he asked.

Not answering, Dade leaned on the railing beside him and said, "Dan, I've got me a problem with this business. Maybe you can help me."

Dan glanced back at the door to the saloon, then gave Dade a hard-eyed stare. "I get it," he said. "First, Olivia. Now, me. Where do you get off?"

Dade laced his fingers. "The French police have asked me to take depositions from all of you."

"Bullshit."

"If you prefer to remain silent—"

"Ask me when the time comes. Ask me officially."

"That might prove embarrassing to you."

"Oh?"

"You told me you never heard of that reliquary." Dan looked at him stonily, not answering. "But it seems to me you've been reading up on it." Dade took the Stimudent from his pocket and showed it to him. "Here's your bookmark. That book is in what they call Special Collections, which means you had to request it. The librarian will be able to identify you."

Dan turned away. Staring out over the prow of the moored barge, he said after a moment, "They call the stretch of water between any two locks a pound, I guess because the waters are impounded. I just found that out."

"Dan . . ."

"All right, all *right*."

"See, I'll have to go on record myself as saying that you knew about it. You can understand that."

"Sure."

"How did you hear about it?"

"From Kate."

"Mind expanding on that?"

Dan took a long breath. "You know from Maggie that Kate was irrational on the subject of Remords. She told me in Paris that their names would be linked down through history because she was arranging to be buried beside him in the Sarlat cathedral. I figured she'd gone over the line and I started to humor her. She said she knew what I was thinking but that they would be glad enough to have her when they found out that she was prepared to make the cathedral a gift of the Remords reliquary.

"When she saw that I didn't know what she was talking about, she said that, for my information, it was a cross set with a priceless ruby which Saint Louis had given to Remords. Just then, Maggie came into the room and they had that crazy set-to, Kate slapped her face, Maggie stormed out and Kate then left in the car with Billy. Well, the next morning I took the early train to Toulouse—Maggie just wouldn't get up at that hour so I went alone. The train got in around one-thirty. I went to the library and looked the thing up. I should have told you the truth, but when she was murdered, I thought maybe it was for that, and I damn well didn't want to be the only one on board who seemed to know anything about it."

Dade said, the crocodile eyes half closing, "But you thought at the time that her death was an accident. That's how you referred to it."

"Well, I didn't think that."

"You telling me you thought all along she was murdered?"

"I damn well knew that everyone on this barge had a motive to kill her."

"What was yours?"

Dan turned and faced him again. "Money. Maggie doesn't know this, but I'm broke. I guess that's why I'm so irritable. And I'll tell you this—if Kate had had that reliquary on her—"

"You might have killed her for it? But you'd be stuck with the difficulty of getting rid of it."

"Yeah." Then Dan said with an effort at humor, "I've got a lot of problems but, unfortunately, that isn't one of them." He gave Dade a thin smile.

When Dade got back to the cabin Ellen was lying on the bunk, her shoes off, reading Apicius on Roman cookery and making notes on a pad.

"What are you doing?"

"Translating a sauce for boiled ostrich."

"Say, once we get home, you're not going to be doing any testing, are you?"

"Aha!" She exclaimed, her nose in her book.

"What?"

"Here's a helpful hint to keep the birds from going bad: 'Cum plumis elixare omnibus malius erit.'"

"You gonna boil them with their feathers on? By God, if you try it—!" Dade had pulled off his jacket, getting ready to wash up. First, he took out his notebook and made notes of what Olivia had told him, leafed back through the other notes he had made and then, tapping his pencil on the pad, he frowned, muttering "Bugger Bognor!" under his breath.

Ellen sat straight up and asked, startled, "What did you say?"

He looked at her blankly for a moment and then replied, "Oh, I was just quoting the late King George the Fifth. Those were his last words."

"Are you serious?"

"Well, his official last words are given as, 'How is the empire?' but what he really said, as I understand it, was 'Bugger Bognor!'"

"Bognor?"

"Bognor Regis!" he said impatiently. "That's that watering-place to which his doctors sent him to recuperate. He didn't, and on his deathbed, his majesty is reputed to have trumpeted out 'Bugger Bognor!' and then expired. It must have been embarrassing to say such a thing and then to realize, in the final seconds of life, that those were to be your last words—and even more embarrassing to have been present at his demise and then have to go out and repeat what he said to reporters assembled from all over the world."

"I still have no idea what you're talking about."

"I'm talking about—or am about to talk about—Lyme Regis, but every time I think of Lyme Regis, I think of Bognor Regis and that makes me think of 'Bugger Bognor!' Now, do you understand?"

"No."

"Of course you do! Lyme Regis is the place where there's a whispering wall, which the gentle Jane happened to use in *Persuasion*, same as the one Christopher Wren built into St. Paul's."

"What is all this about whispering walls?"

"Remember what happened to Kate at Sarlat?" Ellen stared at him. "I didn't tell you?"

"You have told me nothing."

"Sorry!" He gave her a look of chagrin and then summarized what he had found out about Kate laughing to herself and the name Manitoba.

"Maybe it's the punch line of a joke she had just remembered. It's only a guess."

"It's a good one."

"Your turn. Care to make a guess as to who done it? I mean, what's your hunch?"

Grinning at her, he shook his head. "I don't guess."

"Just this once?" He shook his head again. She said with a side-long look, "Your mentioning St. Paul's just reminded me of something."

"Oh?"

"What Charles the Second said when he first saw it. Do you remember?"

"Remind me."

"Make a guess who done it and I will. You're dying to know."

"I am?"

"Yes."

"No."

"All right for you." Seeing something out the porthole, she said, "Here comes Marbeau. We'd better hurry."

Rinsing his face, he asked, "You miss me?"

"No."

"Want to hear what else I've been up to?" he asked, stropping his razor.

"No."

"I suppose the same goes for the dirt about Kate." She sat bolt upright on the bunk, banging her head. "Gotcha," he said.

"What dirt?"

"Keep your voice down. First, I'm going to tell you, then I want you to do some checking up for me." Quickly, he summarized Olivia's story.

Ellen stared at him, incredulous. "Where was Leo during all this?" she asked.

"That's a good question."

"You mean, with a play at stake, Olivia went down there to argue about a *watch*? I don't believe it!"

"That's why I want you to do some checking up. You remember that lorgnette Maggie used to wear, don't you?"

"I think so. Yes. Yes, I do."

"Ask her what happened to it."

"That's easy enough."

"Is it?" He looked at her in the mirror as he shaved himself, pulling the straight razor over his pink soapy chin.

"I'll simply ask her where she got it, saying I want one. When she tells me it was an antique and one of a kind, I'll just say, 'That's funny. I could have sworn Kate had one like it.'"

He smiled at her happily. "Good girl!"

16

At shortly before five-thirty Dade and Ellen went topside, crossed the saloon where the others were all assembled, sitting under the watchful eye of the red-faced Constable Joliet and waiting to be summoned to give their depositions. Going out on deck, Dade and

Ellen made their way along the gunwale aft and then climbed a ladder to the wheelhouse, behind which the deckhand Mike sat at the big wheel, steering the slow-moving barge. They entered the wheelhouse, where it had been arranged that the depositions would be taken. It was a small cabin with a captain's swivel chair behind a kneehole desk. Opposite stood a wooden visitor's chair. Ellen, present as a witness, was seated on Ned's bunk. Marbeau had placed himself in an armchair in the corner between the bunk and the desk, near Ellen, so that she could translate for him. The depositions were to be taken on a tape recorder.

Dade had seated himself. Through the windows opposite the desk he could see along the length of the saloon roof and across the deck to the canal ahead, winding as it followed the contours of the countryside, the water a shimmering green, disappearing under a low stone bridge in the distance as they glided below the fields, nothing visible on either side but the towpath and the dense rows of plane trees.

Shown in by Constable Joliet, Ned seated himself with a flash of a smile through the shaggy beard, Dade turned on the tape recorder, Marbeau administered the oath in French and Ned went on record as saying that the night before, all eight of the passengers as well as the crew—consisting of himself, Mike, Kitty and the chef, Jean-Claude—had boarded the little bus that accompanied the barge and gone off to dinner at seven o'clock. It had taken them perhaps five minutes to drive the country road to the village of Narouze, a mile away. There, all eight of the passengers were let off at the Brasserie Languedoc, where they were to have dinner, while Ned and the crew went off to have the evening to themselves. The bus was to come back to the brasserie shortly before ten to pick up the passengers. When it turned out that all of them had already set out on foot, Ned and the others drove back to the barge, returning at precisely ten that night.

Ned and Kitty had retired immediately. Mike had gone below into the galley with Jean-Claude to help stow some cases of wine delivered late that afternoon—something that took them less than five minutes—and they had both then gone to bed. Jean-Claude, like Kitty, had a tiny cabin all the way forward, reached by a trap door. Mike slept on the little foredeck, just over the prow. He had since reported to Ned that so far as he knew no one had boarded afterward, which led Ned to believe that all the passengers were already on board when the crew returned.

There were nine cabins on the lower deck, four on either side and one aft, now occupied by Dade and Ellen. Ned explained that since there were sufficient cabins and they were all small the couples had all decided on splitting up, so each person would be able to sleep more comfortably.

The arrangement thus ran: Kate, George, Olivia and Leo on the port side, and on the starboard, Maggie, Dan, Billy and Cissy.

"And the empty cabin my wife and I occupy?" Dade asked. "Was that empty?"

"No."

"Who occupied it?"

Ned flushed, embarrassed. "Well, I did, as a matter of fact. You see—" He broke off, sniffing the air. "Smells all right in here now, doesn't it?" Then, when Dade gave him an inquiring look, Ned explained, "Problem with a dead mouse. Bad smell. We found the dead mouse and disposed of same, but the odor persisted and so I just helped myself to the empty cabin for the night. Then, in the morning, I moved my gear back topside and Kitty tidied up. Actually, I didn't say anything to anyone because I thought Mrs. Mulvaney might object."

"Why?"

He made a face. "She objected to everything."

Dade asked him several more questions. Ned's answers were in the negative: No, nothing untoward had happened, no, he did not have the impression that the deceased feared for her life, no, there was no light he could possibly shed on what had happened. Indeed, when the body was found and they said it had been in the lock since at least eleven o'clock last night, he had found that hard to believe, since he himself had been sure she was in her cabin at that time.

Dade, eyes still on him, sat motionless and said, "What made you sure she was in her cabin?"

Ned blinked several times. "Well, I wasn't sleeping well—strange bunk and all—and I was reading when I thought I heard the lady go to the loo."

"What time was that?" Dade asked softly.

"Let's see. Around one. Yes, it was just after one. I remember now because I had just looked at my watch and was thinking that if I didn't get to sleep, I'd have trouble getting up in the morning."

"Tell me what you heard."

"Her door opening."

"You're sure it was her door?"

"Positive."

"You say you just heard her door opening?"

"Well, the door opened and closed and then opened and closed again."

"How long afterward?"

"Oh, just a matter of minutes."

"But it couldn't, of course, have been Mrs. Mulvaney you heard because at one o'clock in the morning she was already dead." Ned nodded. Dade went on, "So that it could be that what you heard was someone coming *into* the cabin, closing the door and then going *out* of the cabin, is that possible?"

"Yes."

"Have you mentioned this fact to anyone else?"

"No."

"Don't." Dade looked at him levelly. "Don't mention what you've told us to anyone, understand?"

Ned nodded slowly. "I understand," he said.

17

The next to be shown in was Maggie. "Am I the first?" she asked. "I mean, of us? Well, of course, I must be." She seemed nettled, as if having to make her appearance ahead of the others deprived her of a star's entrance. Then she said in a matter-of-fact voice, "I think I should tell you that I don't believe my sister was murdered." She held up a hand, as if to forestall interruption. "No, I've thought about it. Her death was a freak accident. Now that I've realized that, I feel much calmer about it."

The inspector had risen. Dade presented him to her again. He kissed her hand and she said with a flawless accent, "*Enchanté, monsieur l'inspecteur.*"

"*Mais, vous parlez français, madame!*" he said, surprised.

She shook her head. "Not at all. I can pronounce it but I can't speak it. Once, I was up for a part in a picture where I had to speak some French, so I got a divine French actor to take me to a restaurant where I knew the director was having dinner and arrange to have the actor talk French to me, you know, tell me stories and so forth, funny anecdotes, and I would laugh and clap. I knew I had to say something, so I had memorized a French menu and I would cry out the name of some dish every time he paused in expectation. I didn't get the part but the actor was another matter." She flashed a smile at them and then frowned slightly. "Was I married then? I think I must have been. I was always married. Dan is my fourth." She drew herself erect with a quick sigh, clasping her hands in front of her, arms extended, and said, "Well, how may I help you?"

Dade turned on the tape recorder. Marbeau put Maggie under oath. Dade explained to her that these depositions were concerned principally with everyone's movements the night before, then asked her what time she had left the restaurant.

"Let me see. Billy and Cissy left before coffee to go for a walk, then George went lurching off to the lavatory and—ah, yes—Kate looked at her watch and said that it was nine o'clock and that she wanted to go. She then left with her doggie bag and we left a few minutes later."

"Were Leo and Olivia still there?"

"Yes."

"Did you and Dan then catch up with Kate?"

"No. She was gone by the time we got outside. Kate walks—walked—much faster than I do."

"And where did you go from there?"

"Back to the barge."

"Know what time you got there?"

"Oh, I have no idea. Wait a minute—yes, I do. I remember Dan thought his watch had stopped or something because it said only nine-thirty, and he asked me the time and nine-thirty it was. You know, on the barge you get sleepy and your time sense tends to get thrown off."

"You see any of the others?"

"No. We went right to bed."

"Did you leave your cabin at any time during the night?"

"You mean, to go potty?"

"For any reason."

"No." She crossed her trousered legs and studied her hands.

"You mentioned a picture you're about to start."

"*Jericho.*"

"Good role?"

She met his eyes. "I couldn't ask for a better part."

"After that go-round about the bishop, you said your sister slapped your face."

"What of it?"

"Couldn't she have had you replaced in the motion picture if she so wished?"

Maggie reddened with anger and exclaimed, "Well *really!*" Dade shut off the tape recorder and started to say something to her. Riding over him, Maggie said, "You told me we were to be asked about our movements the night she was killed! I certainly didn't expect to be cross-examined on my professional life!"

Leaning toward her, Dade said, "You listen here, Maggie. I've got two things to say to you. First, the French authorities have asked me to get these depositions from all of you. These depositions are concerned with establishing opportunity and motive. Second, I'm trying to help you. Think of this as a trial run. These are the questions you're going to be asked by the Public Prosecutor and the French authorities, and I want to tell you something, those boys play rough. This is the time to think your answers through. I'm being a friend. Don't turn your back on me."

Her face softened and her violet eyes met his. "I'm sorry. I overreacted. They make jokes about the kind of part you'd kill for and that's what this is, but of course such a notion in real life is . . . well, it's just unthinkable, that's all. She was my *sister.*"

Switching the machine back on, Dade asked, "Did Kate in fact intend to have you replaced?"

"Yes."

Dade picked up a pencil from the desk and toyed with it. "You and Dan have any other business dealings with her?"

"Dan?" She looked puzzled. "Dan writes thrillers. She had nothing to do with publishing."

"What about *Jericho*?"

"Oh, you mean the money he got from the studio for the rights? Well, Kate did want them to buy it, but she didn't want to pay Dan's price if she could help it. As it happens, the studio had to bid half a million to get it, no thanks to her, she fought them tooth and nail, and when Dan was stupid enough to put half of it in a joint business venture with George—which that damn fool of a financial adviser Billy recommended—and then lose almost all of it, she was delighted, and said that the two of them had gotten exactly what they deserved. So much for Dan's business dealings with my late sister."

Dade studied her, lips pursed. She looked across at him inquiringly. "Have you ever heard of something called the Remords reliquary?"

"You asked me that this morning."

"Now, I'm asking you under oath."

"Well, the answer is still the same. No, I have not."

"All right, that'll do it. Thank you, Maggie," he said, shutting off the machine and getting to his feet.

She rose, adjusting her wimple. "Aren't you going to arrest me?"

"You kill her, Maggie?"

"Goodness, no! But you're so clever, Dade, I'm sure you could make out a case proving I did, and you're so persuasive I'd probably end up believing you and confessing!" She gave him a blinding smile, then sweeping it across Ellen and Marbeau like a searchlight. Dade stepped to the door, opening it for her, and taking her elbow, steered her toward Joliet, who started to help her down the narrow companion ladder.

"Would you be so kind as to ask your husband to join us?" Dade asked.

"Is he next? Oh, I see! You want to talk to him before I get a chance to brief him on what I said! What a clever man you are!" Waving, she took Joliet's hand and started down the narrow ladder.

After Joliet showed Dan in, Dan stood in the doorway for a moment or two, looking at each of them in turn. He had put on a white cable-stitched pullover, which made his deeply tanned skin seem even darker. When Dade greeted him, Dan did not answer at first. Then, abruptly, he said to Dade, "Look, I'm sorry as hell about how I behaved."

"It's all right," Dade said. "This business has put everybody under a strain." Dade introduced him to Marbeau, who placed him under oath, Dan seated himself, Dade turned on the tape recorder and asked him about his movements after he left the restaurant. Dan's account was exactly the same as Maggie's. When asked whether he had left his cabin at any time during the night, he said he had not.

Dade said, "Now, for the record, I'd like you to tell us what you know about the Remords reliquary." Dan repeated what he had told Dade earlier, finishing up his account with the remark, "So, when I got to Toulouse—well, you know, writers go to libraries the way Germans go to lectures. I'm sure you've heard what they say about themselves: when a German dies, if there are two signs, one pointing to Heaven and the other to Lectures on Heaven, the German will go to the second place!"

He broke off, then looked up, a rare smile on his face. The smile was crooked, looking as if he had put it on hastily, and it gave his face a slightly unfocused look. Then, he said, "Anyway, I went to the library and read up on the thing. That's all I can tell you about it."

"Did you go to the library alone?"

"Yes."

"What about Maggie?"

"She stayed in Paris to go shopping and took a later train."

"Anybody else take the train with you?"

"No. Come to think of it, all the others arrived at the hotel in Toulouse alone—I mean the hotel where we met the bus that took us to the barge."

Dade nodded, not saying anything for a moment. When Dan started to rise, Dade said, stopping him, "One last thing: were you on good terms with the deceased?"

Dan's features hardened. He looked at Dade stonily. "You mean, because she was planning to have Maggie replaced in *Jericho*?

What did you expect me to do, sing and dance? I was mad as hell. Both of us were."

"But that just happened, didn't it?"

"It happened in Paris after that bullshit go-round about the bishop, when Maggie referred to him as a prick."

"I meant, earlier. Was there already trouble back in the States between you and Kate?"

"I'd like to know where the hell you get off making assumptions like that!" Angry red spots appeared under his cheekbones.

"It isn't an assumption, it's a question. Were you on good terms?"

"Of course we were!"

"We've had testimony about an investment you went into with George, where the two of you lost practically everything."

"So?"

"We've also had testimony that Kate was delighted and said that the two of you got exactly what you deserved."

"That is what she said." The mouth closed in a firm line.

"I see."

"I hope to Christ that isn't your idea of a motive for murder."

"No, but it does suggest that perhaps you and Kate were not on such good terms as you've told us."

"Oh, *Jesus*—!" Dan's voice was filled with contempt.

Dade leaned forward and pressed a button, shutting off the tape recorder. "Dan," he said, "if an investigation turns up evidence that there was really bad blood between the two of you—which is what her remark suggests—then you're better off just saying so here and now."

Dan looked around impatiently and then gestured at the tape recorder and said, "Turn that thing back on!" Dan had raised his voice. Behind him, Dade could hear a note of indignation in Marbeau's hushed voice as he asked Ellen questions about what was being said and Ellen's rapid, murmured replies.

Dade switched the tape recorder back on, and meeting Dan's eyes, said, "The question is, if you and Kate were on good terms, what was her motive for making such a remark?"

"This is what happened. The studio in which she had a controlling interest paid me a lot of money for *Jericho*. Rather than give half of it to the government, I put it into a tax shelter with George, something Billy found for us. We each put two hundred and fifty thousand into this company—they owned rolling stock and leased it out. Billy told us we'd make money four ways: we'd get ourselves a depreciation allowance, a tax-investment credit, we'd get deductions for interest and then, the actual profit for leasing the stock. You couldn't lose, right? That's what we thought. How were we to know that people would somehow stop leasing boxcars the way they used to? We didn't make a dime.

"Then George came to me, all shook up. He said it was worse than he thought. We were going down the tube. He said somebody had come to him with an offer to buy us out for ten cents on the dollar. He didn't know what the hell to do and left the whole decision up to me. I said the first loss is the best, so we sold out and each of us came out of the whole mess with twenty-five grand." He shifted in his chair. "Makes a nice story, doesn't it? As good old Nigel Dennis says, 'One is always excited by descriptions of money changing hands. It's much more fundamental than sex.' " He sat back, crossing his feet and firmly gripping the arms of the visitor's chair.

"Kate was delighted because Billy had offered her in on the same deal and she'd turned him down cold and then tried to get us to turn him down, too. We thought we knew better. That remark of hers was nothing more than the good old-fashioned 'I told you so.' " Dan gave him a cold smile. "See? No bad blood. Nothing. Satisfied?" Dade nodded, staring off into space, abstracted. Dan said, leaning forward, "You were just off on a fishing expedition, weren't you?"

Dade did not answer for a moment but only continued looking off at nothing. Then, coming back to himself, he turned to face Dan and said, " 'I told you so.' That's very interesting. Yes."

Dan said, leaning forward again, as if trying to get Dade's attention, "But there was something more to it than that. That was all the money George had, I mean, of his own. It was inherited money and Kate couldn't touch it. It was a threat to her. She never wanted George to be independent. Well, that's Kate for you. She played games with people but she never cheated. And she always quit winners."

"Until now."

"Yes. Until now." The eyes hardened again, then shifted away and stared out through the windows at the rippling waters of the canal through which they moved, colorless in the twilight.

18

Cissy Schuyler entered, wearing a white linen dress with blue piping and a sailor's collar and rope-soled blue canvas espadrilles. Her child's face was framed by a broad-brimmed straw hat held on by a blue bandanna tied under her chin.

Dade introduced himself and Ellen and then presented the inspector to her. She smiled at them all and seated herself, folding her narrow hands in her lap. She looked at Dade attentively, as if waiting to be called on by the teacher. Dade sat back, clasping his big hands over his middle. He said. "You look awful young to be Dan's little sister."

"I'm twenty-five."

"No!"

"Yes, I am."

"Well, you look about fourteen."

She giggled, like a child being tickled. "Well, Dan *is* older than I am by, let's see, sixteen years."

"Then you must have a lot of brothers and sisters."

"No, none." Her face sobered. "Our parents wanted more but they were never able to have any—that is, until me. I was sort of an accident, what they call a change-of-life baby."

"But a happy accident, I'm sure."

"No." She looked at him gravely. "My mother died giving birth to me. It broke my father's heart and he followed her a year later."

"I'm very sorry."

"It's all right. I don't mean to sound unfeeling, but I never knew them, of course. Dan is the one who suffered. He loved them both. He was sent away to boarding school and I was reared by my maternal grandparents. They're gone now and there are just the two of us left."

"Is that how come you moved to California, to be near him?"

She shook her head. "I came out because we inherited a little property from about the only relative we had left. I didn't have a penny, nothing but a job as a typist in a title company, so this mattered to me, but I had to get Dan's written consent to sell it and he couldn't make up his mind and couldn't make up his mind—this, please understand, over something worth, as it turned out, only twenty thousand dollars, a fishing shack out in the woods where he could never live, and then finally I got him to say yes and that was that."

"And you stayed?"

"Thanks to Dan. I was staying with him and Maggie, and Dan kept me waiting two or three weeks, and by then I'd met Billy and we were together. We're going to be married. I expect you know that."

Dade nodded. After Marbeau had put her under oath Dade switched on the tape recorder and said, "If we may, I'd like to turn now to your movements last night after dinner."

"Billy and I left the restaurant and went for a walk."

"Where?"

"Oh, around. I don't know. Ask Billy."

"I'd like your account, please."

"Up the opposite way, through the town square and then off somewhere or other where we found a lane we thought would be fun to explore, and we ended up in a ditch and then across somebody's farm with a lot of dogs barking at us and finally back at the towpath."

"You remember what time you got back to the barge?"

"As a matter of fact, I know exactly what time. I looked at this." She opened her purse and took out a pocket calculator with a digital watch showing through a plastic window. "It was twenty of ten."

"Then what did you do?"

"We got on board and went straight to bed."

"You see anyone else?"

"Olivia and Leo."

"As you got on board?"

"A couple of minutes later when I went to the bathroom. They were both coming down the companionway stairs. I said good night to them and went back to my cabin."

"You leave your cabin again for any reason during the night?"

"No. I went right to sleep and waked up around seven the next morning—my God, that was *this* morning! It seems like a lifetime ago! Anyway, I showered, dressed and went upstairs to breakfast." She gave him a childlike smile, putting her hands on the sides of her head and shaking out her red-gold ringlets. "My life and times."

"And Billy, you say he was with you the entire time?"

She looked around, embarrassed, at Ellen and Marbeau. "You mean, did he spend the night in my cabin with me? Yes, he did. We're always together." She gave him a shy smile.

He leaned forward slightly. "But you didn't go with him down to that château, or am I mistaken?"

"When we got to Paris I didn't feel very well, jet lag, I guess, so I stayed on alone in the hotel while Billy drove Kate down to Montalban. I was fine in the morning. I took the train to Toulouse and Billy met me."

"You knew, then, that she was going to visit the tomb of Remords?"

"Yes."

"She talk about Remords in your hearing?"

"Yes."

"She talk about the Remords reliquary?"

She seemed to hesitate for a moment. Then she said, "Yes."

"What did she say about it?"

"Only that she was going to donate it to the cathedral. I mean, where Remords is buried. If they'd let her be buried beside him."

"Did that give you the impression it was in her possession?"

She looked puzzled for a moment. Then, her face cleared and she said, "Oh, I see what you mean. No. She said something about acquiring it."

"What did she say?"

"Just that." Cissy gave a little shrug. "You know how Kate was. She would let things drop and then, if you asked her about them, she got very close-mouthed, so I didn't press her."

"Do you know much about the reliquary?"

"I don't even know what it is."

Thanking her, Dade got to his feet, shutting off the tape recorder.

Cissy remained seated, her head turned slightly, gazing out the window to her left at the tranquil waters of the canal. Then she said, turning to meet his eyes, the child's face serious, "This sounds like an impertinence, but is there any chance at all that you could be wrong?"

"The body was put in the water after she was dead."

"Oh, I didn't mean any chance that she wasn't murdered. I understand that, even though my mind keeps going back to it, as if some part of me didn't yet believe it. No, I meant, is there any chance that she wasn't . . . murdered by someone on board?"

"I'm afraid not."

She nodded slowly, looking at the floor and saying, "I see what you mean. If it had been some . . . some stranger, there'd be no reason for him to throw her body in the lock, that whoever did it wanted to make it look like an accident. Is that what you're saying?" Dade studied her, not answering. She got slowly to her feet and walked mechanically toward the door. When Dade opened it for her, she hesitated, turning toward him, her little girl's face ashen, her eyes bright, a disbelieving smile on her face. "It's . . . horrible," she half whispered. "Horrible!" Then, she went quickly out of the cabin.

After Ellen had translated the substance of her remarks for Marbeau's benefit, Marbeau nodded, saying, "A farmer in the neighborhood reported trespassers last night. He heard his dogs barking and saw two figures hurrying away, a man and a woman. The time was just after nine-thirty."

Dade nodded, silent.

Billy Penrose's deposition corresponded exactly with Cissy's. He sat motionless in his chair, his arms folded. The scarred face was bluish with a heavy shadow of beard. He looked steadily at Dade through his grayish lenses, tinted at the top like the windshield of a car. His eyes were very dark, with long straight lashes and thick straight brows.

Dade laced his fingers, pursing his lips and putting his head on one side, studying Billy. Then he asked, "You leave your cabin at any time last night?"

"Absolutely not. And, for the record, it was Cissy's cabin. We spent the night together." Dade swiveled in his chair, crossing one ankle over a knee, and placing his hands behind his head, stared out the window. After a few moments of silence, Billy stood up. "Well, if that's all—" he began.

Dade straightened up, swiveled back around to face Billy and said, "No, it's not all. Sorry. I have another question."

"Go ahead."

"Sit down, please." Billy sat down on the edge of his chair, resting his palms on his knees. Dade said, "You left Paris with your aunt?"

"Yes."

"And went where?"

"Montalban."

"That's that château?"

"Yes."

"Where is it?"

"Just outside Cahors."

"How come you went there?"

"It belonged to that bishop. She wanted to spend a night in the place."

"They take paying guests?" Billy nodded. "And the next day?"

"I drove down to Toulouse to meet Cissy's train."

"You say you drove."

"We rented a car in Paris. Kate wouldn't drive in France, so I had to."

"You drive Kate to Sarlat?"

"No."

"Why not? You said that château is near Cahors and that's only about an hour from Sarlat, isn't it?"

"She was already gone when I got up the next morning."

"Oh? Was there trouble between you?"

"No. She knew I didn't want to go and I figured this was just her way of letting me off the hook."

"How was her mood at Montalban?"

"Fine." Billy looked at him levelly.

"I should think it would have been. After all, she was visiting the place where her ancestor lived and that was a matter of some importance to her." Billy nodded. "She talk about him on the drive down?"

"Yes."

"Tell you stories about him, did she?"

"Yes."

"She tell you the story of how Saint Louis gave him a reliquary?" Billy leaned back in his chair. "Yes. Yes, she did."

"What did she tell you about it?"

"She described it."

"And?"

"She told me she was in the process of acquiring it."

"And what did you say?"

"Me?"

"Well, you were her financial adviser, weren't you? You must have had some opinion of the investment she was making."

"I thought it was crazy. She was buying it just to give it back to the cathedral so they'd bury her there. She didn't stand to make one dime."

"You tell her that?"

"She didn't want to hear what I thought. Not about that."

"And where was she going to take delivery of the reliquary?" Billy shook his head. "I don't know. She never told me."

Dade got to his feet and walked around the desk. Billy eyed him. Tapping his lips with a thick forefinger, Dade said, "Your account tallies with Cissy's, right down to that business about the dogs barking. By the way, what time would that have been?"

Billy hesitated. Then, he said, "I guess a few minutes after nine."

"A few minutes after nine." Dade was standing in front of Billy, arms crossed, leaning against the desk.

"Maybe I have the time wrong. It was pitch dark." Dade reached over and touched the face of the digital watch Billy wore. The numerals lit up for a moment. Dade withdrew his hand, his eyes still on Billy's. Billy did not look away. "I guess I didn't look at my watch," he said.

Dade said, "The two of you were seen to leave the restaurant shortly before nine. Now, where were you between nine and nine-thirty?"

Billy shrugged. "You know."

"I don't know."

"Guess." He picked at a pimple on his scarred face.

"I can't guess my way through a deposition."

"We were off in the bushes screwing, okay? I don't know what the hell time it was." Through the tinted lenses the dark eyes had an opaque look.

Dade went around the desk and sat down again, rubbing the tip of his nose with a blunt forefinger and squinting at Billy. "Now, for the record, let's come to the matter of your business relationship with the deceased."

"I did some investment counseling for her."

"How long have you been doing that? I ask because I last saw your late aunt a little over two years ago and it seems to me you weren't around at that time."

"No, I've only been working for her the last couple of years."

"You make any money for her?"

"I gave her recommendations. Whether she followed them or not was up to her."

"You give George advice?"

The dark eyes flickered. "You heard about that."

"That company he invested in with Dan? Yes, I heard about it. I heard they both lost their shirts and had to sell out for a dime on the dollar."

"Did you also hear that I told them not to sell?" Dade looked at him sharply. "They wouldn't listen. Six months later the company was back on its feet." He ran the flat of his hand over the sleeve of the rust-colored cashmere sweater he wore, smoothing out the wrinkles. "The stock went through the roof and they got gobbled up by another company at a handsome profit for everybody concerned."

"Except George and Dan."

"Like I say, they were warned."

"Thank you," said Dade abruptly. He shut off the machine.

Billy left the cabin, banging the door behind him.

19

Now, with Leo seated in the visitor's chair, the tape recorder on, Dade said, "We'd like you to give us an account of your movements last night."

"I had just the one, before going to bed."

Dade said, "Leo, we got to be serious about this."

"Suppose I begin by making a full confession?"

"Please—"

"Naturally, I don't expect to be believed." He gave a brief smile, hardly more than a smirk, and the quick tongue moistened the finely carved lips.

"You and Olivia left the restaurant when?"

"Shortly after nine. We then went our separate ways, which is something we should have done years ago."

"And where did *you* go?"

"For a walk. Around the town. Then I headed back for the barge."

"And got there when?"

"I don't know. Ask Livvy. Somehow, we both got back at the same time. Call it fate."

"You see anybody else?"

"No."

"You sure?"

"I didn't see anybody till I got back to the towpath and saw Livvy there."

"I mean, on board."

"Oh." Leo thought. Then he said, "Yes, it seems to me we saw Cissy on her way to her cabin as we went downstairs."

"And then?"

"We both went to our cabins."

"Leo, you get up at any time during the night?"

"I got up once to go to the bathroom. I was pretty groggy and I remember I started to go into the shower by mistake." He started to laugh. "You know, that once happened to us when we were traveling in the Orient years ago? We were on a sleeper outside Hangchow and somebody mistook our compartment for the toilet. Anyway, I did find the john, used it and went back to bed."

"For the record, what was your business connection with your late sister?"

"She was going to back my new play."

"And then?"

Leo looked uncomfortable. "When we got to Paris she told me she was pulling out. She told everybody."

"Could you have gotten other backing?"

"Money is tight."

"So her proposed withdrawal was a serious blow."

"I've always admired your gift for understatement."

"Did you go to Sarlat with your wife to try to get Kate to change her mind?"

"I didn't even know Livvy had gone there."

"You ride with anybody on the train from Paris to Toulouse?"

"Actually, I took the sleeper Tuesday night."

"You what?"

"Livvy and I had a quarrel. I left her a note. I have since learned that she left me one. We had separate rooms. This is the only case I have ever heard of where the husband and wife managed to run out on each other at the same time."

"You spent the next day—that would be Wednesday—in Toulouse?"

"No, I made a side trip to a town about sixty miles away."

"What town?"

"Condom. To buy postcards for friends."

Ellen's murmured translation broke off abruptly. Marbeau looked puzzled. Dade cleared his throat and stared at the ceiling. Then he said, "Leo, returning to last night, I'd like to hear about what happened after you went back to your cabin."

"Nothing. I went to sleep. This morning Livvy and I went up to breakfast around half past seven. I think all of us did. And we just sat around, waiting for Kate to surface." The bald head turned slightly. "I'll rephrase that." The lizard's tongue darted out, moistening the lips again.

Dade said after a moment, "The day before Kate boarded the barge, she made a pilgrimage to the tomb of her ancestor, Bishop Remords." Leo nodded. "She talk much about him?" Leo imitated, with a jerk of his head, bulging eyes and a lolling tongue, the face of a man falling through the trapdoor of a gallows. Pointing at the tape recorder, Dade said, "I'll need a spoken answer."

"Words fail me."

"I take it that means yes?"

"She has been talking about him constantly for the last two years."

"She talk much about his reliquary?"

Leo burst out laughing. Then, controlling himself, he said, "I'm sorry! For some reason, your saying that reminded me of something I read years ago. An eighty-year-old socialite married a girl of nineteen and gave her a fabulous diamond on a chain and some birdbrain society columnist wrote that 'the groom's gift to the bride was an antique pendant.'" Leo guffawed.

"This reliquary isn't a pendant, Leo."

"Oh? Well, I can't tell you anything about it, excepting that Kate said—oh, way back when she first heard about it—that she'd like to buy it, but it seems the damn thing had disappeared. Help you any?"

"Thank you very much."

After Olivia had been sworn in and was seated in the visitor's chair, she crossed her sleek legs and adjusted the thick turtleneck collar of the mauve sweater she wore, leaned back, elbows on the arms of the chair, twisted her fingers together loosely, as if to display the Greek gold rings fashioned into frogs, serpents and dolphins that she wore, tilted back her head and studied Dade through half-closed eyes. The planes of her face, illuminated by the warm light of early evening coming in through the windows, were softened, the skin golden. It was very quiet, the only sounds, the faint whir of the tape recorder and the thrumming of the barge's engines as it swam through the flat waters of the canal. At Dade's request she repeated her explanation of what had happened to her watch and how she had followed Kate to Sarlat to confront her. Asked about her movements the night before, she explained that after leaving the restaurant she and her husband had gone back to the barge separately.

Dade asked, "Why?"

"We were having a quarrel. It's gone on since Paris. It's personal and has nothing to do with all this. That's all I'll say."

Dade sighed. "All right, after you left the restaurant, you say you went back to the barge."

"Yes."

"By what route?"

"Along the main road."

"You see anybody along the way?"

"No. It was pitch dark. Oh, I saw Leo. He got back just moments after I did."

"Then how is it you didn't see him on the road?"

"Oh, *I* don't know!" She was suddenly impatient.

"Where was he when you saw him?"

"I *heard* him. He said my name as I was climbing onto the barge and then climbed on after me."

"Had he been following you?"

"Yes. Yes, he had."

"That's a gravel road, the road back from Narouze. Naturally, if he'd been following you, you would have heard his footsteps."

"Yes, I did. I remember now."

"Then how is it he had to speak your name to get your attention?"

"We were having a quarrel! I was trying to get away from him! Don't you understand?"

Dade did not say anything for several moments. Then he asked, "What time did you get back to the barge?"

"I don't know."

"You see anybody on board?"

"Yes. Yes, we saw Cissy, on her way to her cabin from the bathroom."

"Then maybe I can help you. Cissy says she got back at twenty of ten and went into the bathroom a couple of minutes later. Is that when you think you got back?"

"Yes, that sounds right."

Dade said, doodling with the pencil on the pad, "You said you left the restaurant shortly after nine. That means it took you over half an hour to walk to the barge."

"Yes."

"It's only a mile."

"Well, I . . . I stopped along the way."

"Where?"

"There's a stone chapel on the way at the edge of a little cemetery. The chapel's in ruins. I went in to look at it and—oh, to sit down and think. I guess I was there a short time."

"I see." Dade studied her. "You leave your cabin during the night for any reason?"

"No, I did not."

"Sure?"

"I most certainly am. I didn't leave the cabin until this morning, quite early. Mike was just setting out on his bike to get breakfast rolls in the village and Dan was doing his Air Force exercises on the towpath, which I wish Leo would do but he simply won't."

"Turning to something else for a moment, I'd like to know whether Kate told you much about Bishop Remords."

"More than I wanted to know."

"She mention a reliquary?"

"That thing you asked us about this morning? Frankly, I don't know. I don't remember. When she got started on that subject, I just tuned her out."

"I see." Dade sighed. Then, he said, "Livvy, you want to reconsider and give us some idea what you and Leo quarreled about, just for the record? You know, this is all confidential."

"Sorry. Believe me, it has nothing to do with all this. Besides, we've been quarreling for ages. Really, what we most need is a good long vacation from one another. Say, about twenty years." She gave a short, bitter laugh. "But at this point in our lives, we can't even afford twenty minutes. Which is why we're described in the columns as 'inseparable.'" She gave him what he had once heard her describe as a prop smile. He switched off the machine. She got to her feet, smiling at him again, and this time it was a star's smile.

George stood swaying in the doorway, blinking at them with red-rimmed eyes. Marbeau administered the oath and then Dade seated George, asking him the same question he had asked the others.

George answered slowly, "When I left the restaurant? Well, I got up from the table and I went into the back, looking for the john. I opened the wrong door—it was the back door—and I just went out that way and relieved myself against a wall."

"Why didn't you come back inside?"

George looked around at the three of them, the reddened eyes blinking, a paw of a hand reaching inside his shirt and scratching the pelt of hair on his thick chest. "What?"

"I asked you why you didn't come back inside."

"Well, Kate was gone—"

"But you didn't know that."

"Well, the truth is . . ." he began, "I'd had a lot to drink but I felt pretty sober and then, from one moment to the next, I crossed over that line and I was afraid I was just going to fall down, so when I got outside in the cold air, I stayed outside. I just stood there, leaning my head against the back of the building. There was one of those plaques there that they put up where somebody in the Resistance was killed by the Germans and I remember trying to focus my eyes so I could read it and then figuring out that the French words meant the kid was only seventeen and I thought, Jeez, I'm standing right where he was shot and I tried to imagine how he felt, did he live long enough to know what was happening? I had this fantasy about lying there on the ground in my own blood and thinking, My God, I'm bleeding, I'm bleeding a lot, and feeling, Oh, Christ, I've got to stop bleeding or I'll die. I could even smell the blood, that metallic smell, and I said, Oh, no, and then I couldn't see anything but I could still hear. I could hear footsteps, people running and shooting and voices yelling. All of this seemed to go on forever. I was like two people. I mean, I was me, but at the same time I felt as if I was caught up in someone else's world and I couldn't get out, I felt the way you feel when you have a dream, a terrible dream, and you know it's only a dream but you can't wake up."

He sighed deeply, rubbing his eyes with the heels of his hands. "All of a sudden I was too damn drunk to go back inside. I thought if I did, Kate would start in on me and besides, I wanted to be out in the air, so I just walked. I knew I was staggering, but the night air was beginning to sober me up, so I went on walking as fast as I could. A couple of times, I fell down. When I got back, I was a mess."

"What road did you take?"

"I didn't. I walked through the fields. I didn't want to run into any of the others."

"And did you?"

"No."

"What time did you get back to the barge?" George shrugged. Pointing at the machine, Dade said, "I'll need a spoken answer."

George leaned toward the machine and said, "I don't know."

"You see any of the others on board?"

"No. I just went straight to bed."

"Was the bus back when you got to the barge?"

"The bus?" George thought about that for a few moments. Then he answered, "No, it wasn't back." Dade did not say anything more for a few moments. George continued to meet his eyes, almost defiantly. He shifted his big hulking frame in his chair.

"Your late wife spoke to me on the phone about something called the Remords reliquary."

"I know she was about to acquire it and have it placed on his tomb."

"From whom was she going to acquire it?"

"I don't know. She never told me any of the particulars."

"This morning you told me you'd never heard of it. May I ask why you did that?"

"This morning, I didn't know it was murder and I didn't know I'd be asked questions about it under oath." He had begun to perspire. "Look, I'm her heir, okay? You know that. Well, I damn well don't want to shell out a bundle for some damn souvenir so's I can hand it over to the church in her memory. When all this happened, I thought, By God, if somebody shows up with that lousy keepsake and tries to fob it off on me, saying she arranged to buy it, well, I'm just going to play dumb and say no. I don't want to buy it, I don't want to donate it to anybody and I don't want to hear any more about it, if that's okay."

"How is it you didn't go to Sarlat with your wife?"

"Are you kidding?"

"Where did you go?"

"Straight to Toulouse."

"You take the train with Dan?"

"No."

"Why not?"

George tipped him a wink. "I didn't get out of visiting the bishop in Sarlat only to spend six hours cooped up with Dan."

Dade took a long breath through flared nostrils, nodding. Then he said, "A last question: you leave your cabin at any time during the night?"

"No, I didn't."

Dade looked at him closely. "But when a man has had that much to drink . . ."

George didn't answer. Dade pressed him. Then George flushed and said abruptly, "I pissed in the sink, okay?" Dade rose, shutting off the tape recorder. George struggled to his feet, nodded at all of them and made his way unsteadily to the door, going out and pulling it shut behind him.

Dade sighed, arching his back. Repeating Maggie's reference to the doggie bag, Dade asked Marbeau whether his men had mentioned finding one on the path or in the lock. Marbeau shook his head. "Maybe it was just floating in the lock and went unnoticed."

Marbeau was vehement in his denial. Everything had been noted. He himself had gone over the list in detail. "The answer is no." Marbeau looked thoughtful. "Perhaps the lady finished what she took with her while she was waiting on the towpath and then threw the bag into the canal."

Ellen shook her head. "She hated littering," she said. "We once had a conversation about it. We both felt the same way. She would never have done such a thing, any more than I would have."

"Then the doggie bag should have been found on the towpath where she was killed," Dade said. "Strange." They all looked at each other. Then, shaking his hand, Marbeau thanked Dade for taking the depositions.

Reacting to the word, Dade pulled out his pocket notebook and gold pencil and wrote down a word. "Depose!" he said with a broad smile.

"Depose?" echoed Ellen.

"To deposit for safekeeping or to dispose of!" Dade answered.

Marbeau looked from him to Ellen, not understanding. Dade tried to explain himself, failed, and turning to Ellen, said to her, "You tell him."

"How? You made up the word. It doesn't exist in French."

"Opponym," Dade said to him. "My term for words that mean their own opposites." Marbeau looked blank. Dade said to her, "Can't you think of one in French?"

Her face lit up. "You had one on your last list!" Turning to Marbeau, she exclaimed, *"Merde!"* Marbeau bristled. Ellen covered her face with her hands, trying not to laugh.

Joliet put his head in the door then, to tell them the car was waiting to take them to Bram, so that Dade could place his overseas telephone call.

"I'll just get my coat," Dade said, starting out of the cabin with Ellen. The barge had stopped and Mike was tying it up for the night alongside the towpath.

20

Leaving the wheelhouse, Dade and Ellen went along the gunwale toward the foredeck. The curtains in the saloon were drawn, but through an open window they could hear raised voices, Maggie's, Dan's and Billy's. As soon as Dade and Ellen entered the saloon, silence fell. Maggie, Dan and Billy looked in their direction. There was no one else in the room. With a brief nod at the three of them, Dade led Ellen down the companionway stairs and along the corridor to the cabin.

Back in their cabin, Dade pulled on his overcoat.

Ellen said to him, "What do you think?"

"Dunno."

"Everybody seemed quite straightforward. There was nothing anybody said that struck me as odd. But I do have this hunch."

"Your honor, although I don't have anything much in the way of what you folks call evidence, my wife's got this hunch . . ."

"Very funny." She gave him a cold blue stare.

"I was just teasing."

"After a point, teasing can become cruelty."

"I was only joking."

"I can't always tell." She folded her arms.

"Well, hereafter, when something I say is a joke, I'll hold up my hand." He raised his right hand to demonstrate. She turned away quickly, trying to hide an involuntary smile. He saw it and put an arm around her waist. "Ellen, honey," he said, "it's just my habit of mind. Myself, I've often found that what's called intuition skews the mind. I like to proceed by the rules of evidence. And, as for there not being anything odd—"

"Well, I'll tell you what I'm going to do: I'm going to let my intuition guide me. I don't want you to tell me what you think. And we'll just see who gets there first."

"All right."

"Promise?"

"Promise."

Then, remembering something, Ellen said, "What did you mean, 'as for there not being anything odd'?"

"You said you didn't want to know what I think."

"I want to know facts."

"What's odd is the fact that whoever went into Kate's cabin at one in the morning didn't knock. That suggests that whoever it was must have known she wasn't there."

"The murderer! Searching for the reliquary!"

"In the first place, there's no evidence that she ever had it in her possession. In the second place, the police have searched the barge and the passengers and there's no sign of anything like that on board. No one has left this barge since last night—remember, all the footprints show people returning to the towpath, none leaving it— no one, that is, except Olivia, and I had her under observation the entire time she was gone. And, apart from everything else, I can't imagine myself killing a woman for a priceless ruby and then pawing through her effects hoping to find it. So why did whoever it was go into her cabin at one in the morning? In search of something? What? One other thing puzzles me."

"Which is?"

"That 'I told you so.'"

"Dan said it. She played games with people."

"That doesn't explain it."

"Dade, of course it does! I think you're trying to make something out of nothing."

"Don't you bullyrag me! When a man's been sucking the hind tit for twenty years and married to Hetty Green in the bargain, for him just to fly in the face of her warning and go into something—and I don't mean just take a flier but go whole hog with everything he's got—well, I just don't see that."

"Why, Dade, it's the oldest story in the world. It's human nature. It's called, 'I'll show *you*.'"

"So you think he just kicked over the traces?"

"Lots of men his age do."

"That's so, that's so. I'm blessed if I know what I'd do without you to keep me honest." He stopped in his tracks, staring at her.

"What is it?"

"Blessed!" He pulled out his notebook and his gold pencil. "Blessed, blessed! Consecrated or cursed! Five down, five to go!" He glanced at his watch, said, "I make it eleven A.M. in Los Angeles," gave her a kiss and went out, meeting Marbeau, who waited for him on the towpath in a police car. Dade and he were driven quickly to the nearby town of Bram, then down a dark street lined with shuttered buildings toward the blue light of the town's police station, a small stone building with barred windows.

Inside, they found themselves in the usual reception room, the drab walls covered by a large map of the vicinity and a bulletin board with an assortment of colored pieces of paper, the countless carbon copies of the notices and receipts endlessly churned out by officialdom.

A lieutenant was waiting for them, a swarthy man with dark morose eyes and a pencil mustache. Shaking hands with them, he seated Dade at a desk, handing him a telephone. Dade placed the call. The operator told him the circuits were busy. Marbeau took the phone from Dade, and identifying himself, told the operator he was sure that she would be able to get through. A few moments later they heard the number ringing. Marbeau handed the phone back to Dade.

After half a dozen rings, the number answered and a woman's voice said, "Manitoba."

Dade's eyes narrowed. He said, "I'm calling you from France. This is an urgent matter. May I speak with someone in charge?"

"I'm sorry," the voice said, "but there's no one in the office at this time. If you'd care to leave your name and number—"

"It's after eleven o'clock in the morning there, isn't it? What time is someone expected?"

"Just a moment, please." She left the line, leaving it open. He could hear her answering other calls. Dade waited a long time. Then she came back on the line, a shade breathless, saying, "I'm terribly sorry to have kept you waiting. No, I really can't answer that question."

"As I say, this is urgent. I'm calling at the behest of the French police."

"You say you're from the police?"

"Do you have a number where you can reach anybody in an emergency?"

"One moment, please." He waited again. Finally she came back on the line, saying, "No, I don't. I'm very sorry."

"Look, this is important—"

"I realize that. There just isn't anything I can do."

"Is this an answering service?"

"Yes. Yes, it is."

"Well, let's just think about it for a moment. These people must pay their bill or you wouldn't be answering their phone."

"Who is this, please? I mean, you don't sound French."

"My name is Cooley and I'm calling you from a French police station. What address do you have for Manitoba?"

"I'm sorry. I'm not authorized to answer any questions."

"All I want to know is their address."

"I really am sorry."

"I'm also an attorney, young woman, this is a case of murder and you wouldn't want me to have the authorities there charge you with obstructing justice, now, would you?"

"Look, I don't really know who you are—" She sounded frightened.

"You look in your file and find out their address."

"I'm all alone here and I have to answer a lot of calls."

"You hear what I said to you? Now, this comes first."

There was a pause, then she said in an altered voice, surrendering, "All right. But you'll have to wait a minute." He waited for a long time. Finally he heard her voice again. "Sir," she said. "Sir, I don't want to get into any trouble with anybody—"

"You're not going to get into any trouble."

"The address we have is 13 Victoria Place, Suite 4, Winnipeg, Manitoba 92349."

Dade repeated it, then asked, "What's the full name of the firm?"

"As I said, Manitoba."

"That's the full name, Manitoba?"

"Well, Manitoba, Inc."

"Inc.? You mean, incorporated?"

"Yes, sir. That's all the information I have."

"That'll do nicely. Good-bye, young lady."

He broke the connection, got hold of the operator and put a call through to a firm of attorneys in San Francisco, asking for someone called Jacob Cohen and insisting that they call him out of a meeting.

At last, an irritable man's voice came on the phone and said, "This is Cohen. What seems to be the trouble?"

"Jake? This here's Dade."

"For Christ's sake, the girl said Dooley and all I could think of was Finley Peter Dunne. What's up?"

"I'm in France, Jake."

"How's the weather?"

"Threatening. This here's a case of murder."

There was a whistle at the other end of the line, then Jake's voice asking anxiously, "Dade, you in some kind of trouble?"

"I'm not in trouble, Jake."

"Well, I'll do what I can but we're corporate lawyers. I don't know anything about—"

"Jake, Jake, just listen. There's a corporation called Manitoba, like in Canada, got that?"

"Manitoba, right."

"Take down this information." Dade gave him the phone number of the answering service and the address. "Now, you find out everything you can about that corporation, who runs it, what their line of work is—and you get back to me at this number." Dade took out the card Marbeau had given him and repeated the telephone number printed on it. "You get hold of somebody there who speaks French, have them call this number and say they have an urgent message for Inspector Marbeau"—he spelled it, trying to keep the impatience out of his voice—"and get me that information as fast as you can, will you do that, Jake?"

"I'll try. You don't happen to know where they're incorporated, do you? See, that's the thing—"

"Just go right down the line."

"They could be offshore—the Bahamas or something—and then I wouldn't be able to find out a damn thing."

"Sully in town?"

"Come *on*, Dade—! I can't go to the IRS with a question like that. It's unethical!"

"Who said anything about the IRS? I just mentioned Sully. He owes you. He owes both of us. Now, if you were to have a drink with him, say in the next ten minutes—"

"It's eleven-thirty in the morning!"

"An Irishman, he don't ask the time of day. Now, if you was to say to him, Sully, I've got this great investment opportunity just come along and Dade, he says to ask you whether you wanted to come in on it with us—tell him that on the phone and he'll get back to you with a yes or no in no time at all."

"It's unethical as hell."

"So is murder. You do like I say."

"I'll have to think about it."

"I'll hold the line."

"All right, all *right*!" Jake banged down the phone.

Dade handed the instrument back to the lieutenant, they shook hands and Dade and Marbeau left the station and got back in the police car.

21

When they returned to the barge it was a quarter to eight. Marbeau got back on board but Dade stayed on shore, wanting some exercise. He walked toward the next lock. The dark waters of the canal were perfectly still, and overhead the black sky was thick with stars.

A voice whispered, "Hey, mistair—you want have good time?" Ellen materialized out of the darkness.

"What I want is to stretch my legs, then go in and get drunk."

"If your flask isn't empty, we can do both at once."

He pulled it out of his pocket, unscrewing the top and handing it to her. She took a short swallow, gasped and handed it back. He helped himself generously, then put the top back on, pocketed the flask and the two of them began to walk briskly toward the next lock a short distance away, identified by a sign over the lock keeper's house as ÉCLUSE DE LA CRIMINELLE. Dade noted the irony with satisfaction and then began to inspect the full lock in the dark, beginning with the end nearest the lighted barge, which was moored a few hundred feet upstream. This lock was very much like the one where Kate had been murdered. He walked past the cords of wood neatly stacked at the side of the path in front of the plane trees, then up and down in the deep clearing that paralleled the towpath for about a hundred feet alongside the length of the lock and ran back perhaps ten feet from the edge of the towpath to the bushes.

Then, taking a small log from the pile of wood at the upstream edge of the lock and walking into the clearing with it, he stopped at the bushes and said, lifting the log in the air, "I'm the murderer. I bash in her skull. She falls to the ground. Now, I'm going to dump the body into the lock, trying to make her death look accidental. But she didn't die instantly, according to the coroner, and there was no water in the lungs. That means I waited. Why? Only possible reason I can think of is that somebody comes by. Almost catches me. I hide. From here I can see the lights of the barge. I wait until whoever it was walks away from me toward it. Now's my chance. I drag the body over to the lock and ease it over the side into the water, which at this point is only about a foot below the stone lip.

"Just then, I discover something: *those glasses*, they're not on the body. They must be in the clearing near the bushes where I killed her. I search. I find them. The chain isn't broken. That means they must have gotten caught on something, a rock or a branch, when I dragged her body across the clearing and the path to the lock, and her head must have been pulled right through the loop of the chain. They have got to be in the lock along with the body if this is to look like an accident."

He stepped closer to Ellen. They looked at each other's shadowy faces in the dark. He could see her eyes gleam. "All right," she said, "but then why carry them over a hundred feet downstream in the other direction and then throw them in?"

"I hear something—" he began.

"Footsteps again? Then you'd lie low, as you did before." Dade hesitated, thinking. "Maybe you *see* something," she suggested.

"What?"

"Oh, I don't know—" Then, something struck her and she said, "*Lights!* That's what you see! The lights of the bus!"

"Bull's eye!" he said. "Here I am, over next to the bushes, a good fifteen feet away from the lock, and all of a sudden I see the lights of the bus just as it starts to turn and come down the slope to the towpath. As soon as it swings around, those headlights will pick me up if I so much as set foot on the towpath at the upstream end. The only chance I've got of not being seen is to stay off the towpath and *run the other way* through the clearing, hidden by bushes, until I get to the *downstream* end of the lock, where the plane trees will screen me from view, and *then* cross the towpath and throw the glasses in there! That's how I hide! And that's why the glasses were found down there, at the other end!" Then his expression changed. He turned and looked at her narrowly in the dark. "But that means she had to have been killed just about ten o'clock last night and every goddamned one of them was back on board then."

"Well, then, the murderer has to have gotten off the barge after they were all in their cabins and gone to the towpath expecting to find her," she said.

Dade put an arm around Ellen's shoulders, at the same time reaching across her to rub the tip of his nose with his knuckles. "Let's see, let's see," he said. "She leaves the restaurant at nine o'clock, obviously in a hurry, not even waiting for her husband to come out of the john. She walks quickly. Maggie and Dan say she was already out of sight when they came out of the restaurant just a minute or so later. At a good clip, she would have walked the mile back in, say, twenty minutes. Now, she wasn't on board when Maggie and Dan got back to the barge at nine-thirty and nobody seems to have seen her after she left the restaurant. All of that suggests that she came directly here to meet someone."

"The murderer," Ellen said.

"But why? Hold it, I've got three whys coming up." He took his arm from Ellen's shoulder and ticked off his points on his thick fingers. "One, why was it so urgent? Here, we've got eight people all having dinner in a restaurant in Narouze. Suddenly she has to leave to meet one of them. Why? Two, all these people are on the barge together. Couldn't she meet whoever it was in Narouze, say, or back on the barge on deck or in her own cabin? Why does this meeting have to take place in the dark, in a clearing next to the towpath beside the lock? And three, it's one thing to have a date with your murderer. It's quite another *to wait forty minutes* for him or her to show up and do you in. *Why?*"

"I don't know."

"Never mind, honey. That stroke of genius about the lights just earned you an Award of Merit."

"You mean, a badge?"

"I'm sure we can get you a badge."

"I want a badge, Dade." His expression changed. She could see him set his jaw in the faint light. "What's the matter?"

"At ten o'clock, they were all back on the barge."

"I just said—"

"*And Mike, he was bedded down on the deck.* So, if our murderer killed her just before ten and was then trapped by the lights of the bus, as you say, and ran to hide, *how did he or she get past Mike to get back on the barge?*"

"I'd just stay here until he was asleep."

"You'd take that chance? All he'd have to do is wake up as you boarded and you'd have sealed your fate, no question about it."

"Maybe they're all in it together."

"If they are, it's the only thing they've ever agreed on. Apart from the fact that none of them cared for her." He stopped in his tracks, scratching his head as if trying to remember something. Then, his face lit up, and turning to her, he began to sing in his deep ringing voice, at the same time waving his arms and lumbering up and down on the path before her, dancing like a bear:

> *The master, the swabber, the boatswain and I,*
> *The gunner and his mate*
> *Loved Mall, Meg and Marian and Margery,*
> *But none of us cared for Kate;*
> *For she had a tongue with a tang,*
> *Would cry to a sailor, Go hang!*
> *She loved not the savour of tar nor of pitch,*
> *Yet a tailor might scratch her where'er she*
> *did itch:*
> *Then to sea, boys, and let her go hang!*

Holding the last note, he balanced on the ball of one foot, arms outstretched.

"That's shocking!"

"That's Shakespeare!"

"Not him, you!"

"Well, hell's bells! She was salty as Lot's wife, Kate was! What's the harm of a joke?"

"I'm going to tell you something about Kate. I asked a few questions while you were gone. She wasn't always like this. Not at all. She was a wallflower with a sister who was a beauty. She married George because she was in love with him, and frankly, I don't think it ever occurred to her that he might be marrying her for her money, and she only began to let herself go after he was blatantly unfaithful to her over and over and over again, did you know that?"

"No, my dear, I must confess, I did not." He was suddenly quiet, falling in step with her, thoughtful now, as she spoke.

"Well, it's as if she were daring him to leave her and, if he did, he wouldn't get a penny, because she'd made all her money long before she met him. Nobody cared for her! I think she knew that. It must be very painful to be in the bosom of a family who only care about you for your money. Yes, it's true enough, Dade. Nobody cared for Kate." She broke off. "I think it must be getting on for dinner time. I don't think we should stay away much longer."

He caught his breath. "Hold everything!"

"What?"

"*Stay!*"

"Stay?"

"To stop from a course of action or to continue with it, as in staying with a project."

"Dade, I'm not altogether sure—"

"You want that merit badge or don't you?"

"All right, stay." She made a face.

From the lighted barge they heard the thin sound of a dinner bell, summoning them.

22

Dinner was about to be served. The tables had been placed end to end to form a refectory board, which was covered with a snowy cloth reaching to the floor. The places were set with the barge's best china, crystal and silver, four on each side and one at each end. Jean-Claude stood at the end nearest the galley, his long white apron covering him like a surplice, his meaty reddened hands clasped in front of him as if he were about to utter a prayer. Under his white chef's hat the heavy features of the red face sagged and the pale, watery eyes looked sadly around at all of them, now clustered in a group at the bar, as if he were going to announce not dinner but some fresh catastrophe. He seated them, putting Ellen at the end where he himself stood and Dade at the other end, and to Dade's left, as if with an instinct for the welfare of the stranger in their midst, separated from them by the double barriers of language and occupation, he placed Marbeau.

There was a stir and a murmuring. When they were all seated, Jean-Claude clapped his hands together, his features at the same time lifting into little crescents of pleasure as he broke into a broad smile of welcome.

"*Eh bien!*" he said. "Permit me to tell you the menu for this evening's dinner." Mike moved from place to place, opening bottles of Corbières, as Kitty carried in a steaming platter from the galley and began serving all of them. He gestured at Kitty's platter. "Mrs. Mulvaney had written from the States asking that I prepare a first course from the Middle Ages as a taste of history, something the Bishop Remords might have dined on, and I had the good fortune to discover his favorite: *animelles de mouton frites.*"

Ellen put down her fork hastily. Her eyes met Dade's.

"What is that?" Maggie asked.

"*Animelles* of mutton, fried. We remove the skin and cut each one into eight pieces, put the pieces into an earthenware bowl with salt, pepper, tarragon vinegar, olive oil, a little thyme, bay leaf, sliced onion and parsley. We cover the bowl. After about one hour, they should give out their liquid. We drain them, put them back into the bowl and sprinkle with the juice of lemon. Then we dredge them with flour and fry them until golden."

"Delicious," said Olivia. All of them except Ellen and Dade began eating with pleasure.

"Mutton," repeated Maggie.

"*Exactement, madame!*"

"But what are *animelles*?" Maggie asked.

"Balls," said George shortly.

"Don't be vulgar," Maggie said. "If you don't like them, you don't have to eat them." Turning back to Jean-Claude, she gave him a winning smile, asking, "What are they, exactly?"

Jean-Claude hesitated, looking around for help. Ellen studied her hands. "Down here," Jean-Claude said, making a deliberately vague gesture. "You understand?"

"I told you," said George.

"Oh, my *God!*" Maggie's fork clattered to the floor.

Everybody stopped eating except George, who picked up his plate and held it out, saying to Kitty, "Another ball, please."

Olivia said uneasily, "Pardon me, but is the rest of the dinner going to be—?"

Before she could finish, Jean-Claude shook his head vehemently, saying, "Madame, the rest of the dinner will be classic French cuisine."

They were then served a *consommé à la Colbert*, made with fresh tiny spring vegetables, which Jean-Claude said were grown specially for him by the wife of the lock keeper back at the Ecluse de la Méditerranée, right at the side of the lock. They all turned and looked at him. Aware suddenly of the indelicacy of his reference to the fatal lock, his face flushed. "Excuse me," he said. The soup went uneaten.

When the dishes had been cleared away, Jean-Claude struggled to begin again. "For the fish," he said, "we will have *brochet farci à la mode du Velay*. To begin with, it is necessary to procure a fine pike—the shark of fresh waters. Some grow as large as a hundred pounds. Ours tonight is fresh from the Garonne. How do we know he is fresh? The eyes, they are bright, the gills, bright red, and when we touch him, he is firm as if still alive. Myself, I would prefer the live fish and to kill him myself. I will tell you how. Do not kill with the knife. Oh, no! It must be done, as in the case of *truite au bleu*, with a sharp blow delivered to the head. I will demonstrate." He picked up a heavy knife-sharpener, brandishing it.

Cissy began to choke. Maggie let out a cry of dismay. Dan slammed a fist down on the table angrily. Olivia pushed her plate away and Ellen cleared her throat, seeking Jean-Claude's eyes. Billy's face was a mask. Leo, seemingly oblivious, went on drinking his wine. George sat forward, elbows on the table, his face in his hands. Jean-Claude, breathing heavily, his face glistening with perspiration, looked around, more at a loss than ever.

Kitty served the fish. Except for Marbeau, who ate ravenously, making little sounds as if talking to his food as he consumed it, few of them had any appetite. After the fish, Jean-Claude, by now demoralized and trying not to show it, said, "For the entrée, I now present *poulet aux quarante gousses d'ail*, which in English you will call Chicken with Forty Cloves."

Ellen said to him in a whisper, "Of garlic."

"Certainly of garlic," Jean-Claude answered. Kitty carried in a large earthenware dish, the aroma of chicken and garlic filling the saloon, and began serving. Jean-Claude said, "I will now explain how he is created. We cut up chickens as for a sauté. These chickens will be two months old, not older. These chickens have also come from Madame, the good wife of the *éclusier* at the Ecluse de la Méditerranée. You probably saw them eating the rich grains on which they are fed as you took your promenades yesterday on the towpath—yes, they are right there, running free, as you go along your way!—and all of them were killed only last night—a thousand pardons." He had tried to catch himself but too late. Maggie buried her face in her hands. Jean-Claude pulled out a red bandanna and began blotting his face. Maggie lifted her face, now reddening, and began to laugh uncontrollably. Jean-Claude stared at her.

"I'm sorry!" she gasped, looking back at him, trying to control herself. "We just don't seem to be able to get off the subject of killing!"

"Alas, madame!" Jean-Claude said to her, "we must kill to live! Yes, it is so, madame. We must kill to live."

"Nobody knows that better than all of us," Leo said with a sigh.

Maggie dissolved in hysterics. Dan sprang to his feet as Maggie rose from the table, choking, laughing, tears in her eyes. He put an arm around her, his face full of concern. Waving him away, she mumbled excuses, hurrying toward the companionway with tiny steps and then vanishing from view.

They had all just begun to eat, to Jean-Claude's relief, and Jean-Claude was speaking of the salad of wild greens, herbs and morels that was coming next, as well as cheese from the region, such as chèvre, which, as legend had it, graced the tables of the caesars in Rome, when the air was shattered with the sound of Maggie's screaming. Dan sprinted toward the companionway.

All of them scrambled to their feet, a new wave of fear sweeping over them. Dade strode toward the companionway and clumped down the stairs. The screams were coming from the last cabin on the left, Maggie's. The door was open and Dade could see Maggie, her back toward him, her hands to her face, Dan beside her, his face livid. Dade stepped quickly into the cabin and then saw what had happened: her toy dog lay on the bunk, a paring knife thrust into its body and what looked like blood was smeared all over the woolly torso.

23

Dade took hold of Maggie by the shoulders, moving her aside, then put a finger into the sticky red substance, smelled it and put it to his lips. "Ketchup," he said. Dan looked at him, incredulous. They turned, hearing an uproar. Behind them, all of the others were crowded in a shocked group in the corridor.

Maggie elbowed Dade aside. She said, "You dirty bastard, you did it!" Pushing past George, she thrust an accusing forefinger at Billy's chest. He looked at her, shocked. She gave him a bitter smile. "Don't pretend with me! You did it as a warning, didn't you? To keep me from saying anything! Well, I don't scare that easily!" Whirling on Dade, Maggie said to him, "You know why? I'll tell you why!"

"My God!" said Dan, staring at Billy. "My *God!*"

"Last night, after I had gotten ready for bed," Maggie said, "I started hunting for the book I was reading. I must have turned that cabin upside down before I remembered that I'd left it up on deck, so I put on my robe and went up to get it. Well, just then the bus came back and the crew got off, and since I don't like being seen without my face, I hid in the shadows. When the coast was clear I made a dash for it and you know who ran past me?" She pointed at Billy. "*He* did! He wasn't even watching where he was going! He almost knocked me down!"

She took a step toward Billy. "You know it's true! Don't try to deny it!" She turned back to Dade and said, breathless, "This morning, after they told us Kate had been murdered, Billy said to me, 'Let's not say anything about seeing each other on deck.' He said it would just mean a lot of questions and we might both end up looking bad. I was so rattled, I agreed.

"Well, when I told Dan what I had done, he said I absolutely had to tell the truth—that I had lied under oath and that made me look bad—so I told Billy I was going to tell you, to give *him* a chance to tell you first and he warned me not to." She turned on Billy with a malevolent smile. "You remember how you warned me not to, Billy? You remember that, don't you?"

"I don't know what you're talking about," he said.

She turned quickly back to Dade. "You heard us arguing! That's what was going on when you walked in on us! And now, *this!*" she said, gesturing toward the open door of her cabin. "My sweet little Alfie!" Suddenly she turned and slapped Billy's face with all her strength, leaving a red welt on the bluish cheek. "You murderer!" she yelled. "You killed her and now I know it!"

Billy looked at Maggie, his face expressionless. Then abruptly, he strode toward his cabin, yanking open the door. Cissy, a shocked look on her face, stared at Maggie in disbelief, then turned away and, hurrying after Billy, went into his cabin and closed the door quietly behind her.

Maggie watched them go, wide-eyed, the others all crowded together in the narrow corridor staring at her. Turning to Dan, she said in a weak voice, "My little Alfie!" She buried her face in his shoulder. He put his arms around her protectively, his face set.

The corridor was silent now, except for the soft sound of Ellen's voice murmuring a translation of what had been said to a grave Marbeau, who stood there, head bent, listening and nodding, hands clasped behind his thick back. Abruptly, George banged his way into the lavatory, Olivia, excusing herself to the air, went into her cabin and Leo went quickly into his.

Dade said to Maggie, nodding his head in the direction of the companionway stairs leading up to the saloon, "May I have a word with you, please?"

Maggie looked at Dan as if for permission. He nodded at her. Excusing himself, Dade brushed by Ellen, Marbeau and Joliet, leading Maggie back up the stairs, Dan following. The saloon was empty now, the table set for salad and dessert.

Rubbing his palms lightly together, Dade asked, "Maggie, you got any witnesses for what you've told me?" When she only shook her head, looking at him wide-eyed, Dade took a deep breath and said, "I have to warn you that you're in a very difficult position. You've made an accusation. Billy denies it. You have no witnesses."

"Dan knew about my having seen Billy! I told him!"

"And are you now willing to change your deposition, even

though that means admitting that you lied under oath?" He looked at her from under his eyebrows. She gave a little cry, hands to her mouth.

Dan said angrily, "Here we go again! What are you trying to do, intimidate her?"

"I'm trying to warn her that this new statement of hers could be self-incriminating." Maggie gasped. Dade said, speaking without emotion and looking alternately at Dan and Maggie, "What you're doing is placing yourself very close to the scene of the crime at almost exactly the time your sister was murdered."

Dan said, the deeply tanned face mottled with anger, "What the hell is all this? My wife tries to tell you the truth and you treat her like this?"

Dade walked a few steps away from them, and speaking slowly, his eyes on the floor, he said, "Put the case this way. Maggie lied under oath." She started to interrupt in a strangled voice but Dade held up a hand, saying, "Let me finish, please. Maggie was not in her cabin, as she said. At the time of the murder—at *precisely* the time of the murder—she was up on deck, *perhaps even on the towpath.*" Maggie looked up at him with horrified eyes. "After making her statement, she discovers that someone saw her, someone who, for reasons as yet unknown, has not yet come forward. Maggie is trapped. Maggie now knows that she must change her story—before someone else changes it for her. Maggie makes up a story about a book she'd gone looking for, and to turn suspicion away from herself, tells us she saw a man on board at just that moment, a man you yourself, Dan, told me all of you dislike, and a man who denies what she says and has an alibi."

Dan said, putting an arm around Maggie, "Where do you get off, will you tell me that?" He tried to lead Maggie out of the saloon.

Blocking their way, Dade asked, "When did you tell Dan you had seen Billy?" Maggie's eyes moved toward Dan's but Dade took a quick step in front of Dan. Dade made her look at him. "Answer me," he said.

"This morning." She tried again to look at Dan but Dade held her eyes.

"And did he try to get you to tell the truth *then*?"

"We were all so upset—"

"In other words, the answer is no." She averted her face. Dade turned suddenly and stared at Dan. "You knew you were putting your wife in jeopardy by insisting she change her story later. Why did you do it?"

Dan flushed an angry red. "I was afraid. For Maggie's sake. Because of what I'd found out about Billy. From Kate." Then, turning aside and thrusting his hands into the back pockets of his denim trousers, he said, "I'd better explain. Kate told me to get Cissy away from Billy. I don't have any control over my sister and I told Kate that. She said if I knew what was good for me, I'd find a way."

"She give you a reason?"

Dan took a long breath. Then he said, "Kate told me Billy had been bilking her out of a fortune with some oil scheme, that she'd found out about it and had enough on Billy to send him to prison."

"Kate told you this when?"

"Yesterday! The first time we were alone together on the barge. And you know why? Kate was very big on family and hated scandal. I told Cissy, of course, but she wouldn't listen. She said I had no proof. Well, I didn't have, and once Kate was dead, it was only my word against Billy's.

"When . . . when Maggie told me what she said about seeing Billy when she did—well, Christ, I didn't want Maggie mixed up in something like this. I mean, suppose he'd killed her when he found out what she was going to do? I told her to keep her mouth shut!"

He stepped closer to Maggie, putting a protective arm around her. His expression changed. He turned his head away, looking sideways at Dade. "Then, tonight I thought, Wait a minute. What the hell is the matter with me? If he killed Kate and Maggie saw him—I mean, when he got back on board—well, Christ, she has to say something! I just wasn't thinking. I said to myself, Once she's told them, then he'd have no reason! That's why I told her she had to tell you!"

Dade looked at him for a long time. Then he asked, "Kate, she happen to tell you anything about this oil scam?"

Dan shook his head. "No, nothing. You know, Kate was secretive. She said, 'Now, I've given you fair warning.' Then she said something about this company he was using to cheat her."

"How do you know she was talking about a company?"

"Well, she referred to it by name."

"What name?"

Dan frowned, thinking. Then he looked at Dade and said, "Manitoba."

24

A few minutes later Dade went back downstairs and knocked on Billy's door. Billy opened it. Cissy, her mouth set and her eyes hard, was standing behind him. Dade said to Billy, "Let's you and me take us a little stroll together, what do you say?"

Cissy took Billy's arm and said to Dade in a low voice, "He was with me." Her eyes moved. Then, she said in a half whisper, "That woman is vicious."

"You telling me she made all this up? Why would she do something like that?" Dade asked.

Cissy looked at Billy briefly, then turned back to Dade. "Oh, she has a reason. She has a reason for everything she does."

Taking Billy's arm, Dade said to her, "I won't keep him long."

Cissy stepped into the corridor with them, closing Billy's door behind her. "I'll be in my cabin," she said to Billy.

Dade and Billy went topside, climbing down the gangplank, which led from the moored barge to the towpath. One of the constables guarding the barge immediately intercepted them, turning his flashlight on their faces and then, recognizing Dade, touched his cap and stepped aside, allowing them to pass. Together, Dade and Billy walked ahead on a graveled stretch of dark path, no sound but the rhythmic crunching of their shoes. They strode on in silence, keeping pace with one another. When they got to the next lock, Dade gestured at the catwalk and then made his way along the narrow iron walkway to the center, Billy following him. At the center Dade stopped, peering down into the next lock where the water shimmered in the dark some twelve feet below them.

Billy stood next to him, facing across the catwalk to the opposite bank, hands in his pockets. He threw a quick glance at the deep, almost empty lock on his left, then reached out and grasped the railing to his right against which Dade was now leaning. Dade folded his arms and stood there in silence for some moments. Finally, he turned his head and looked at Billy.

"Well?" Dade said. "What have you got to say?"

"She never saw shit."

"Sure?" When Billy said nothing but only continued to look at Dade with an opaque glance, Dade said, "Just for the sake of argument, let's pretend that she did. Now, let's consider Cissy's position. I'm Cissy, see? I wasn't with Billy at all at ten o'clock last night. But he says I was. So, he's my alibi. And I'm his.

"Now, all of a sudden, some woman comes along and says, 'Here, I saw Billy board the barge right after Kate was murdered!' I'm Cissy, understand? And if it turns out that my alibi was actually off murdering Kate when I said the two of us were in the hay together on the barge—well, I'm in a trap. You can see that, can't you, Billy? I'm in a trap and I've got to 'fess up and quit playing alibi before it's too late and what they start thinking is that we made this thing up between us *because we both killed her*."

Billy turned toward him, his glasses glinting in the faint glow of the barge lights behind them, a surprised look on his face. Then he burst out laughing. He said, "Just what the hell reason would *I* have to kill her?"

"Because she threatened to put you in prison," Dade said, watching him. Billy remained standing where he was, not moving. His face was expressionless. He turned away then, staring into the dark water far below them.

After some moments, Billy said, "So that's why she sent for you."

"An oil scam, wasn't it?"

Billy turned to face him. "I don't know what you're talking about."

"You build a high line, you know that, sonny?"

"What's that supposed to mean?"

"Polite way of calling you a damn liar. Now, let's have your version."

Billy continued to meet Dade's eyes for a long time without say-ing anything further, as if trying to read his thoughts. Then he took a deep, uneven breath and said, "I was Kate's investment coun-selor. I put her into a little company—wildcatters."

"Manitoba?"

Billy nodded. "It went under. Kate told me she'd had an audit run on it. I don't know what they came up with, you know, those people can take things and twist them, they don't understand, they don't want to understand—" He broke off, turning away.

When Billy said nothing more, Dade asked, "When did you find out that she knew?"

"At Montalban. She told me that they had grounds—you know, to prosecute."

"And so you went looking for her last night, is that what hap-pened? That's how it's going to seem to the French police." When Billy did not answer but only stood there rubbing his palms to-gether slowly, Dade said softly, "When you know a man's going to find out something anyway, that it's just a question of time and a little digging, why not make him a present of the information and come up smelling like a rose?"

Billy exhaled slowly through his teeth. He looked at Dade, his eyes searching Dade's face for a long time. Then, nodding to him-self, Billy said, "She . . . said she was going to give me a chance to . . . straighten things out. All day the next day I tried to get with her, to talk with her, but she wouldn't let me. So last night I said to Cissy, I've got to talk to her, and I didn't go with Cissy the way I said, Cissy went off by herself somewhere and I went back alone to the barge and waited for Kate, only she didn't show up. I waited and waited and she didn't show, and then I got off the barge and went walking along the towpath looking for her and, oh, Jesus, I tripped over her body in the dark!

"She was just lying there, and at first I wasn't even sure it was Kate, I couldn't see, and I bent down to get close to her face and then I got up and ran like hell out of there and I swear by Al-mighty God that that's the whole truth! Oh, Jesus, don't you see why I couldn't say anything? And if it wasn't for that bitch Mag-gie—! She pulled that stunt with the dog . . . she pulled it on her-self, you know that, don't you? Comedy isn't the only thing she can play. And she did it so she could turn on me!"

"Why would she do that, Billy?"

"She saw me. I saw her. *She's* the one who said not to say anything. It was *her* idea. Well, she was afraid I might change my story and that would get her in a lot of trouble."

Dade asked softly, never taking his eyes off Billy's face, "Why would she think you'd do a thing like that? Is there something else she's afraid you know?" Billy gripped the railing, stretching his arms and lifting his chin. When he did not answer, Dade said, "Maggie accused you of killing Kate."

Billy gave Dade a slight smile, not much more than a sneer. "She doesn't think that!"

Dade said, "You make it sound as if you think Maggie herself killed Kate." Billy nodded slowly. Dade said, "Why would Maggie do a thing like that, Billy?"

Billy stared at him. "Don't you know? George! She used to be married to him! This is twenty years ago. George went bankrupt, they had a big fight, broke up, and after the divorce Kate married him. Bought him, I should say. It's one of those things we never talked about. Not if you wanted to stay friends with Kate. Maggie wants him back. She's always wanted him back. And what I think is, she saw her chance and took it."

"She's got a husband."

"Dan?" Billy gave vent to a short, brutal laugh. "Don't you know why she married him? To protect her investment! She saw *Jericho* in manuscript, knew it was a winner and made Kate's studio shell out a small fortune for it and then got them to let Dan do the screenplay, which she worked on with him, to give her the single greatest part of her life. Now she's got him working on a sequel. She only married Dan so she could control him. And he married her because he's nothing but a goddamned starfucker. Get the picture?"

Dade grunted, touching his palms and tapping his fingers together, not saying anything for several moments. "All right," he said finally, "we'll correct your statement and have you sign it."

"And tell Cissy what?"

"It's not for you to tell her anything. Let me give you a piece of advice, may I do that? In your place I would keep to my own counsel. You understand me, boy?" Dade studied him through half-closed eyes. Then he said, "I think we'll go back now." Together the two of them walked up the dark towpath in silence, this time, slowly.

As they approached the barge, Marbeau stepped out of the shadows, blocking Billy's way and looking toward Dade for some explanation.

Dade told Marbeau what Billy had admitted, saying, "We'll get an amended statement from him tomorrow." He hesitated, then adding, "As a matter of fact, we'll get us three amended statements."

Marbeau did not say anything. He remained standing where he was, blocking Billy's way, eyeing him. Then he stepped aside, nodded at Dade, and walked away, hands clasped behind his broad back.

25

The lights were on in the saloon but the curtains were drawn. Billy climbed up on the foredeck, then went down the few steps to the saloon door and opened it. Over his shoulder, Dade could see the others gathered around two tables playing poker, their faces intent in the lamplight.

Dade watched Billy enter the saloon, closing the door behind him. As if preoccupied with their cards, the others did not look up. Billy stood there, irresolute, for a moment. Then, slowly, Maggie lifted her head and gave him a hard stare. Billy, his jaw tightening, turned away abruptly, crossed the saloon and clattered down the stairs.

As Dade went into the saloon, Dan's eyes met his. Getting to his feet, he went up to Dade. "Well?" he said, his voice low.

"Let's talk about this another time, shall we do that?" Dade tried to walk away from him.

Stopping him, a hand on Dade's arm, Dan said, "I want to know what he said. I've got a right."

"Another time," Dade repeated.

"Tell me this one thing," Dan insisted. "Are you satisfied now that Maggie saw him?"

"Oh, she saw him, all right. Excuse me." Dade walked a few steps away from him. Dan rubbed his knuckles in his palm. Then he went back and sat down at his place.

Dade looked around the saloon. Cissy was not there. At one table sat Maggie, Leo and George, at the other, Ned, Dan and Olivia. The air was thick with smoke.

Maggie said, surprised, "Leo? You're not going to give George your play?" Leo shook his head, a smile on his lips.

George said, "We have a deal, Leo. Remember?"

"I had a deal with Kate."

"You're going to another studio?" Maggie asked.

"Over my dead body," George said.

"I can't think of a nicer way of doing it," Leo said.

"Why?" Maggie asked.

"In my opinion," Leo answered, "George has set nepotism back a hundred years." Leo said, smiling at George, "I'd add, that's just one man's opinion, but it isn't."

"Deal," said George. His florid Irish face showed no change in expression.

"I don't like you, George," Leo said. "Now that Kate is dead, I can tell you the truth. I don't like you and I never have."

George looked up at him and said mildly, "I know that, Leo. I've always known that. See you and raise you."

Dade went over to Kitty at the bar and ordered Calvados.

Serving him, Kitty said, "Your wife is in the cabin." Dade nodded, then turned, resting his elbows on the bar and leaning against it.

Ned said to Dade, gesturing, "Come on. Join us."

"No, it's all right."

"More fun with four," Ned persisted. He and Olivia looked up at Dade expectantly. Dan studied his cards, not looking up.

"All right," Dade said. "Next hand." Carrying his snifter over, he sat down heavily, sighing.

"Deal," Dan said to Ned.

Ned shoved stacks of chips from the bank over to Dade and said, "Ten dollars, okay?"

"Fine."

Olivia looked at Dade's snifter. "Calvados," she said. "In Normandy they tie bottles on the branches of trees with the buds inside and get the fruit to ripen in the glass, so that you end up with a whole apple in the bottle. The first time I saw it, I thought it was a trick."

"You always think people are trying to trick you," Dan said.

"Not always." She picked up her cigarette, inhaling it. "But sometimes."

Dade took out his pipe, stuck it between his teeth and then patted his pockets for matches. Ned pulled a folder of stiff French matches from his pocket and offered them to Dade, who opened the folder and broke off a match. A paper ticket was stuck in the matchbook. Dade looked at it. It was a parking chit from a lot in Aigues-Mortes and the date on it was May 13, Wednesday, at one twenty-five in the morning. Dade started to light the match, at the same time reaching out for his stack of chips and knocking over his Calvados in the process. Unnoticed, Dade slipped the matches and the parking chit into his coat pocket as Ned took a napkin to the spilled drink. "Goddamnit," Dade said.

"Kitty," Ned called out.

She hurried over, quickly blotting up the Calvados and picking up the glass. "I'll get you another," Kitty said.

"Nope," Dade answered. "I did it and I deserve to be punished."

"Get him another," Ned said.

"Right away," Kitty said. She hurried away.

Retrieving the matches from his pocket, Dade said to Ned, "I'm sorry. Yours."

Ned said, holding up a hand, "Keep them."

Dade pocketed the matches, looking around at all their faces. At the next table the game went on in near silence, interrupted only by the low-voiced bets. Leo pantomimed a conversation with himself, gesturing at his cards, moving his lips, but making no sound. George thrust his fingers between the buttons of his flannel shirt, scratching the thick matted hair on his chest. Maggie studied her hand as if it were a part she was memorizing, arm arrested in midair, her rings sparkling.

Interrupting Olivia, who was shuffling the pack of cards, about to deal, Dade said, "Ned, could I have a word with you?" Ned got to his feet. Dade indicated the door with a dip of his head. They went out on deck together. Dade said, "Mind telling me where you got those matches?"

Ned looked at him, puzzled. "I just picked them up."

"Where?"

"From the bar." He gestured toward the saloon. "In there."

Dade's eyes held Ned's. "When?"

"A few minutes ago."

"That bar was used as a serving table for dinner. Any chance the matches could have been left there, say, by one of the constables?"

"Oh, no. The bar is wiped clean before we set up for dinner. They had to have been put there sometime after that."

"When everybody was there having drinks?" Ned nodded. "Everyone boarded the barge around five-thirty on Wednesday, that's so, isn't it—except for Mrs. Mulvaney, who was late?"

"Yes."

"Where was the crew the night before that? Tuesday."

"Up at La Vache, on the other side of Toulouse. We spent the night there and most of the next day getting her shipshape—"

"All of you?"

"Yes. And then we got under way to meet the party at Toulouse."

Dade said, "All right, now you keep our conversation to yourself."

"Don't worry." The white teeth flashed in the brown beard.

"I'm obliged to you." Dade left him then, making his way back through the saloon and downstairs.

In the cabin he found Ellen stretched out on the bed, poring over Fodor's *France*. On his pillow were four picture postcards of the barge, stamped and addressed and a note reading, "Write to the children before coming to bed. This Means You!" Still reading, she stretched out a hand toward him. He took it and kissed it. She seized him by his thick hair and pulled his head down close to the note.

"All right," he said.

She sighed. "I couldn't stand it up there," she said. "The cabin is so close and they all smoke. All of them."

"Speaking of smoking, take a look at this." He handed her the book of matches. She looked at it. "Well?" He took the receipt from his pocket and handed it to her. "This was inside."

She sat up. "A chit from a parking lot." She reacted with surprise. "Aigues-Mortes? Home sweet home to our long lost reliquary?"

Indicating the parking chit, he said, "And this had to have been brought on board by one of the group." He told her why he thought so. "Now, look at the date on it."

She frowned. "That's the date everybody boarded the barge."

"And, please note, one twenty-five in the morning on Wednesday. This is stamped. And it says the charge is eight francs. That means there had to have been an attendant on duty at that hour. Probably to keep an eye on the cars."

Ellen said slowly, "The reliquary disappeared in Aigues-Mortes in 1970. Well, it must have turned up there again because Kate told you that's where it was. Maybe somebody else went racing down there in the middle of the night to get there first, and when Kate found out about that, she called you the next day!"

"Well, it's possible."

"But Dade, why else would any of them have made that trip? Aigues-Mortes is just a tiny medieval town, way out of the way. Hardly anyone goes there. It's really something like a museum. Well, who would visit a museum in the middle of the night?"

"That's what I'm going there to find out. Tonight. According to their accounts, all of them came straight down to Toulouse from the north. Aigues-Mortes is due *east*. And it's a hundred and fifty miles out of the way. But the funny thing is, they all traveled *alone*, so there's no corroboration for any of their stories."

Suddenly she was apprehensive. She said to him, her eyes searching his face, "Dade, this isn't for you! You told me you were just going to help them get statements but now, you're going around questioning people, getting *involved*—"

"Course I am."

"But this is murder. If you start getting close to the truth . . . well, anybody who's killed once won't stop at twice."

"But that anybody isn't going to be anywheres near me. That anybody is going to be right here on the barge, while I'm a hundred and fifty miles away in Aigues-Mortes." He reached for his coat.

"Just a minute. You write those cards."

"Tomorrow I'll write those cards."

"Just write, 'Love, Papa.' I want the children to have something to remember you by." He took out his gold pencil and began scribbling a note to each of them. "How on earth do you plan to get there?"

"I'm hoping I can rent me a car, although at this hour and on a holiday weekend . . ."

"You could do what Asclepiades did. He made the first Grand Tour on the back of a cow and lived off her milk. It's just a thought."

"You don't mind if I repeat that to Marbeau, do you? I'll need his help and after he finds out what kind of a wife I really have—"

"—he'll take pity on you, of course!" Getting to her feet, she took a raincoat from the hanging space and handed it to him. He looked at it.

"That's not mine, that's yours."

"Yes. I was hoping that you'd help me into it. The nights can get chilly."

"Ellen . . ."

She eyed him. "And so can I."

"I don't want anybody to know I'm gone. If I'm not back for breakfast, I want you to go upstairs and tell the others I had a bad night, that I'm sick abed on two chairs, and then I want you to bring a tray down here to me and stay in the cabin with me, so to speak."

She helped him into his raincoat, then, holding on to him she said, "You be careful."

"I promise." He squeezed her, kissing the top of her head.

Opening the little door of the cabin and ducking under the low lintel, Dade stepped out into the companionway. Joliet, sitting in a wooden armchair, had now stationed himself there. In answer to Dade's question, Joliet said the inspector was out on the towpath, taking his evening constitutional. Dade thanked the constable, went down the hall, climbed the stairs into the saloon and, going to the bar, asked Kitty for another Calvados, meanwhile lighting a cigar. Then, making his way past the preoccupied card players, a snifter

in one hand, a lit cigar in the other, he went out onto the deck and
climbed down off the barge, walking past the lighted windows of
the saloon, the picture of a man out for an evening stroll.

Catching up with Marbeau on the towpath, he told Marbeau
what he had discovered. Marbeau let out an exclamation of surprise. Dade explained what he wanted. Marbeau said, slapping
away the gnats that circled his head, "Joliet must stay on board
with me. Orders from Paris. In Bram, they have only one police car
and it must remain there."

"A rental car is fine. I thought if you used your influence, perhaps telephoned, although I realize that it is late, it may be that
someone could deliver one to me in, say, the next hour?" Dade
handed him the snifter of Calvados. Marbeau thanked him.

"So that the others will not know you have gone, is that it?"
Dade nodded. The inspector turned slowly toward him, eyeing him
and taking a sip of Calvados from the snifter. The glass eye, catching a light from the barge, flashed at him briefly like a tiny beacon.
"I will use the radio telephone and have a constable bring my own
car from Castelnaudary. It will be on the road above the towpath,
just there"—he pointed to a spot above the Ecluse de la Criminelle—
"in a short time." Marbeau touched Dade's arm. "Take care," he
said. Then he walked briskly away.

26

Minutes later Dade was driving east in Marbeau's car. The land
was flat and the white center line was scrawled across the dark
plains like chalk on a blackboard. After about a quarter of an hour,
the highway was bisected by another, running south. A sign read
BARCELONA. To his right he could see the dark hulking range of the
Pyrenees. He had not remembered how close he was to Spain.

At Narbonne he went northeast, the road following the curve of the Golfe du Lion, the landscape a gray monotone. Now, the names of the towns all belonged to an ancient past, Celtic Ensérune, which flourished long before the Romans came, Agde, once a Phoenician seaport, Roman Sète, its harbor now silted up, a town like a ship, built on a long narrow spit of sand stretching out to sea, past Montpellier, then on into the Camargue.

Here, surrounded by sleeping waters, was a land of gypsies and bulls, the air full of the scent of strange herbs. It was the domain of the *gardians*, the French cowboys who rode western style and raised fighting bulls. He had wanted to show Ellen the Camargue, the endless salt marshes, where a sudden loud noise, splintering the stillness, filled the sky with pink clouds of flamingos, purple herons, long-legged cranes, the blue ibis from Egypt, all of them mirrored in a thousand still ponds.

But now he could see nothing but gray wastes, a vast plain with lagoons, like a mirage. He opened the window. He could smell the sea. Sleepy, he tried to rouse himself by conjuring up visions of what he had seen there—farmers walking on stilts so that they could keep an eye on their herds of sheep in the flat land—no, that was wrong, that was up near Médoc, in Landes. He said to himself, I must stay awake. It was just after midnight.

He drove now along a kind of causeway. A sickle moon came out from behind a cloud. Ahead of him were the walls of Aigues-Mortes, built like the hollow square of an ancient Greek army, a tower on each corner, four on each side, not a rooftop visible above the fortifications. In the moonlight the golden limestone walls were a ghostly white. Nothing else was visible anywhere. Beyond was only the sea and Africa. It was as if he had taken a wrong turn and driven somehow straight into the past. Here was the town of Saint Louis himself: Aigues-Mortes—in the ancient dialect of Languedoc, the language in which 'oc' meant 'oui'—Dead Waters.

He drove alongside the east wall, past the swamp where the Crusaders who had died before embarking lay buried under water in full armor. Turning right he went across the lowered draw-bridge, under the raised portcullis in the huge arched opening in the walls and then straight ahead, down a narrow deserted medi-eval street that, in less than a quarter of a mile, opened into the lit-tle town square.

On his left was the church where Saint Louis had prayed before embarking on his last Crusade, on his right, a hotel facing the square and built into the ramparts, the Donjon.

There were still a few late customers at the tables of its sidewalk café. Dade parked his car in that part of the square reserved for the hotel. He got out and stretched, taking a deep breath of the fresh night air. An old man in a rumpled uniform came out of a kiosk and limped toward him, holding out a ticket. Dade took it. The ticket was the same as the one he had found in the matchbook Ned had given him.

"Eight francs, monsieur," the old man said in English. His face was twisted, as if in a permanent grimace of pain. Dade saw a pin on his lapel, which signified that the man had been crippled in the war. Dade took coins from his pocket and paid the man, then handed him Marbeau's card. The man read it, expressionless, then handed it back. "How may I help you, monsieur?"

Dade pulled out the receipt for parking he had found in the matchbook and showed it to him, indicating the date and the time: one twenty-five in the morning. "Were you here then?" he asked.

The old man thought for a moment, then said, "No, monsieur. I was ill and could not report for work."

"Can you tell me who was?"

"I regret to say that I have no idea, monsieur."

Dade took out a ten-franc note, held it in his fingers and shook hands with the attendant, pressing the note into his palm as he thanked him. The old man took the money, nodded, silent, and limped away. Dade looked toward the hotel, sure someone there would know the whereabouts of the man on duty Tuesday night. He walked toward the café, and crossing through it, entered the lobby. He went to the desk.

A middle-aged concierge, with a carefully trimmed thin blond mustache and filmy hazel eyes magnified by the thick lenses of the glasses he wore, said in English, "Good evening, sir. How may I help you?"

"Good evening," Dade said. He took the inspector's card out of his pocket and handed it to the concierge, who looked at it closely, then put it down on the glass-topped counter, sliding it across to Dade, removed his glasses and looked around apprehensively.

"Is something wrong, sir?"

"An American used your parking lot on May thirteenth. I would like to know where I can find the attendant who was on duty that night."

The concierge was sorry he could be of no help. "The parking lot has nothing to do with the hotel, sir. It is a concession."

Dade sighed with vexation, pinching the bridge of his nose. He would see whether the police station could help him. He was about to ask directions to it when he looked back at the concierge, who stood there with his hands flat on the counter. Between them lay the hotel register. "I'm a damn fool," Dade said to himself under his breath. The answer was right in front of him. "I wonder whether this American person rented a room here on that date. May I?" He reached out both hands, swiveling the register around on its base so that it faced him. He checked the names for Tuesday night: a couple from Sweden, a family from Italy, two women from Spain and then, what he had come so far to find, the name of the barge passenger who had been there: Cicely Schuyler. Dade lifted his head, meeting the hazel eyes of the concierge. Turning the register back around to face him, Dade said to the concierge, pointing at Cissy's name, "Do you remember this woman?"

The concierge tapped a forefinger to his lips, as if prompting himself to remember, to speak. Then, he said, "A young woman, yes, monsieur."

"Was she alone?"

"Oh, yes. Definitely. She told me her name and said she had a reservation."

"And how was it made?"

"I do not know, monsieur. I found her name on our list."

"Did she make any calls?"

"I will check. Excuse me, please." Returning after a few moments with a book, he shook his head. "No. The lady made no calls at all, monsieur."

"Did she receive any calls?"

The concierge shook his head and answered, "No, monsieur, the lady—" and then clapped a hand to his mouth and said apologetically, "Monsieur, I forgot. The lady did receive one call. I remember now that it was made in the small hours of the morning and I was reluctant to put the call through, but the voice on the telephone said it was urgent."

"Was the voice a man's or a woman's?"

"A man's, monsieur."

"Do you know where he was calling from?"

"The lobby." Dade reacted with surprise. The concierge nodded. "The call came in on the house phone."

"Did you see the caller?"

"No, monsieur. The house phone is there." He indicated an alcove around the corner, near the hotel's front door.

"Can you tell me anything at all about the call?"

"It was very brief. And then afterward, I heard footsteps and I saw the lady hurrying past the desk through the lobby."

"Was she gone long?"

"Only a few minutes." He hesitated, trying to remember what had occurred. Then he said, "It seems to me I heard what sounded like an argument. Then, having given him whatever it was he had come for, she went back to her room."

"How do you mean, 'whatever it was he had come for'?"

"I am sorry. I did not remember to tell you. As she went by, she was taking something out of her purse."

"What was it?"

"Something in brown paper." He measured a space in the air of six or eight inches. "About this size."

"I'll be damned," Dade said softly, almost no expression in his voice, his eyes fixed on the concierge. The concierge was startled. His gesture was arrested in midair, and now he seemed to hang before Dade, motionless, like a puppet on strings. Dade leaned across the desk and asked in a half whisper, "Was it a package?"

"I do not know what it was, monsieur."

Dade turned away from the concierge and leaned his elbows on the desk, his eyes filmed with thought. Then, swinging around and placing the palms of his hands flat on the edge of the glass-topped desk, he asked, "Between the time she arrived and the time this man called, did she ever leave the hotel, to your knowledge?"

"I was at the desk the entire time and I can assure you, monsieur, that she did not."

Dade said, half talking to himself, and at the same time shaking a finger at the man, "That means that when she walked into this hotel, she had this whatever-it-is with her . . . I don't care if she stole it or picked it up in the street or won it in a raffle, she had it with her. She wasn't by any chance carrying it when she came into the hotel, was she?"

The concierge shook his head. "All I saw was the one suitcase brought in by the cab driver."

Dade said, startled, "What cab driver?"

"Just . . . just a cab driver, monsieur." He edged away, as if the look on Dade's face made him uneasy.

"You didn't tell me anything about a cab driver!"

"I . . . I didn't think of it. Not every little thing seems important, monsieur."

"Then the car belonged to somebody else," Dade said under his breath. "It belonged to the man."

"Pardon?"

"Nothing." Thanking the concierge, he asked for directions to the police station.

27

The préfecture was in an ancient stone building constructed, from the look of it, at the same time as the thirteenth-century walls. Dade stepped into a large rectangular courtyard surrounded by buildings, their doors and windows completely shuttered except for what looked like a porter's lodge on his right. There, a light shone through a window and a sign on the small iron-banded door read PRÉFECTURE. Dade rapped on the door, then opened it. He found himself in a room with a linoleum-covered floor and large uncomfortable-looking desks and chairs. A kerosene heater warmed the room; the air was heavy with its fumes.

Behind a cluttered desk, a young constable, uniformed but with his tie loosened, sat filling out a report with the stub of a pencil, which he moistened with his tongue repeatedly. In his left hand, a cigarette had burned down almost to his nicotine-stained finger-nails.

He talked to himself as he wrote, reciting the words under his breath but speaking with animation, emphasizing phrases such as, " 'The suspect then said'—no, 'asserted, asserted' "—and " 'I, for my part'—no, no—'I, the investigating officer'—ridiculous, they know that"—erasing this last phrase and, aware of the presence of a visitor, waving at the air, his eyes still on the paper, and saying, "one moment, one moment, if you please," then continuing until he got to the end of his sentence, which was—" 'that he knew nothing about the matter at all'—wrong. 'That he knew nothing about the matter whatsoever.' Wrong again. 'That he knew nothing at all about the matter.' There we are!"

He finished the phrase with a flourish of his stub of pencil, then threw himself back in his chair, satisfied, and grinned at Dade, exposing a row of yellowish teeth. "How may I help you?" Dade took out the inspector's card and handed it to him. He read it and then handed it back, his face assuming a serious air. "Constable Aristide Brunel at your service," he said.

"Constable," Dade said, "I want to talk with the parking attendant who was on duty in the square opposite the Hôtel Donjon last Tuesday night."

"Tuesday night?" The constable reflected for a moment, then said, "Ah! The man you are looking for is the day man. When the night attendant did not come to relieve him, he worked that shift, too. I know because I myself am on duty at night, and when I made my rounds, he complained to me about having to work so many hours in a row."

"If you could tell me where I might find him—"

"It is one in the morning, monsieur. The poor man is asleep."

"This is a capital case."

"A capital case? I see."

"If you could just telephone him—"

"A parking attendant does not have a telephone, monsieur." He fixed his tie, clapped a helmet on his head, and striding to the door, opened it, saying with a gesture of invitation, "If you please." Dade stepped out of the office. The constable turned off the lights, hung a sign on the door that read CONSTABLE ON PATROL, closed the door, locking it with a large, rusty key and led Dade out into the street.

He escorted him down the road that ran along under the thirty-foot-high crenellated walls and then turned right into a maze of narrow alleys, where the houses on either side were so close together that in some places flying shores had been erected, crossbeams that were wedged between the houses as braces to keep them from falling in on one another. At one point, by stretching out his arms, Dade could touch the walls on either side.

Finally the alley widened into a tiny square with a pump and great stone washtubs beside it. Bending down, the constable picked up a handful of pebbles, took aim and threw them at the shutters of a window on the second floor of a stone house. When nothing happened, he did the same thing a second time. Again, nothing happened. Whispering to Dade that if he rang the doorbell, he would waken everybody in the household, the constable picked up a third handful, hurling it at the shutters just as someone in a nightshirt had thrown them open. The pebbles clattered into the room behind him, several of them striking the figure, so that he threw up an arm to protect himself, crying out at the same time, "Who are you and what do you want, you piece of shit?" The figure glared down at them over what seemed to be a bandage across his face just under his nose.

The constable called out, "Constable Brunel!" The man then hurried away from the window, and moments later they heard him unlocking the front door to the house. He opened it, barefoot and in his nightshirt, and stood behind the door modestly, peering out, blinking at Brunel, a puzzled look on his face, a hand shielding the lower part of his face like a woman trying to keep someone from seeing her without her false teeth. "An American visitor has an official question to ask you," Brunel said, gesturing at Dade.

"One moment, monsieur," the man said. He disappeared again behind the half-open door and they could see his right elbow going up and down, like a semaphore. Then the face appeared once again, now unbandaged, exposing a magnificent pair of long, curled mustaches, which he evidently tied up at night in a kind of snood. He nodded gravely at Dade.

"May we step inside for a moment?" the constable asked.

"Certainly," said the man, gesturing. They entered and he drew a tattered sheet around him like a toga. The man, who was middle-aged and bald, with an extraordinarily long nose that plunged down through his mustaches like a cleaver dividing them, looked at Dade and said, "And you, monsieur, you are . . . ?" Dade pulled one of his cards from his card case.

When the man made no move to take it, the constable said to him, "He's offering you his card, Maurice. Take it."

The man then reached for the card so quickly that he lost his grip on the sheet and it began to slide down to the floor. Hastily he put Dade's card between his teeth, wrapped himself once more in the threadbare dignity of his bedsheet and said thickly, Dade's card still in his mouth, "I am Maurice Rodier, at your service." Dade bowed, murmuring the name and expressing pleasure at their meeting. Mollified, Monsieur Rodier asked how he could possibly be of help.

Dade said, taking out the photograph, "I wondered whether a person who parked in your lot at one twenty-five in the morning on Wednesday could be one of these people."

Monsieur Rodier struggled to free his right hand from his wrappings without again losing his grip on the sheet, then, taking Dade's card out of his mouth, he wiped it on his sheet and gestured with it as he turned to face Dade. Now, in the dim light of a street lamp coming through the open door, Dade saw the milky film on Rodier's pupils that meant cataracts. "Unfortunately, faces to me are only a blur, monsieur."

"I'm sorry," Dade said.

Rodier stroked his mustaches. "One twenty-five in the morning? People leave at that hour, but to arrive then is most unusual. I remember a man leaving at about that time, a most generous man— ah!" His face brightened. "But *he* had only arrived minutes before! That must be the man!"

"Minutes before," Dade repeated. He hesitated, thinking. Then, he sharpened his glance. "You said generous?"

"He gave me a ten-franc piece. One remembers that."

"Did you do some particular favor for him? Carry suitcases, for instance?"

"No, monsieur."

"May I ask when he gave you this ten francs?"

"When he was leaving."

Dade rubbed his nose in thought. "One pays in advance, is that not the case?"

"One pays in advance."

"And one locks one's car?"

"It is true."

"So that when he returned, all he had to do was unlock his car, get into it and drive away, isn't that so?"

"Yes, certainly."

"And late at night, there would be no reason for you to leave the comfort of your kiosk and go out into the damp night air when someone returned to pick up his car, am I right?"

"None whatever." His face, which had worn a bewildered expression, now lit up. "I remember now! He summoned me!"

"Summoned you?"

"To ask directions."

"To where?"

"He needed gas and few places are open so early in the morning."

"And where did you send him?"

"There was only one place he could go. Aigues-Mortes is a peninsula. To leave here, one must drive back to the main highway at Montpellier. You yourself must have come that way, monsieur."

"Yes, I did," Dade said.

"Well, there at the crossroads, just outside Montpellier, half an hour from here, there is a truck stop which is open all night. I told him so, and at that point he gave me the ten-franc piece and drove away, not even giving me a chance to thank him." Monsieur Rodier stiffened, drew away from them and sneezed loudly.

Dade took out a twenty-franc note and pressed it into Rodier's hand, saying, "But I thank you very much indeed, Monsieur Rodier."

Rodier held up a hand, refusing it. "I do not take money for assisting the police, monsieur."

"Certainly not, monsieur," Dade said. "But I am afraid that in doing so, you may well have caught cold. This money is to buy you Cognac, which I find an excellent preventative."

"Take it, Maurice," Brunel said, adding in an undertone, "and next time, watch out who you call names, you turd in the punch bowl!" Maurice Rodier bristled, the mustaches twitching. The constable turned, letting himself out the front door. Dade nodded good night to Monsieur Rodier and followed Brunel out into the street. The constable had taken out a notebook and was scribbling in it, reciting his words as he jotted them down. "'The distinguished gentleman—'" he began, then breaking off and asking Dade to spell his name for him. Dade obliged.

Above them, a shutter banged open and a voice called down, "Constable!" Brunel looked up. Rodier's voice called out loudly, "I am sorry I called you a piece of shit!" The shutter banged shut.

Brunel's vexation showed in his face. Then, turning back to Dade, he shook hands with him, after which Dade strode away in the chill night air, damp from the marshes, and made his way back to the square where the car was parked. Montpellier was on his way back to the barge. Maybe he would be lucky. Maybe someone else would remember the generous man.

He passed the little church. The façade was modern and undistinguished and gave no hint that the building itself dated from the thirteenth century. To his surprise, the door was ajar and light came from inside. He climbed the shallow steps and pushed the heavy door open wider. The altar was still decorated for Ascension Thursday. By the glare of a work light, a charwoman was scrubbing the floor. He remembered that this was where Saint Louis had prayed before setting out with his wife and children on his last Crusade. Dade glanced around. To the left of the altar there was a statue of the saintly king on a pedestal, one hand holding his sword upended, the other, which had once held the reliquary, now empty, clutching at nothing.

28

Dade drove for half an hour back along the peninsula through vineyards and olive orchards, from Aigues-Mortes toward the main highway. Reaching the crossroads at Montpellier, he pulled into the truck stop, got out and stretched while a wiry old man in overalls filled the tank, meanwhile talking to himself under his breath. He had a broad, flat nose and long wisps of hair that grew only on his scrawny neck under his chin and jaw, giving him the appearance of a yak. When the old man had finished, Dade took the inspector's card out of his pocket and showed it to him.

He reacted with alarm. "Is something wrong, monsieur?"

"I just wanted to ask you a question or two."

"Yes, monsieur?"

Dade looked up and down the highway, which ran east and west from Toulouse to Avignon. There were no cars in sight. He turned to the old man and said, "It appears that not many people come here at this hour."

"Very few, monsieur."

"So that you would probably remember those who stop here late at night?" The old man nodded slowly, looking at Dade. Dade asked, "Do you remember a man stopping by here at about this time Tuesday night—that is, to be precise, Wednesday morning? An American?"

The old man looked at him for a long time. Then, nodding slowly, he pointed up the road that came from Aigues-Mortes, crossed the highway and continued north. "He went in that direction, monsieur." The old man stuck out his lips and gave Dade a hooded look. "He was going to Montpellier-le-Vieux! Think of that!" Dade frowned. The name seemed familiar. The old man took a step closer and said, gesturing at the road, "Does monsieur know of it? Some distance up that way there is a dense forest. In the old days it was almost impenetrable. There, in that forest, is Montpellier-le-Vieux! The city itself is completely abandoned, deserted, inhabited only by wolves. At night it is a very dangerous place." The old man drew even closer, touched a long, bony finger to the tip of his nose and then touched Dade's, as if establishing a mysterious communion between both of them, a kind of brief spell in which it was safe to utter certain words, then he whispered in a low voice, "They say the place is haunted by the Devil!"

"And this man we're talking about, he was going *there*? He told you that?"

Ignoring Dade, the old man made a little questioning gesture, as if exempting himself from the responsibility of having made so serious an accusation, carefully repeating the words, "They say." He took a breath, looking around warily. Then, he said, giving Dade a veiled look, "After all, why was the town abandoned? Why has no one lived there in memory? They say it does not even have a *graveyard!* Think of that!"

Then, suddenly, Dade remembered. Montpellier-le-Vieux was not a town at all, nor had it ever been. It was a chaos of rock, huge boulders worn away in prehistoric times so that they formed a kind of labyrinth of seeming streets, alleys, buildings and courtyards, a mock-ruin of an ancient town. For a hundred years, the truth had been known about it but the legend persisted.

"One warns people, monsieur . . ." He made a fist, placing his thumb between forefinger and third finger, a sign to ward off the evil eye. "One warns people, monsieur, but if they won't listen, am I responsible? That will be eighty francs exactly, monsieur."

Paying him, Dade asked, "What gave you the idea he was going there? Did he ask you directions?"

He turned aside, his yak's beard bobbing up and down as he spoke, and said in a whisper, "He paid me for the gas and got back in his car and studied a map. When I gave him his change I saw his finger on the spot where the map says Montpellier-le-Vieux." He fixed his eyes on Dade's.

Taking the group picture out of his pocket, Dade held it in the light so the old man could see it. "Was the man you speak of one of these people?"

The old man narrowed his eyes as he stared at the picture. Then, letting out a little cry of surprise, he pointed at the photograph, saying hoarsely, "That woman! Her picture has been in all the newspapers! They say she was murdered!"

"Is the man's picture here?"

The attendant looked at him with a peasant's cunning. "Perhaps the man you speak of murdered her. And perhaps this man is fleeing from the police. Yes, and perhaps this man would come looking for anyone who had information about him. It is lonely here at night, monsieur. I am by myself. And I am an old man."

Dade said, "These people are all in protective custody, so if the man who came here is among them, you have nothing to fear."

The old man answered, "In cases like this, a man who does not remember has nothing to fear."

Dade took a hundred-franc note out of his wallet, and grasping it between two fingers, held out the photograph with his other hand. "You do not have to say anything," he said. "Just point."

Fearfully, the old man came nearer, looked closely at Dade, then at the hundred francs and then at the picture, finally pointing with a bony finger at one of the faces: Billy's. Dade's eyes narrowed. The old man snatched the bill from Dade's hand and, backing away, cried out, "I said nothing! Remember, I said nothing!"

Getting back into the inspector's car, Dade said Billy's name under his breath, picked up the map and scrutinized it. A glance told him why Billy's finger was on Montpellier-le-Vieux. The road forked there, one branch going on north to Vichy, the other going straight west to Cahors. And, in the outskirts of Cahors was Montalban, where Billy and Kate had spent Tuesday night.

He took out his watch and looked at it. It was just after one-thirty in the morning. He had two choices. He could call it quits for now and drive back to the barge, or else he could drive all night, get to Montalban at dawn, and another three hours' drive south would get him back to Bram, where the barge was moored. Well, hell, he said to himself, the night is young. Ahead of him lay four hours of mountain driving. Every town would be shuttered. There was no coffee at the truck stop. Even a piece of candy would be welcome.

Wondering whether the inspector had children, he opened the glove compartment to search for something, anything. He felt what he thought was a flashlight, but it was warm. Puzzled, he pulled it out and found that it was a thermos with a note pasted to it reading "Bon voyage, M. Cooley!" in a feminine hand. The inspector's wife, he said to himself. Steering with his elbows, he managed to open the thermos and gulped down steaming café au lait. At the back of the glove compartment was a bag with palmiers in it. God bless you, madame! he thought. He suddenly felt better.

He drove north, the window open so the cold night air would keep him awake. Now, crossing a stone bridge over the gorge of the Tarn, he raced through the night between pastures, treeless except for scrub oak, separated by low stone walls. Now and then there were farmhouses built over a lower floor housing livestock, with an outside stone staircase leading up to the living quarters and, above that, to a dovecote.

He caught himself on the verge of sleep. He told himself he

should pull over to the side of the road and rest for a few minutes, but instead, he said to himself, "Dovecote, dovecote. What is it I remember about dovecotes?" He thought he could keep awake by talking to himself, and remembering that he had read that these dovecotes had been built not so much to keep pigeons as to collect their droppings, he said loudly, "Goddamnit, that pigeon-shit was so valuable, when somebody died, they divvied it up same as the hens and sheep among the heirs. Now, how do you like that, Noah?" He was addressing his second-born son now. "How'd you like it, Noah, if I kicked the bucket and you had to tell your friends your daddy left you a bag of shit, don't that beat all get-out?"

Rubbing his eyes, he thought of Ellen. When this was over, maybe he would rent a car and drive up a few miles north to the old town of Grignan, where Madame de Sévigné had sat in her cool grotto writing about partridges fed on marjoram and thyme. Ellen, he said, I've got a surprise for you. He was very tired. He drove on mile after mile, seeing no one, fighting sleep. The accelerator was hot through the sole of his shoe. Hours went by. He was on a plateau now, megaliths and dolmens everywhere in the stony fields. This was truffle country and there, in the mist, he could make out the white truffle oaks and smell lavender and acrid juniper. The sky was beginning to pale, the stars disappearing. He pulled out his hunting watch again and opened it. The time was a quarter of six.

Now there was traffic on the road, carts, bicycles, trucks and occasional cars. The signs pointed straight ahead to Cahors. Just before he reached the town, he saw a sign pointing south: Château de Montalban, 5 km. He turned left onto a rutted dirt road and bumped along slowly, not wanting to damage the suspension of the inspector's car.

He felt refreshed. It was as if sleep, the terrible siren-song of sleep, were somehow an emanation of the night, its power dissipated with the coming of dawn. He jounced along the deeply rutted road, which was lined with pleached plane trees, relics of what had once been an avenue. Through them came the dappled light of morning.

Then he was in the clear. Below him, in a little valley, he could see the quadrangle of Remords' château, built around a courtyard, round squat towers at the corners and a garden in front of it laid out in dark green geometrical forms, with graveled walks surrounding a pond.

Well, here it was, the keep, home to Kate's boy bishop, the one person she had felt it safe to love, which, of course, had turned out not to be quite the case.

29

He entered the courtyard of the château. Against the side, a scaffolding had been erected and a good deal of the stone facing of the wall lay on the ground. The center of the courtyard was littered with debris. There was a large cart there with huge wheels, looking like a tumbrel from the Revolution. Piled against it were ancient farming implements. Suddenly, a gaggle of geese charged toward him, honking.

An English girl's voice called out, "It's all right, I'm just feeding them." He turned and saw a girl in her teens standing by a well and scattering grain. She was barefoot, her long blond hair uncombed. "We're not open yet," she called out, then, evidently not sure that he understood her, she repeated her words in French.

Dade looked around. To his right was a line of open sheds built into the walls and stacked floor to ceiling with the rubbish of centuries. He started to speak to the girl. The sound of a window banging open interrupted him.

He looked up and saw two boys of about her age climbing out through an open casement window and onto the scaffolding. They wore jeans and T-shirts and tennis shoes without socks. The first one carried a long board as he made his way along the scaffold, balancing it. The other followed him. The first boy turned to look down at them, at the same time swinging the long board around so that it caught the other boy in the middle, almost knocking him off the scaffold. He yelled out in English, "Watch it! Do you want to kill me?"

"Is it that obvious?"

Dade took out Marbeau's card and showed it to the girl. She glanced at it and then looked at him steadily, not saying anything. "My name is Cooley," he said, giving her one of his own cards.

"Mine is Clive-Hansford." She glanced down at her dirty feet and shooed away a goose pecking at her toe.

From the scaffolding above them, the sound of hammers striking stone rang out. Gesturing in that direction, she said, "Those are my brothers. My half-brothers, I should say." She looked up at them and made a face. "Mother should have let well enough alone."

"May I ask who's in charge here?"

"Comte de Remords. But since he's away, I suppose we are."

There was a yell from above and a stone crashed to the ground close to where they were standing. Taking Dade's arm, she pulled him away. Looking up at the scaffolding, where the two boys were now climbing back in through the window, Dade asked, "Just what the hell is going on around here?"

"My brothers and I answered an advertisement which offered us transport and room and board to work in a château 'helping to restore damaged works of art' and here we are, not even able to afford the fare home." She gestured around at the château. "A mess, isn't it?"

Nodding, Dade looked at her and said, "I want to ask about two Americans who arrived here Tuesday."

"Oh, yes. She was an odd-looking woman. From the way she was dressed, she looked right at home in this pigsty. Must have felt that way, too, because she went around touching everything, running her hands over the stones in the walls and actually patting them, as if they were dogs."

"I particularly want information about the man. So far as I can tell, he took off sometime that night, drove all the way to Aigues-Mortes to pick something up and then drove all the way back, arriving here just about this time in the morning. Now, it's very important to find out what that something was. Anything that either of them might have said to you or to one another might be useful."

"I'm afraid I can't be much help. We go to bed early and they arrived after I was asleep, so I just got a brief look at her in the morning, when she was taking her leave of the château, so to speak."

"Your brothers happen to talk with them at all?"

"Not so far as I know. Can you tell me what's the matter?"

"Mrs. Mulvaney was murdered the night before last."

"Good heavens!" Then, her expression changing, she said, "Wait. I just remembered. My brother Gerald drove her into Cahors when she left in the morning. I'll take you to him."

She led Dade up a broad flight of stone stairs to the second floor. A door to a corner tower room was open. "This is where Mrs. Mulvaney stayed. Her nephew was down the hall." Dade entered the room. It contained nothing but a bed, some broken furniture and a fireplace, which lacked both fire dogs and a screen. "Bathroom's next door," the girl said. "There's only one for the wing, though there is a *pissoir* built into the stone wall on the ground floor. We're quite authentic here."

She left him alone. Dade walked over to an embrasure and looked out the windows at the overgrown garden below, on the far side of the château. In a few moments the boy who had carried the board entered the room, offering Dade his hand and introducing himself as Gerald Pomfret.

He was thin and dark-haired, and his narrow face had a serious expression. "My sister told me," he began. "She said 'murdered.' Are they sure?"

Dade nodded, then saying, "I understand you drove Mrs. Mulvaney into Cahors on Wednesday morning."

"Yes, that's quite right."

"At about what time?"

"Seven. She wanted to leave before breakfast."

"What about the nephew? I know he was gone all night. You drive her because he wasn't back yet?"

Gerald seemed to hesitate, then shook his head. "No," he said. "He was back by then."

"You see him come back?"

"Yes, I did. He returned around six. I saw him running across the courtyard and then he went charging up to her room."

"When you saw him, was he carrying a package of any sort?"

"He had a manila envelope in his hands, do you mean that? An envelope about this long." He indicated a space between his hands about eight inches. "I saw it when he took it out of his jacket as he crossed the courtyard."

Dade frowned. "An *envelope?*"

"Yes."

"And you say he went straight to her room? At that hour?"

"Well, she was expecting him."

"How do you know that?"

Gerald clasped his hands behind his back, like a boy who has been trained not to fidget, and said, "One doesn't want to go around telling tales, but when you say murder . . ." He frowned, staring at his shoes. Then, after a few moments, he said, "That night, I went down the hall to the loo before turning in—"

"What time was this?"

"Around half-past nine, I would guess. Anyway, it's right next to this room and I could hear them talking—Mrs. Mulvaney and her nephew. They kept their voices down but he was angry, I could tell that much."

"Was she?"

"No. No, as a matter of fact, once or twice, she laughed."

"She laughed?"

"Oh, yes."

"What did she say?"

"I just heard the occasional word, do you see, not whole phrases, and I wasn't really paying any attention. I did hear her say one thing."

"What was that?"

"'I want it tonight.' That's how I knew she was expecting him."

"'I want it tonight'?" Dade echoed. "Were those her exact words?"

"Absolutely."

"What else?"

"That's all."

"So all you heard was what sounded like an argument, with the woman laughing."

"There was a little more to it than that. You see, the loo was broken and I was going to mend it in the morning. It wouldn't flush. Well, I'd put a bucket of water in there. Someone had used it and the bucket was empty, so I took it and went down to the courtyard to the pump to fill it up, then got a second bucket and staggered back upstairs with both of them, like the Sorcerer's Apprentice in that film, went back in the loo and did my business, and just then the door to this room opened and someone came out, him, I guess, and now I could hear their voices because we were just separated by the door to the loo and not by stone walls, and I heard her say, 'I wouldn't want anything to happen to you.'"

"You're sure of that?"

"Yes. Reason I'm sure is that she sounded . . . well, you know, sort of *concerned*, and one would have expected him to say something like, well, Thanks, or That's awfully decent of you—that sort of thing—but instead, he called her a filthy name."

"Go on."

"That's all. And then she said, in that same sort of gentle voice, 'Get rid of her. Understand?' Then the door closed and I could hear him walking down the passageway to his room and the door opening and closing. It was most extraordinary. I went back to the room I share with my brother—it's a cell, not much bigger than a priest's hole—and I told him about it—and I said, 'What's going on?' but Fred said it couldn't be serious because she was laughing earlier and to go to bed and that was that.

"I was kind of shaken up because Fred hadn't heard it, and to be quite honest, I didn't know what to think, and as I was standing at the window wondering about it, I saw the fellow come out of the far end of the château—there's a little circular stone staircase just outside the room he stayed in that goes down to a door leading to the courtyard—and he crossed the courtyard and went out of the gate to where the cars were parked. Well, I opened the window and listened, I heard a car start up and drive away and I thought, My God, maybe I ought to call the police. I don't know why I didn't. Well, yes, I do. Nobody had actually threatened anybody. What could I have told them?"

"I see." Dade's eyes were half closed in thought.

Eyes searching Dade's face, Gerald asked, "Would it have made any difference if I had?"

"No," said Dade. "No, I'm afraid it wouldn't have." Then, galvanized, he thanked the boy, ran down the flight of broad stone stairs and hurried back to his car.

30

Minutes later Dade was bumping along the road back to Cahors. Crossing the bridge that spanned the Lot, its arches mirrored in the river in the morning light, he turned left onto the highway and drove south until he reached the canal and then took the country road that skirted it and got to Bram just before nine. The barge would already be under way. He drove along, keeping an eye on the canal below him, until he spotted the barge. He parked the car by the side of the road. Then, recognizing a constable who was riding his motorcycle up the slope from the towpath, Dade hailed him and gave him Marbeau's car keys. Dade scrambled down the towpath and walked quickly to the lock the barge was just entering, making his way down the slope, and as the water was let out of the lock and the barge sank to its new level and entered the canal again, climbed aboard.

Olivia, sitting reading in a deck chair, looked up and saw him. She reacted with surprise. "You're out walking?"

"Just a little."

"I thought you were sleeping in. Ellen said you had a bad night."

"I'm better now."

"Too much rich food. Billy's under the weather, too."

He went into the saloon, where he saw George and Dan sitting at separate tables having coffee. George had a script spread out in front of him and was making notes on it. Dan was reading a book. They both looked up and greeted him.

"Well," said George, his florid Irish face creased in a smile, "you feeling better?"

"I'm fine," said Dade.

Dan said to Dade, "Listen to this: 'If once a man indulges himself in murder, very soon he comes to think little of robbing; and from robbing he comes next to drinking and sabbath-breaking, and from that to incivility and procrastination.' De Quincey. *On Murder Considered as One of the Fine Arts*. Here's another—"

George lifted his head. "I'm working, okay? I've told you that already."

"Ahh, fuck off," Dan said to him in disgust.

Walking away from them, Dade sat down at another table. Kitty brought him some coffee and a roll. Sipping the coffee, he picked up the roll, broke off a piece and buttered it. Then, looking up, he saw the inspector coming up the companionway. Dade got up and went over to him, steering him back down the stairs into the corridor and saying into his ear, "I think we'd better have a little talk with Billy."

"Too late." Dade stared at him. "Early this morning, Constable Joliet found him dead in his cabin."

"Oh, Christ!"

"The throat was cut. And the weapon is not in the cabin." He glanced upward. "The others, of course, know nothing. Except for the murderer, clearly one of the party, since there are guards posted at the towpath." Dade heard a sound in the lavatory and drew the inspector away down to the far end of the corridor. "They think he is ill with the same misfortune that befell you."

Dade passed a hand over his face. "Christ," he said again.

"This being the Ascension Day weekend, there have been so many accidents that we are having trouble getting an ambulance." He opened his hands. "Those who can still be saved must of course come first. Meanwhile, I have told my men that we will keep the barge under way, so as not to attract any further attention, until Paris tells us what we are to do." He blew out his cheeks, his eyes round with disbelief. "The incredible thing is, Joliet saw the murderer."

"He what?"

Marbeau nodded. "Joliet only left his chair in the hall once, to go to the lavatory, and returned just as someone he thought was the late Mr. Penrose came out of Mr. Penrose's cabin to go to the shower. This person was wearing the long, multicolored bathrobe of Mr. Penrose, a towel over the head. This was about two hours ago. The murder was evidently timed to coincide with the hour that the others customarily use the lavatories and the showers, and Joliet, sitting in the corridor, was aware only that all the other passengers were going from their cabins to the bathrooms and then back again.

"After everyone had gone to breakfast, Joliet realized that he had not seen Mr. Penrose go upstairs. He checked the shower. Finding the robe there but not Mr. Penrose, he went to the victim's cabin and found him dead, whereupon he summoned me." Dade whistled with surprise. Marbeau said, "Extraordinarily clever, to commit a murder right under the eyes of a constable, but I fear that the only thing Paris will find extraordinary is our carelessness." Studying Dade, Marbeau said, "You look very tired."

"All I need is a shower. Then we'll talk."

"They tell me an ambulance should be here in half an hour. Meanwhile, the cabin of Mr. Penrose is locked."

"All right."

Marbeau went slowly upstairs and Dade walked down the narrow corridor to his own cabin and opened the door.

Ellen jumped up from the bunk and embraced him, pulling him into the cabin and closing the door. She said, "Are you all right?"

"Got a taste in my mouth like I'd had dinner with a coyote. You?"

"With you out all night?" Still clinging to him, she said, "I did my best. I was almost too successful with my story about food poisoning. Somebody—Leo, I think—said, 'He is just away,' as if you were dead."

"I'm not. But Billy is." He repeated what Marbeau had told him.

She looked at him, horror in her eyes. Then she sat down suddenly, pressing her cheek against his hand. "Poor Cissy!" Suddenly, she looked at Dade with surprise and asked, "But where *was* Cissy?" Dade tapped a finger to his lips as he looked through their porthole, seeing the mossy bank sliding slowly by them. Ellen went on, saying, "Well, they had separate cabins and even though they were sleeping together, maybe last night, for some reason, they weren't." She hesitated, reflecting. Then, she said, "But how would a murderer know that? It's not exactly what one would be dying to let everyone know—" She broke off, seeing a sudden light in his eyes. "What is it?"

"Let!" Pulling out his notebook and gold pencil, he exclaimed, "Permit or obstruct! Hold 'er, Deacon, she's a-headin' for the barn!"

"Dade, 'let' used as 'obstruct' is obsolete!"

"As in a let ball in tennis?"

"Damn you, Dade!"

"What's wrong? I play fair."

"Not damn you for that. Damn you because I asked an important question and you rode right over me with your silly game! *How did he know?*"

"Or she."

They looked at each other. "The only person who had to know was Cissy."

"Good girl," he said softly.

31

Dade told Ellen what he had learned about Kate's quarrel with Billy at the château and Billy's all-night drive to get an envelope from Cissy in Aigues-Mortes, then showered and shaved and was just getting into fresh clothes when they heard the klaxon of an ambulance approaching. With Ellen, Dade hurried out of their cabin and up the companionway into the saloon, where all the others watched motionless, bewildered, as the ambulance made its way slowly down the towpath. The barge bumped to a stop. Mike jumped ashore, a coil of rope in his hands.

The driver and his assistant got out of the front, opened the rear doors of their van, and pulling out a stretcher, came toward the barge and climbed on board. The others turned as one person, watching Ned lead the green-coated attendants through the saloon and down the stairs. At that moment Marbeau arrived in a police car and boarded the barge with another constable.

Olivia said, "They must be taking Billy to the hospital."

"My God!" Maggie said, "I didn't know he was that sick!"

Dade looked at the inspector, who returned his inquiring look with a brief nod. Dade paused, eyes on the floor. Then, he looked up at her and said, "Well, he's dead. Billy, I mean. You'll find that out soon enough."

"Dead?" echoed Maggie. There was a murmur of disbelief from all of them.

Then Cissy said, dropping her cup and spilling hot coffee down the front of her dress, at the same time lunging at Dade and seizing him by both arms, "He's not dead!"

"Take it easy, Sis," Dan said, stepping quickly forward and putting his hands on her shoulders. His eyes met Dade's, searching them for confirmation. Dade nodded. Dan's mouth gaped open in disbelief.

Cissy, seeing this, yelled out, "He's not dead! He can't be!" She began to struggle with both of them, hysterical.

As Dan tried to quiet his sister, Maggie said, "How do you mean, he's dead? We all thought he was sick, like you. An upset stomach. You mean food poisoning? Oh, but that's absurd. We all ate the same thing. If that were the case, we'd all be dead, wouldn't we? Or in the hospital." She looked around at the others with a frightened smile.

Olivia said, looking at her, "So it can't be food poisoning, can it, Maggie?"

"Why are you looking at me like that?" Maggie demanded.

"I was just following your train of thought," Olivia answered. "You're always so quick about everything."

"I don't care for your tone."

Cissy had grown strangely quiet. She turned away from Dan, her eyes glazed. The others watched her. Patting her brother's arms, as if by way of thanks, she took a step away from him and then turned suddenly and said in her little girl's voice, "I think I'm going to be sick."

Ellen took Cissy's arm. "Let's get you outside in the fresh air." She led Cissy toward the steps. Cissy walked slowly, unsteadily. Ellen got her to the railing and they could all see her holding onto Cissy as she leaned over the side.

Mike jumped back on board and hurried along the gunwale, going aft. Through the windows, Dade got a look at his face. It was very pale and the eyes were wide with fear.

Dan walked over to the bar and poured himself a stiff drink. Ellen came back inside just then and, taking the glass from his hand, said, "You're very kind." She turned and said to Kitty, who was standing behind the bar, saucer-eyed, "Oh, and a damp cloth, if you would." Ellen went back outside, carrying the drink. Kitty stood where she was, her eyes following Ellen. Then, coming to herself, she rinsed out a tea towel and hurried out on deck with it.

Dan poured himself another drink. Maggie asked timidly, "I don't suppose there's any hope it was suicide? Oh, wouldn't that be wonderful!"

"I should explain that my sister has a death wish," Leo said. "Unfortunately, it is always directed toward others."

Dan, his face contorted in sudden fury, said to Leo, "You do that to my wife one more time and I'll break your neck!"

Maggie stepped between them, taking one of Dan's hands and patting it. She said in a quavering voice, "I only meant, if it were suicide, that would mean he'd killed Kate and now he's sorry and this whole awful mess would be over and we could go home."

"Remorse," mused Leo, hands behind his back. "It never occurred to me."

"Shut up, Leo," Olivia said.

Breaking free of Maggie, Dan took a step toward Leo, eyes blazing. Quickly, Leo pulled a hand from behind his back and held it up, showing crossed fingers. "King's X!" he said. Then he added, "But it is an odd way of making amends. I mean, to cut one's own throat and then hide the knife—" He broke off, aware that they were now all staring at him, incredulous. Turning his palms upward, he looked at Dade and said, "The fatal slip. Now, you know."

Dade said, "I know that there was somebody in the lavatory when the inspector was talking to me in the hall."

"Spoilsport," said Leo.

Maggie stared at him. "You mean, you knew? Why on earth didn't you tell us?"

Leo answered, "Well, here's an interesting thing. I came back up here and I thought, They don't know. At least, all but one of them doesn't. So, when they find out, I'll watch their faces."

"And what did you learn?" Maggie asked.

"That if I didn't watch my step, I'd be number three. By the way, do they still have the guillotine in this country?"

"It's a damn shame they don't!" Dan said to him pointedly.

George stared out a window at the green water. His voice, when he spoke, was flat, unemotional. "I read that during the Revolution, there was so much blood spilled around the guillotine that the ground could not absorb it and the earth there became as soft as a quagmire."

"You stop it!" Olivia yelled at him. "I want you to stop it!"

"Excuse me," Dade said. He had caught the inspector's eye and followed him out on deck and then down onto the towpath.

Marbeau reached into a vest pocket and took out a folded piece of paper, which he handed to Dade. "During your absence, the following message was telephoned to me from San Francisco to give to you from a Mr. Jake Cohen."

Dade opened the paper. The message read: "Manitoba California-based. Personal corporation in name of Cicely Schuyler. Assets in millions until quite recently. At present, nil."

Dade looked up and saw the inspector's good eye fixed on him. In a low voice, Dade translated the message.

Marbeau said, "I think we now have grounds to detain her."

Dade reflected. "Suppose I can get her to tell me the whole story?"

"You are suggesting that once we have the young woman in custody she will have no motive to say anything?"

"Something like that."

Marbeau opened his hands. "Talk to her."

32

As Dade entered the saloon he saw the group gathered together. They were standing in a tight knot, huddled in conversation, but the low murmur of their voices ceased the moment he opened the door. He came down the steps into the big cabin. No one met his eyes. As he looked at them, one after another, each of them looked away. Eyes averted, their heads turned, almost as if this collective gesture were a dance movement they had rehearsed together. George's red face was set, the jaw clenched. Dan, hands in his back pockets, looked steadily at Maggie. Olivia, her bare, rounded arms folded across her chest, looked pointedly at the floor. Leo, trying to control the animation of his face, moved his lips slightly, as if talking to himself in a voice only he could hear, following this with his brief, flickering smile. Maggie, who was wearing half a dozen strands of different-colored beads, played with them, adjusting their arrangement on her throat, and reaching behind her neck, checked the clasp. Cissy was not with them.

Dade said flatly, "I'm looking for Cissy." When nobody said anything, he looked out the window, up and down the towpath, then he started to turn away, saying, "Must be down in her cabin, right?"

Olivia took a short step toward him. "She isn't feeling well."

"That's too bad." Dade started toward the companionway.

Olivia added, "She asked not to be disturbed."

"I guess that's what we'd all of us like, wouldn't you say?" Dade searched their faces.

Then, as if this were something that had been agreed upon beforehand, Maggie stepped forward, twisting her ringed hands in front of her and said, casting a glance at the others with her violet eyes and then looking at Dade, "All of us feel that you're, well, setting us against one another and we don't like it."

"Is that so?" Dade looked around the group.

Maggie went on in that same unsure voice, like an actress trying to remember a line accurately, "We're . . . we're all family. I know we quarrel and say spiteful things, horrid things that a stranger might not understand, but we need each other—at a time like this, more than ever—and your suggesting that one of us killed Kate and I suppose Billy . . ." Her voice quavered off-key as it trailed away.

"That's the view of the police, that they were killed by one of the party."

"Well, we don't agree," Olivia said flatly.

"We think some stranger did it! Some lunatic!" Maggie interrupted, raising her voice.

"The police have already explained that that is impossible."

"Oh, the police!" Olivia cried out, exasperated. "When my house was robbed, do you think the police found out who did it? They did not! The police are fools!"

Indicating Dade with a slight movement of his head, Dan said, "He keeps watching us. All of us." Turning to Dade, he said, "Don't you?" When Dade didn't answer, Dan said, "Can't you answer me? That's surprising. I've always heard you described as an eloquent man."

"The only words that come to mind are, Excuse me." Dade nodded to all of them and walked away. He started to descend the companionway stairs. Then he stopped, hearing a door banging open somewhere below and the sound of men's voices speaking French. He stepped back into the saloon, saying, "Let's clear a path here."

For a moment it seemed as if they didn't understand him. Then they reacted to the sight of two ambulance attendants coming up the steps of the companionway, carrying a sheeted body strapped to a stretcher. All of them moved away from the bar and the steps leading up to the foredeck, their attention riveted on the stretcher. The man bringing up the rear had lifted his end high over his head, arms upraised. Eyes on the stretcher over his head, he missed the last step, tripping, and almost lost his grip. Quickly, he recovered himself, moving so suddenly that the body strapped under the starched green sheet rolled abruptly to its right, exposing a naked arm, the right hand clutching at the air as if at an assailant. Maggie stifled a scream. Olivia buried her face in her hands. The attendants carried the body out on deck.

As they climbed off the barge a constable rode up on a motorcycle. Marbeau came along the gunwale, returning the salute the constable gave him. The two of them stood framed in one of the windows, the constable leaning forward to speak into the inspector's ear, the inspector nodding gravely.

Dade went out onto the deck and the inspector, hands on the low roof of the saloon, edged sideways along the narrow gunwale and came up to him. "It is Paris. When they learned we have been unable to find the murder weapon, they ordered a team of experts to make an exhaustive search of the barge, as well as that part of the canal where we were tied up at the time of the murder. Everyone on board must get off for the next few hours."

"And go where?"

Ned, who was standing on shore with the coroner and his men, glanced up at Dade and Marbeau, then jumped up onto the deck and came toward them, looking from one to the other. Marbeau explained. Ned said, "Oh." He gestured toward the village in the distance. "Not much of a town, but there it is."

Ellen came along the gunwale toward them, walking as if on a tightrope, arms outstretched, at the same time pointing up at the sky over the stern. "Look!" she said.

They all looked up. Coming toward them was a multicolored disc, like a child's painting of a sunrise. It came slowly closer, traveling toward them with the gentle prevailing wind that blew from the west, hovering perhaps a hundred feet in the air as it drifted toward them, and now it began to assume dimensions, not a disc but a sphere, its gaudy colors flashing in the sunlight. Now they could see a propane jet that heated the air inside it being shut off. The balloon began to lose altitude as it drifted toward them.

The others inside, seeing their upturned faces, hurried out on deck, looking up at the blue sky, pointing and talking with animation.

"What is it?" Maggie asked.

"It's coming right toward us!" Olivia cried.

"It's a balloon!" Maggie exclaimed. "It's a balloon, a balloon!"

Leo said, " 'Toto, I have a feeling we're not in Kansas anymore.' "

The balloon came rapidly closer, descending swiftly, and now they could see its pear shape and the rattanlike gondola swinging from the ropes visible beneath it.

"Wave, everybody!" cried Maggie, smiling and waving at the sky. "Look, there's a man in it taking pictures!"

"All people crowd together, please! Look this way!" a man's voice from above called out to them in heavily accented English.

"It's the press!" Dan cried out, grabbing Maggie's arm and pulling her away.

"Well, I'm terribly flattered!" she said, throwing back her head and giving the photographer a dazzling smile.

"Flattered!" Disgusted, Dan pointed at the ambulance, where the men were loading the stretcher carrying Billy's body into the rear. "Now you're going to end up on the front page of a tabloid with that in the picture! Boy, they sure timed this right!" He looked up at the gondola, now directly above their heads, and gave the grinning photographer the finger.

"They'll print that, too," Dade said, stopping him.

The police began making futile gestures for the balloon to move off, while the young photographer and a girl assistant hung over the side as he switched cameras and went on shooting pictures of all of them as she changed film. Then a sudden gust of wind swept the balloon away and they watched as it vanished over the trees.

Hastily, the inspector shooed them all back inside. "Paris will not be happy," Marbeau said to Dade. "We must at all costs think of Paris!" Suddenly Marbeau's Paris became, for Dade, the striding woman in the ankle-length filmy robe on all the French coins he had ever seen. Marbeau said, "Paris wants no publicity! None! What is to be done?"

"I'd keep them out of that town," Dade said, nodding toward the village nearby.

"We could all just stay inside," Ellen said.

"No, we can't," Dade answered, explaining about the search.

She shrugged, turning toward Ned. "Montagne Noir," she said. She looked at Marbeau. "The excursion they were supposed to have had yesterday."

Marbeau said, "Perfect! Perfect!"

Ned said, "I'll have Jean-Claude pack a picnic lunch for everybody. Give me half an hour." He hurried away to give orders.

The others were all listening.

George asked, "What's Montagne Noir?"

"It's where the reservoir is that feeds the canal," Ellen explained.

"Is it up one of those picturesque twisting mountain roads?" Maggie asked.

"Well . . ." Ellen said.

"I'm not going." Maggie was decisive.

"If you stay here," Dade said, "it will have to be in a holding cell in the local jail. Make your choice." Excusing himself, he went below and knocked on Cissy's door.

33

When Cissy answered the knock, opening the door a fraction, and saw it was Dade, she said, "I'm sorry but I'm just not up to anyone now."

"I understand. But the alternative might be a lot more unpleasant. May I come in?" Reluctantly, she opened the door wider. Dade came in, closing the door behind him, gestured for her to sit down on the bunk, then pulled up a stool from under her vanity and seated himself opposite her. After offering Cissy his condolences, Dade looked at her as if the thought had just struck him and said, "You told me you and Billy shared sleeping accommodations. If that's the case, why weren't you together last night?"

She wet her lips. "We were having trouble."

"That generally known?"

"Everything with these people is generally known," she said pointedly.

"Inspector Marbeau is curious about a couple of things. Now, if you can just answer one or two questions, perhaps I can set his mind at rest."

"All right."

"You told us you were working for Billy. You much involved in his affairs?"

"I really wasn't much more than a secretary. It was just a polite way of giving me money to live on until we were married."

"You do office work for him?"

"Yes."

"Keep books?"

She hesitated for a fraction of a second and then said, "Well, to some extent. Billy handled a lot of things by himself."

"Did you know he was bilking Kate?"

She met his eyes and said levelly, "I suspected it."

"You in on it with him?"

"Don't be ridiculous."

"Then how come he drove all the way from Montalban to Aigues-Mortes in the middle of the night to get that envelope from you for Kate?"

He had caught her off-guard. She went on looking at him with wide eyes but her face seemed to crumple. Finally, she said, "He told me he had to have it."

"What was in the envelope?"

"I don't know." He looked at her closely. She said, "I don't expect you to believe me, but I don't. He gave me the envelope in Paris for safekeeping."

"Safekeeping?"

"Kate snooped. He was going off alone with her for the night and he didn't want her finding it because it was—well, incriminating, I guess. All I can tell you is, as soon as the body was found, he went to her cabin, got hold of it and destroyed it."

"Destroyed it how?"

"He burned it in an ashtray."

"When did he go to her cabin?"

"When they found the body and everyone was up on deck."

"I see." Dade gave her a veiled look. Then he said, "You say you suspected him of bilking Kate. He know that?"

"I told him so back in California. He denied it, of course. I warned him that Kate was smart and bound to find out. When he came to see me that night in Aigues-Mortes, he told me she had. He was frightened."

"What did you say to him?"

"What could I say? The only course open to him, really, was to go to Kate and throw himself on her mercy, offer to make it up. I said something like that."

"By make it up, you mean, make restitution?"

"Well, yes, if he could."

"What did he do with the money he took from her?"

"I have no idea."

"Any chance he hid it in a firm called Manitoba?"

She tried to go on looking at him with the same frank, mildly surprised look, but all the color left her face. She twisted her thin hands together and shivered slightly, as if she were cold. Taking the pink cashmere sweater she wore around her shoulders, she put it on, then, adjusting the collar of her blouse, she found a pulled thread of yarn in the sleeve of her sweater and began fidgeting with it, trying to roll it up and tuck it back in. Finally, she said, "I really don't know what you're talking about."

"What was the source of Manitoba's funds?"

"I don't even know—"

"Before you embark on yet another lie, I should tell you that I already know that Manitoba is a personal corporation in your name. I also know that, at present, Manitoba is devoid of funds."

"If you're trying to tell me I'm broke, I already know it."

"You were broke when you came to California. At that time you were willing to sit around waiting for weeks to get your half of a twenty-thousand-dollar inheritance. But you sure weren't broke a few months ago when Manitoba had assets in the millions. Care to tell me what happened to that money?"

She turned quite pale. Getting to her feet, she said, "I don't mean to sound rude but I've been through quite a good deal. All of us have. Now, if you'll excuse me . . ."

"You better hear what I got to say first." She sat down slowly, a wary look in her eyes. "The following case can be made out against you: that you and Billy bilked Kate out of a fortune, that she found out and threatened to send you both to prison, that you killed her, that Billy was afraid he'd take the fall for what you'd done, and when you saw that he was about to tell the police everything he knew to save his own neck, you killed him, too."

Her eyes were wide now, her mouth hung open, and when she finally spoke, she tried to keep the emotion out of her voice, but it was hoarse. "I have an alibi, remember? At the time Kate was killed, I was with Billy, no matter what Maggie says. And he's on record as having made a statement to that effect. He told me so himself."

"He changed his statement, Cissy."

"He what?" From the strain, her face now assumed a pinched look.

"He confessed to me that what he told us about his whereabouts was a flat-out lie and agreed to amend the statement he'd given us. Unfortunately, he was murdered before he could do so."

She gave him a thin smile. "Then we just have your word for it that he somehow changed his story, is that it?"

"I think you'll find that my word, as a disinterested witness, counts for quite a good deal in a case like this."

"It can't be true!"

"It is true, which will lead the French police to conclude that you found out last night that he was going to change his statement and that you killed him to stop him."

"I didn't kill Kate! I didn't kill Billy!" Her face had grown suddenly haggard.

"Then don't try to protect yourself with lies."

She walked up and down the small cabin, taking little, measured steps with her narrow, bare feet. Finally, she said, "I'll have to think about it." She turned and looked down at him with her frightened child's face. "You'll have to give me time to think about it."

"It's not mine to give."

"What do you mean?"

"The inspector, he knows everything I know. We're going to be in Carcassonne tomorrow, to meet with Monsieur Sartie, the Public Prosecutor. Now, Inspector Marbeau can do one of two things, knowing what he knows: one, he can just bide his time and then hand everything over to Sartie and go home to his wife; two, he can make an arrest immediately."

"He can what?"

"Oh, yes. We're still under his jurisdiction, don't you forget that. Marbeau is a policeman. Man's got a family. Got a career to think of. This case is notorious. If he makes an arrest, it'll make page one of every newspaper in France, complete with his picture. Once he makes up his mind he's got a case against you, he can march down those stairs and have them put you in handcuffs and there isn't one thing in the world that I or anybody else can do about it. That's what I mean when I say, it's not mine to give. *There is no more time*. Now, as things stand, the lies you've told are going to put you in jail. If you're not guilty, Cissy, turn to the truth. It's the only weapon you've got to protect yourself with."

At that moment there were footsteps in the corridor and Cissy's eyes darted toward the door, terrified. The footsteps passed. Cissy sagged with relief. She twisted her hands together, then snatched up a handkerchief from the bureau and began wiping them, and Dade could see the perspiration glistening on her palms.

She said in her small voice, turning to him with an imploring look on her face, as if begging him to believe her now, "Billy and I left the restaurant together and then he went back to the barge alone to wait for Kate, so he could talk to her privately. He waited a long time. When she didn't return, he was sure she was avoiding him. He was afraid, so he left the barge and went out searching for her. He fell over her body in the dark. That scared him to death.

"Then, when he got back on board and Maggie saw him, he ran downstairs to my cabin and both of us tried to think what to do. First, he got the envelope and we burned it."

"And was that the next morning, as you said?"

She answered in a small voice, after a moment, "No, it was that night. We were both afraid we'd be seen, so we waited till we were sure everyone was asleep. I guess he got it from Kate's cabin around one in the morning. He was afraid because Kate had threatened to send him to prison, and if anybody found out he was on the towpath where the body was discovered, well, you can see how it would look." She blinked a few times and then rubbed her eyes with her fingertips and her cheeks with her palms.

"Billy is all I ever wanted. And he wanted me. But Billy wanted something more than me. He wanted money. Oh, God, he wanted money. And there he was, Kate's nephew, her financial adviser, and there were all those millions and millions of dollars just out of reach. He couldn't touch anything, couldn't hope to inherit anything, and couldn't get anything out of her if he tried to strike out on his own. She wanted him near her. She owned him and that's all there was to it.

"One day he told me he had this idea and that if I'd be patient, we'd be rich. He had a corporation set up in my name: Manitoba. Manitoba was supposed to be a company that invested in wildcatting. These wildcatters were perfectly legitimate oil men and the wells they sank were perfectly real. Billy persuaded Kate to invest in Manitoba as a tax shelter. He told her she would be able to write off what they call the intangible drilling cost, that what she was investing was really the government's money, money she would have had to pay out in taxes anyway, so she couldn't lose; the worst that could happen would be that she wouldn't make any money and the best was that one of the wells would come in big and she'd make a fortune.

"Well, Kate had to give him some leeway to keep him tied to

her, so she kept letting him make investments in Manitoba. So far, all the wells Manitoba had backed had come in dry, but, as Billy said, it was only a question of time before she hit it big. And that was the risk—that one of those wells he kept telling her Manitoba had invested in *would* turn out to be a gusher and then he'd be stuck and have to come up with her profits himself—*because the money she was investing in Manitoba wasn't going into oil wells at all, it was going straight into Billy's pockets* and meanwhile Kate, knowing nothing, was just writing everything off as a tax loss. That's why he set up Manitoba as a blind trust owned by me, so that if anything happened, Kate's money could never be traced to him.

"After we had rather a lot, I said to him, It's enough. But by then, it was—he was—I don't know, like a compulsive gambler. He couldn't stop. Just once more, he'd say. Just this once. And we were so safe. We were so safe, until Billy happened on a sure thing—I don't even know what it was—I could never keep track of his manipulating—and had me draw all the money out of Manitoba and give it to him to invest and he lost every penny! That meant everything was going to go on just the way it had, Billy would go on belonging to Kate and I would just go on . . . well, being there.

"All that happened just before we left for Paris. By then, I wasn't sure how I felt anymore—about him, about anything. I didn't want to go anywhere with Billy, let alone Kate. Well, he was desperate. He said we had to talk and there was no time. He said he had business the next morning in Aigues-Mortes, and if I'd meet him there, we could try our best to work things out.

"Tuesday, as soon as he left Paris with Kate, I got on the Mistral, you know, that luxe train with a store on it and everything, took it to Avignon, went sightseeing there, then took a train to Montpellier and then found out there wasn't even a bus at that hour, and for some crazy reason I'd come to Europe without my driver's license and couldn't even rent a car, and I was so mad I just took a cab to the hotel at Aigues-Mortes, to spend the night there. By then I'd made up my mind to call the whole thing off, go to Marseilles in the morning and fly home from there.

"Well, Billy showed up in the middle of the night. He was beside himself. He said that Kate had found out and we absolutely had to face her together, and meanwhile his only salvation was that envelope, so I gave it to him." She took a quick breath. "There. That's the story."

Looking at her closely, Dade said, "But she had told him to get rid of you."

"Yes, I know that. He was honest about it. But you see, he loved me. My feelings had changed but not his, and he kept believing that somehow we could work it all out. There was also some question in my mind about whether she might not decide to send *me* to prison even though I hadn't done anything but let *him* use my name, so I thought I'd better go to Toulouse and make sure Kate understood that."

"I see." Dade made a pyramid of his hands.

Her shoulders slumped. She let her hands fall into her lap. "It's all been too much," she said. Her voice was very faint. Tears came to her eyes and began to run down her face. She turned slowly toward him. "I didn't kill either of them," she said in a whisper that sounded like tissue paper being wadded up.

Dade took a long breath, then said, "You want me to tell Marbeau what you've told me?"

"Why not?"

"You decide." His eyes were expressionless.

"All right," she said. He turned to leave. She got up slowly, following him. "I think I'll go up and be with the others," she said.

"Don't do that," Dade said sharply. "And don't talk to anybody about this. Just go on about your business as you have been. That's my advice, and I want you to take me very seriously, you hear me?"

She looked at him for a long time, her face drawn, older. "All right," she said.

34

Going out on deck and finding Ellen, Dade said to her, "Cissy's alone in her cabin. Stay with her. My guess is she'll make every excuse under the sun to get away from you. Don't let her. I don't want her talking to anyone alone." She looked at him, taken aback. "I mean it," he said. She hurried toward the companionway stairs.

Finding Marbeau, Dade had the inspector drive him into Bram. On the way, Dade told him about his interview with Cissy, adding, "Myself, I don't think she's told us all she knows."

"You think someone else is involved?"

"If so, she's bound to try meeting with that person, to protect herself," Dade said.

"Then we must keep her under surveillance."

"Yes," said Dade. "Exactly."

They went into the préfecture together and Dade placed a call to Arnolphe Motke in San Francisco. An answering machine said, "Motke," followed by a beep.

"Arnie!" Dade said loudly into the receiver, "pick up the phone!"

After a moment there was a whine of the tape as the machine was turned off and Arnie's voice said, "Dade? That you?"

"Arnie, wake up."

"Dade? Hey, it's one o'clock in the morning."

"I make it ten."

"Wind your watch."

"I'm in France, Arnie."

"I'm in bed."

"Rise and shine. I want to know about a firm called Manitoba." Dade told him what he knew, then said, "Go to Winnipeg. Right now. I don't care if you have to charter a plane. Look for oil. Find out everything you can, then get back to me at this number—the only French you'll need is the name Cooley." Dade gave him the number of the préfecture at Bram.

"It'll cost."

"It already has." Dade put down the phone. They hurried back to the car.

Kitty and Jean-Claude had been allowed to go off to the village. The rest of them boarded the bus, including Marbeau, Joliet and the new constable, Lebrun, a man with a jutting jaw, slitted eyes and coarse black hair. Ellen boarded, her arm linked with Cissy's. The constables took seats in the rear. Maggie and Dan sat down in front on the left side, Olivia and Leo across from them. Behind Olivia and Leo, Cissy took a seat by the window. Marbeau promptly sat down beside her. She ignored him. Dade and Ellen chose places across the aisle from Marbeau and Cissy, and George sat down behind them.

Ned put the engine in gear and followed the road paralleling the towpath west for a few kilometers, taking them back in the direction from which the barge had just come and then turned abruptly north onto a narrow dirt road, saying, "There are hundreds of bicycles headed down this way, cars parked everywhere. The local version of the Tour de France. We'll have to take back roads. Fortunately, the press can't get through to follow us because the highway's closed."

The bus rode swiftly on the hard-packed dirt for a few kilometers more, through a grove of ancient olive trees, their branches bending over the road, the way spattered with sunbeams. Then the road emerged from the trees, Ned shifted down and they began climbing along a narrow shelf cut into the face of the foothills. They drove through powdery soil, and clouds of dust rose, engulfing the bus, so that they had to close the windows hastily. Maggie put her wide blue chiffon scarf over her head, letting it hang down over her face, and put her straw hat over the scarf to hold it in place and rode jouncing along under it like a Chinese noblewoman carried veiled in a litter through the dark mountains.

The road narrowed, becoming not much wider than the bus itself, a rocky escarpment rising on their left. To their right the road teetered on the edge of a chasm. It climbed higher until they could see nothing but the forest-clad slopes of mountainsides wherever they looked, below them, plunging straight down, an ever-deepening gorge.

When Olivia, who was by the window on the gorge side, said, "I feel faint," Leo reached across to open her window and give her air. "Don't!" she cried. "If you do, I'll jump!"

"The perfect wife," Leo said. "She'll do anything to oblige me."

"Why don't we all sing?" Maggie suggested. She began "Frère Jacques" and most of them joined in, turning and singing to Marbeau and the constables.

When they finished, Leo said, "Murderer Sings at Last to French Police but Which Is He?" then added, "I thought I'd prepare a collection of headlines to distribute to the press when they catch up with us." Nobody laughed.

Dan leaned across Maggie and said to Leo, anger darkening his face, so that it looked almost like a clenched fist, "Why don't you knock it off?" Maggie shushed him, patting his cheek and making him sit back in his seat. Leo stared across at him with raised eyebrows.

Their heads together, Ellen whispered to Dade, "In answer to your question, Maggie found her lorgnette years later, when she was having that classic Mercedes she keeps hanging onto reupholstered. The lorgnette had fallen off the chain and slipped behind the seat. The lenses were broken. When she went to have it repaired, she found it wasn't gold and it wasn't antique, which is the real reason she stopped wearing it. Well, what do you think?"

Dade whispered back, "I knew Olivia was a hell of an actress but I had no idea she also wrote her own lines." Putting an arm around Ellen, he whispered, "Do something for me."

"What?"

"When we get to wherever it is we're going to have lunch, I want to have a word with Olivia. See if you can run interference for me."

"Meaning what?"

"Charm Leo away," he said. Dade watched Cissy. She continued to stare out the window, oblivious of all of them.

35

Shortly after one o'clock, Ned steered his way onto a graveled parking strip outside the ruined walls of a little cloister, saying as he opened the door and jumped to his feet, "St.-Papoul. Eleventh-century monastery. If you'd like to poke about in the ruins a bit, we'll get luncheon set up in the courtyard."

All of them got off the bus. Dade and Ellen watched as the group trudged toward the open gates leading into the cloister and then began to disperse aimlessly, all of them disconsolate, out of sorts, like spoiled children on a field trip.

Olivia squared her shoulders, adjusted the strap of her bag, and striding toward the chapel, called out to the others, "Well, come on, let's get it over with." They all converged slowly on the doorway leading into the ancient building, Maggie, her nose in a *Michelin*, saying, "Only the transept dates from the eleventh century."

They all filed slowly into the chapel. It was in ruins. Broken statues lay like martyrs on the floors of their shrines. The clear glass windows had, for the most part, been boarded up, and what light there was streamed in shafts filled with dancing dust-motes through a hole high in the wall behind the altar.

After a while they began to make their way back out into the thin sunlight, going toward the stone benches where Ned and Mike were setting out the plates and glasses and food for the picnic. Dade saw Ellen take Leo's arm. Olivia lingered in the chapel. The heavy, leather-padded door swung shut with a muffled thud.

Dade remained standing in the gloom, watching Olivia as she walked over to a niche where a statue stood. The statue's face was shattered, so that it could no longer return the gaze of the faithful. The arms still reached out, as if in a blind effort to bestow grace, but now they were only stumps, the hands gone. Little remained but the drape of the blue plaster gown, the Virgin's blue. Olivia placed a hand on one of the broken arms. She stood there for a long time. When Dade realized that she was crying soundlessly, he went over to her and touched her shoulder.

She turned quickly, startled. He offered her his arm. There was a side door in the chapel opposite the one they had entered through the cloister and Dade steered her toward it, opened it and led her out into an oblong surrounded by the ruins of the abbey buildings. She looked around for the others. Dade said, jerking a thumb in the opposite direction, "They're out that way." He eyed her. Then he said, "Livvy, I'm afraid you're in a certain amount of trouble."

"Trouble?" The luminous gray eyes widened slightly. "What do you mean?"

"Let's put it this way—now, I'm talking from the point of view of the French police, understand? A man and his wife are flat broke and they're having a rough time with their marriage. Well, we understand that. Married people with money problems often have trouble. The man's written a play, and when his rich sister offers to back it, looks like they're going to end up on easy street. Then he learns that his sister, she's pulling out. He tries to get her to change her mind but he can't. He's pretty upset.

"The next day the wife follows the rich sister to Sarlat, they have a bitter argument, the sister won't change her mind and then, the following night, before this rich lady has had a chance to have the necessary papers drawn up to pull out of the project, why, somebody kills her and the wife's watch is found near where she was killed, and when she's asked about it, she makes up some cock-and-bull story, oh, very clever, never dreaming it'll blow up in her face. Then a witness—that would be Billy—tries to blackmail both of them and he gets his. Oh, it's quite a case. And the most damaging evidence of all is what you tried to cover up by lying." He told her what Ellen had found out about Maggie's lorgnette.

She looked at him, composed, controlling herself so completely that the only indication of her surprise was the slight involuntary dilating of her pupils.

"You lied to me," Dade said. "It's that simple."

"I had to."

"Why?"

Instead of answering, she looked around fearfully, her eyes going toward the door to the chapel. Impulsively, she put a hand on his forearm. "Walk with me," she said. "That way." She led him toward a hedge at the far side of the courtyard and drew him behind it, out of view of the chapel. Then, rubbing her bare arms as if she were cold despite the warm sun, she moved away from him, walking back and forth and picking her way through the rubble of the ruins as she spoke.

"I never understood," she said. "All these years, I just lived with it but I never understood until I read *Swann in Love*. Do you know what I mean?" She looked at him steadily.

He studied her. Then, he asked, "Pathological jealousy?"

"Yes. He hides it. Nobody knows. Only I know. Only *I* hear about it." She glanced again in the direction from which they had both come, then back at Dade. "He knows we're together. We both went into the chapel. We were the last inside. We didn't join the others in the cloisters. We came out this way. Why? It won't matter what I tell him. He *knows* why, do you see what I mean? It's gotten worse. When I go to the market—did I really go to the market? I am questioned endlessly, every day, every night. *There are no right answers.*" Her face was white and drawn, her eyes hollow.

"That's why I made up that story about Kate's taking things. I couldn't bring myself to tell you the real reason I went to Sarlat. I told you that story because I was trying to protect Leo." She began to cry. Impatiently, she brushed away her tears. She said quietly, "It was all Kate's doing. George plays around. You must know that. Everyone does. It's gone on for years. Well, somehow Kate got the crazy idea that he was now playing around with *me*, and when we got to Paris she went to Leo and told him. She said if he wanted the play done, he was to keep me away from George.

"Leo was beside himself. He believed her, of course, and accused me of destroying not only him but his career! Well, I didn't think I had any feelings left, we'd been through this so many times, so many, many times, so that my reaction came as a surprise to me. I went out by myself and spent the day alone in Paris, trying to decide what to do. That night I was so angry I couldn't sleep. I blamed Kate. I pitied Leo, but at that point it was Kate I hated. She was the one I wanted to hurt. I lay awake all night trying to figure out a way to get through that armor.

"Then, in the morning, it came to me and I packed my things and took the early train to Sarlat. It takes forever, what with having to change, and I almost missed her, but I managed to catch up with her in the cemetery just as she was leaving. You want to know what I said to her, Dade? Make a guess. Pretend you're a woman. A woman would be able to guess, Dade. You should ask Ellen!" She gave him an unpleasant smile and then leaned toward him and whispered harshly, "I told her it was true! Yes, Dade! I told her it was *true* and that the only reason George stayed with her instead of coming away with me is that we were both broke and needed money. *Her* money! I gave the best performance of my life! I made her believe me, and, by God, I hurt her! I hurt her the way she'd hurt me!" She took a quick breath and stared at him with glittering eyes.

Then she swallowed, hands to her long throat, and, closing her eyes, walked a few steps away from him. In a low voice she said, "Afterward, on the barge, I told Leo about what I'd done to Kate. He was furious. Do you know what he said? He said, 'Why couldn't you keep your mouth shut? If you hadn't said anything, she wouldn't ever have been sure.' Can you believe that? We had the worst quarrel we have ever had. That's why we went our separate ways that night, after dinner."

"I see. I see." Dade pinched the bridge of his nose, nodding to himself, took out his own pocket watch, and snapping it open, glanced at it, started to say something about their luncheon, then interrupted himself, tapping on his watch crystal with the nail of a forefinger, as if trying to arrest the flow of his thoughts, to remember something. Then he gave her a veiled look. "You're not wearing your watch."

"The clasp is broken."

"You think that's how you lost it, that the clasp gave way?"

"Yes. Yes, I'm sure that's what happened."

"But you didn't tell anybody. You value it, and yet you didn't say anything."

"The idea that my watch was found on the towpath where she was killed—"

"But you wouldn't have known that when you discovered you'd lost it. And there's more: when I asked you what happened to the watch, you were ready for me. That story was more than plausible, it had a kind of attention to detail that made one believe it. That story took time. And that story about Kate would have worked, if Maggie hadn't found her lorgnette years later in her own car, *which you didn't know.* That story served a purpose. What purpose?" He brought his big head close to hers and squinted at her.

She drew back, looking quickly around. "I think we should go back now," she said.

He jabbed a forefinger at her. "The clasp was broken, huh? What if it was *already* broken? What if you knew *when* it broke? Say, in the restaurant. If that happened—"

"Dade, all this has simply exhausted me and I . . ." She leaned back against a pillar.

"If that happened—why, a woman would give the thing to her husband to put in his pocket, now, wouldn't she? Is that what happened and is that why you made up that story—'cause you think it fell out of Leo's pocket when Leo killed her?"

She tried to speak, to protest, but all that came out of her mouth was a helpless sobbing. Pulling a handkerchief out of his breast pocket, Dade handed it to her. She blotted at her eyes and blew her nose.

He stood in front of her, hands behind his back. "That's why you didn't hear his footsteps in the gravel behind you. *There were no footsteps.* Because he wasn't behind you, was he, Olivia? But you said he was to give him an alibi. I think that you boarded the barge alone, went to your cabin and that you have no idea at all when Leo boarded."

She gasped, her hands involuntarily clapped over her mouth, as if trying to stop herself from making any answer at all.

They heard a rustling. Dade swiveled around and saw Leo coming toward them around the hedge, Ellen hurrying down a path after him. Leo looked from Dade to Olivia, studying their faces. Then he turned to Dade and said, "I was eavesdropping, as usual. The truth is, I ran into Kate that night in the dark on the towpath and tried to get her to change her mind. She wouldn't. She started to walk away from me. I grabbed her arm. She wrestled free of me. That must be when I dropped it." Taking Dade's arm and starting away, Leo said to him, his brief smile flickering on and off like a loose bulb on a Christmas tree, "Incidentally, my wife has many talents, not the least of which is an unappreciated but quite real gift for fiction."

36

After luncheon, while Ned and Mike repacked the picnic hampers, putting them back on the bus, Marbeau went into the caretaker's office at the entrance to the cloister to telephone and returned shortly afterward, sighing and slapping his sides with his flipperlike arms. No, he said to Dade, shaking his head, they could not return to the barge just yet. All the roads were still closed for the bicycle race and furthermore, Castelnaudary was swarming with members of the press, all of them looking for the little bus, there were reporters watching the side roads, there were some searching the countryside in helicopters, and he had been given orders that under no circumstances were the celebrated Americans to be interviewed by the press and every effort was to be made to keep them out of the range of television cameras.

Well, there was nothing for it but to get back on the bus and go by back roads to the Bassin de St. Ferréol, the vast reservoir that supplied water to the Canal du Midi, a magnificent place "where you will all be ravished," and where they could take their ease, stroll about and admire this grand result of the collaboration of man and nature, proceeding in perfect security, since he, Marbeau, had been assured that road blocks had been set up to keep out the curious and no one would molest any of the friends of Mr. Dead Cooley, while they waited for word that they could at last return to the barge.

Told by Dade of what the inspector had planned, the others sighed, exchanging looks. Slowly, they got back on the bus. After starting the engine, Ned turned around in his seat and said to all of them, "I just want you to know that this isn't my idea. I mean, taking this route."

"What's the matter with it?" Cissy asked in her piping voice.

"It's a little . . . well, I like to take my passengers on the most scenic routes and this road is a bit—well . . ." Turning to Mike, Ned asked, "What's the word I'm looking for?"

"Hairy."

"That settles it," Maggie said, getting to her feet. Dan made her sit down again, pointing out that there really wasn't any choice.

Marbeau demanded that someone translate for him. Ellen did. He waved aside their fears, saying, with Ellen translating, "It's a back road. Nothing more. There is nothing to fear. Remember"—he gestured upward, lifting his eyes to the heavens—"remember, there is someone watching over."

"God?" asked Maggie.

"The French police. In a helicopter," Marbeau answered.

They began climbing an even steeper grade than the one they had come in by, and in worse repair. Maggie, suddenly finding herself on the cliff side, began to whimper and begged Olivia to change places with her, at the same time getting to her feet and climbing over Dan, not waiting for Olivia to answer, and when the bus at that point ran over a boulder in the road and lurched suddenly to the right, Maggie lost her footing, took a few staggering steps down the aisle, which was now on the same steep angle as the road, and fell into the inspector's lap.

Leo said, turning in his seat, "Famous Actress in Hands of Police at Last." Dan glared at him. Olivia laughed, trying not to. "Oh, poor you!" Cissy exclaimed, leaning across the inspector and murmuring what sounded like words of comfort to Maggie. Wailing, Maggie covered her eyes with her hands and would not look at anything, not even when the inspector struggled to his feet and gently helped her back to her place.

Dade caught sight of Ned's scowling face, eyeing all of them in the long rearview mirror. Half turning, Ned said, "Look, I'm *sorry!*" and then, in an aside to Mike intended only for his ears but which all of them heard, "Cripes, if they don't mind killing off each other, they shouldn't grumble if I have a go." Ned let out the clutch and the bus suddenly jerked forward, down a secondary road for a short distance and then headed north on a road as rough as a washboard that cut through a forest.

Olivia, poring over Maggie's *Michelin,* looked up and said, "This road isn't on the map."

"I don't blame it," said Leo.

The skies darkened suddenly, there was a roll of thunder and a glint of lightning in the distance. It began to rain heavily. What had been a washboard now turned to mud. Ned drove very slowly.

"How far is it?" George asked him.

"Fifteen miles or so. At this rate we should be there in about two hours."

Olivia let out a cry.

Leo said, "I've got an idea! Let's all kill ourselves! That way, they'll never find out who did it!"

"You first," Dan said. He took a pack of cards out of his pocket, squatted down in the aisle and shuffled them, saying, "While Leo is getting up his courage, let's play a few hands. Who's in?" George and Leo squatted down on the floor with him. Cissy took out a paperback book and began to read. Olivia covered herself with her raincoat and scrunched up in a corner. Impatiently, Maggie got up, climbed over the three men on the floor, and going to the back of the bus, stretched out on the upholstered bench at the rear and tried to sleep. Ellen knitted. Dade folded his arms and sat with his eyes half closed, lost in thought. After about fifteen minutes the rain stopped abruptly and the driving got easier. Altogether, it took them an hour and a half to reach St. Ferréol. It was just four o'clock when they got there.

All of them stumbled wearily out of the bus. Before them stretched half a mile of reservoir set in a large, verdant park and surrounded by huge trees. The skies were overcast and a heavy mist rose from the water, slowly blanketing everything. While the inspector went to a booth to telephone, the others went in search of the lavatories.

Dade met Marbeau a few minutes later. Marbeau explained that from here, an excellent highway would get them to the barge in a short time, with a police escort to keep the hordes of press people away, but the highway back was still blocked by the bicyclists and it was impossible to leave there for another half hour.

Marbeau sighed, apologizing, then saying that the members of the party should take advantage of this opportunity to stretch their legs, walk around and look at the scenery. The waterspout ("sheaf of water," as he called it) shooting seventy feet into the air was just that way, yes, just a short walk on paths carpeted with pine needles leading past a series of springs and waterfalls down through a garden of ferns.

A multilingual sign pointed toward the waterspout. With a cry, Dade seized Ellen's arm and pointed at the German: *Zu dem quellen.* "Quell! To spring up or to put down!" Taking out his notebook, he patted his pockets for his gold pencil.

The others were beginning to return from the lavatories as Ned called out, "Half an hour rest stop, everybody!"

The mist was rising. Maggie and Dan, arm in arm, started down the path toward the waterspout, Dan striding, Maggie running along beside him, protesting that she couldn't walk that fast, Dan answering that it was the only way to keep warm. Lebrun, Olivia and Leo followed them. George went on alone, hands shoved deep in his pockets, the bearlike figure leaning forward as he walked, Joliet a few steps behind, all of them disappearing into the mist, which now swirled more densely up from the reservoir, enveloping everything.

Dade found Ellen shivering in the thick fog outside the caretaker's cottage. Going up to her, he wrapped his arms around her. Hugging him for warmth, she asked, "Tell me something."

"What?"

"Who done it?"

"Anybody could have."

"Oh, Dade . . . !" Her voice was impatient.

"Fact. Every one of them had motive and opportunity, and as the Bible says: 'the imagination of man's heart is evil from his youth.'"

"I asked you a simple question."

"I thought you were going to figure this out on your own."

"Why won't you ever tell me anything?"

"Ellen, I tell you everything I know!"

"Except whom you suspect!"

"Don't you chivvy me! The fix I'm in—" He broke off, pulling away from her.

Hanging onto him, she said, "Please, I'm freezing!"

"One second, honey." He pulled out his notebook and gold pencil. "Fix!" he said. "Help or trouble! Nine away, one to go." He put away his notebook and pencil, saying, "Reason I can't answer your question is my daddy, he taught me to think before I speak and I'm not through thinking." He looked around, trying to get his bearings. In a matter of minutes the fog had thickened, now so heavy that it was condensing on the branches of the trees and they could hear the intermittent sound of dripping. From where they stood, the reservoir was now invisible, shrouded in the swirling mist. "Where's Cissy?"

"In the ladies' room."

Marbeau came out of the cottage. Suddenly, a middle-aged woman in a blue smock came running out of the cottage and up to Marbeau, gesticulating and calling something out to him. He turned to her. They had a brief excited exchange. Then, turning away from her and hurrying toward Dade, he said, "She is gone!"

"What?" Dade said sharply.

"She asked to use the lavatory and then complained to the attendant that there was no paper. The attendant was sure that she had just placed a fresh packet in the cubicle. She looked. There was none. She went to fetch more and when she returned, she found the window open and the young woman gone!"

Wringing her hands, the attendant cried out to Marbeau, "I did remember the paper! I saw the packet I put there in the wastebasket. She lied to me! I am not responsible!"

Waving her away, he called out, "Joliet!" Then, wheeling around to face Dade, Marbeau said, "There are roadblocks everywhere. There is no escape."

"She mustn't be allowed to go near the others!" Dade said sharply. "Get hold of her! Now! And while we're looking for her, let's round everybody up."

37

With a quick, apprehensive look, Marbeau blew two short blasts on his whistle. After a few moments Joliet came hurrying out of the fog, looking around. Marbeau strode toward him, taking his arm and speaking in a rapid undertone. Then, Joliet saluted, turned on his heel and began running down the path, footsteps crunching in the gravel.

The three of them stood where they were, waiting, listening. Then they had a sudden blurred vision of Leo, who had caught sight of them and was loping toward them. As he came closer, he called out, "What's going on?" He was out of breath.

"We just want everybody back here," Dade said.

Leo looked around, trying to see through the drifting fog. "Where's Livvy?"

"You weren't together?" Dade asked.

"At first. I wanted to go down to have a look at the waterspout and she didn't want to try it in those shoes she's wearing. What's going *on*?"

All of them looked up, seeing something. Leo broke off, turning around. Through the mist Maggie came toward them like a revenant at a seance, seeming to materialize out of the fog, arms outstretched in front of her. "Yoo hoo!" she called out.

"Over here!" Leo called back.

"I can't see a thing in this fog." Taking tiny steps, she made her slow way up to them.

"Try wearing your glasses," Leo said.

"I am wearing them." Fumbling for something in her purse, she said, "I wear contact lenses. When they first came out, I thought they were a godsend because I could see my way around the set. You know, I found out that before that, the grips used to make bets on whether I'd hit my marks—" She broke off, nose in her purse, still trying to find something in the near darkness, then said, "They make marks on the floor because that's where the camera is focused and when you walk into a shot, you have to end up there and not somewhere else, if you expect to end up on the screen. Well, anyway, I thought they were a godsend until I saw the first takes and there I was with this glittery, glittery look, like somebody on cocaine, so that was the last time I ever wore them in pictures. Are we ready to go?"

"We're just waiting for the others," Dade said. He stared toward the path, a frown deepening the lines on his face, hands clasped behind his back.

Maggie said, looking up at Leo with a trace of annoyance, "I don't think you have any idea what it's like to wear them. They say the new kind can be worn day and night for days, which is equally true of a catheter, but I don't think that's any reason for saying—"

"All right, all right," Leo answered shortly.

"What's got into you?" She had found what she was looking for, a roll of mints.

"Nothing." He continued to stare past her into the mist.

Maggie said, popping a mint into her mouth, "What happened to Dan?"

"There he is," Ellen said, pointing.

Dan came striding toward them, his face set. "Son of a bitch," he said under his breath. He turned to Maggie. "Bastard pushed me."

"What bastard?" Maggie asked.

"One of those constables. Guy caught up with me and motioned me back this way and when I went on anyway, trying to explain that I was looking for you, that bastard pushed me! Joliet," he added, remembering.

"Oh, poopsie, we're just all on edge." Maggie took his arm, hugging it.

"Bastard," he said again. He turned away and saw Dade still staring in the direction of the path. "What's the matter?" When Dade didn't answer, Dan asked Maggie, "What's wrong with him?" Dan looked up. "Here comes George," he said. "Over here!" he called out.

George turned, waved and came slowly toward them, Joliet running after him. Joliet looked around at all of them, as if taking roll, then turned and ran back into the enveloping folds of mist.

Maggie shivered. "Why don't we all go get back on the bus?" she asked.

"I think we'll all just stay together here," Dade said to them.

Maggie shrugged, folding her arms. Finally, she turned and walked over to the shelter of the cottage. After an indecisive moment or two, the others followed her.

George said, irritated, "If it's all right with everybody else, I'd like to get the hell out of here." A look of annoyance on his big, dark Irish face, he clapped his sweatered arms around himself in an effort to get warm, marching over to join the huddled group.

Dade and Ellen remained standing with Marbeau by the path. Dade pulled out a briar pipe and his pouch. He cleaned the bowl carefully, scraping it with the blade of a small, gold-encased knife and then reaming out the stem with the coarse bristles of a pipe cleaner. He filled the pipe bowl slowly with pinches of tobacco held between his thumb and a thick forefinger. Marbeau watched him, as if Dade were about to perform some sleight of hand. Two or three times Joliet reappeared, looking questioningly in their direction, then, when Marbeau answered his look with a slight shake of the head, running off again.

Dade took out a box of matches, struck one and then held it to the wide bowl of his pipe, puffing steadily on it. When he was wreathed with smoke swirling in the fog, Dade took out his watch, opened up the case and looked at the time. They had been waiting almost fifteen minutes.

Then, Lebrun appeared in the distance, running, breathless, and called out, pointing, "They're in the bus! The missing ladies are waiting in the bus!"

Marbeau motioned at the others and all of them together walked back toward the parking lot. Ahead of them a pair of headlights was suddenly flashed on, they heard the familiar grinding sound of the engine and then, from far across the parking lot, the bus came lumbering directly toward them. Maggie, shielding her eyes with her forearm from the glare of the headlights, took a step backward. There was a loud squeal as the bus braked. The door banged open and Mike jumped down, followed by Ned.

"Got her all warmed up," Ned said. "Nice and toasty inside."

All of them moved toward the door, joined by the two constables, who ran up behind them. Olivia's face appeared at a window, hollow-eyed, unsmiling. They heard her voice as she called out, "I thought you'd never get here."

Maggie and Ellen were helped aboard by Mike and Ned. Dade climbed quickly on behind them, looking around. From her window seat, Olivia looked up at them blankly.

Dade said to her, "What happened to Cissy?"

Olivia turned in her seat and looked behind her, as if she half expected to see Cissy there and that something in Cissy's appearance would explain Dade's question. Then, seeing nobody, she turned back toward Dade and said, "What do you mean?"

"Where is she?"

"*I* don't know."

"How long have you been here?"

"Me?" She shrugged. "Twenty minutes, I think."

Ned glanced at his watch. "Ten," he said.

"All right, ten," she said.

Dade got hurriedly off the bus and went up to Marbeau, speaking to him in an undertone. "She's not there." Marbeau snapped out an order at the two constables. Dade looked up at the bus, and through the dimly lit window, saw Mike half turned in his little jump seat, talking to Olivia, saw Mike's mop of red curls, the earring in the left ear, the girlish features. That was what the constable had seen, breathless from running, squinting through the fog, before turning and sprinting back to tell Marbeau that the two ladies were already on the bus.

Maggie climbed slowly down from the bus and said to them, "She isn't here. Cissy, I mean." Then, when they looked at her, not answering, she took a step toward them and said, "She's not here. Did you hear me?"

Ellen got off the bus, her expression apprehensive.

Marbeau said, "I have had them put out word on the radio. As I told you before, all the roads are blocked. She has no chance of escaping."

Ellen put a gloved hand on Dade's arm. He patted her. She and Maggie got back on the bus to keep warm. Dade walked up and down with Marbeau. They got back on board every so often to warm up. The vigil lasted an hour.

At the end of that time, Joliet ran up to them, saluting. Marbeau turned aside as Joliet spoke to him softly. Marbeau issued orders. Joliet ran off again.

Marbeau turned to Dade, clapping his arms to his sides. "They have found her body at the foot of a cliff. She must have fallen in the fog, trying to run away."

Ellen got off the bus and asked, "What is it? What happened?"

Dade squeezed her hand and said, "Cissy."

Joliet ran back toward them, Marbeau excused himself, turning away. There was another hasty, whispered exchange, then Joliet once again retreated and Marbeau came back toward Dade and Ellen and said in a very low voice, "They say she could not just have fallen. There are the signs of a struggle."

38

Ellen put her face in her hands. Marbeau made a helpless gesture. Dade nodded, as if he had expected to hear such news.

Marbeau said, "They will stay with the body until the ambulance comes. Then we will return. Will you tell the others? And tell them they are to remain on the bus."

Dade nodded at Marbeau, then he and Ellen climbed back on board. Mike was sitting on the jump seat beside Ned. They were playing cards. Dade stepped behind them and then stood in the aisle, stooping under the low roof. He could see five pairs of eyes looking up at him. On his left were Olivia and Leo, on his right, Maggie and Dan, all of them sitting in the seats they had occupied before. George sat alone in the seat behind Leo.

Dade said, "Dan, I'm sorry to have to tell you this way, but they found her body at the foot of a cliff."

There was absolute silence. Then, Dan said, "My God!" He stared at Dade, his expression frozen in shock. Slowly, Maggie sagged in her seat. Her face crumbled. For a moment it was the face of an old woman. Olivia's luminous eyes widened in disbelief. She sat motionless. Leo half rose in his seat, his mouth open, his expression incredulous, then he sat down heavily, still staring up at Dade. Mike closed his eyes and sighed delicately.

George said, in the voice of someone whose throat is so dry he has trouble making any sound, interrupting himself with a sudden fit of coughing, "She's—she's dead? What happened?"

"Somebody pushed her," Dade said.

They all looked up at him in shock, as if he had just pulled out a gun and pointed it at them.

Dan's eyes were fixed on Dade's. His face looked as if all the expression had run out of it, like a man who cannot quite absorb what is being said to him. "Somebody *what*?" he asked.

"There were signs of a struggle," Dade said.

"Oh, my God," Dan said. "Oh, my *God!*" Maggie seized his arm, gripping it.

Dade looked slowly around at the five of them. "That's all I'll say for now," he finished. He turned to leave.

Ned was swiveled around in his seat, his face pallid, the eyes like the eyes of the others, fixed on Dade's, the eyes of a mendicant begging for some explanation.

Dade stared at Mike for a moment, then touched his shoulder. "Come this way," he said. Mike looked at him, taken aback. Dade said, "Come on. I want to ask you something." He took Mike's arm and pulled him off the bus.

Still holding Mike's arm, Dade drew him toward the hood of the bus, then leaned against the warm engine, arms folded. Dade's eyes tried to penetrate the fog swirling in the headlights of the bus. "You know, I been watching you." He shot Mike a glance from under his thick eyebrows. In the dim light he caught a flicker of fear on Mike's soft round face. Then Mike blinked it away and his expression showed nothing. Dade straightened up, putting an arm around Mike's thick muscular shoulders, squeezing the right shoulder with a heavy hand. "You want to know what I saw?"

"I don't know what you mean." The boy searched Dade's face. His eyes were watchful, open a fraction too wide.

Dade released him, scuffing as he walked away, then turning to face him, hands behind his broad back, the big face peering closely into the boy's. "When the lady was killed—Mrs. Mulvaney, I'm talking about—you just couldn't believe it. I got a look at your face when you saw that body in the bottom of the lock. You looked around as if you thought somebody was playing some kind of trick on you. Incredulous, that's what you were. Stamped all over your face. Am I right or wrong?"

"I never saw anybody killed in my life, sir. I mean, saw anybody after they were killed. It was like it wasn't real when I saw it, do you know what I mean, sir?" Mike looked at him earnestly, bringing his young face even closer to Dade's, the frank blue eyes round with wonder at the memory.

"Yes, that's what I saw in your face. No doubt about it." Dade clenched his jaw, his eyes narrowing. Suddenly, he brought a hand from behind his back and startled Mike by jabbing a thick forefinger into the brawny chest. "But this morning, when you heard Billy Penrose was dead—his throat cut—I got another look at you and, you know what? You were scared to death, face all pasty, breathing hard, your eyes darting back and forth. I was watching you. Scared to death. Why?"

"Wh-who wouldn't be? A thing like that, well, cripes!"

"I wasn't scared. I can't say as I like things like that happening around me, but I wasn't scared. What scared you?" Mike, still meeting Dade's eyes, shook his head, swallowing, and made a helpless gesture. "Well?"

"I was just scared, is all, sir." He wet his lips. "I got a right, haven't I? His throat cut in the middle of the night in his cabin and me all the while sleeping up on deck. It could've been me, you know, sir?"

"No, I don't know. What motive would anyone have to kill you?" Dade frowned. "That's right, you were sleeping on deck, weren't you?" Mike nodded, swallowing again. "You hear something?" Mike shook his head, that same flicker of alarm in the blue eyes. "See something, maybe?"

"No, sir. I swear to God—"

Dade interrupted him, jerking a thumb back at the bus. "A few minutes ago, when I let everybody know that the girl had been murdered, you know what you did?"

"I don't know anything about all this, sir, honest."

"You sighed. Fact. You closed your eyes and sighed. How come?"

"I . . . I was saying a prayer, sir. That's it. Just a little prayer."

"I don't have that impression."

"You don't, sir?" Mike looked at him, his frank open face filled with surprise. At the same time a muscle in his cheek twitched.

Again Dade put a hand on Mike's shoulder, squeezing it. "The old Greeks, they used to say that words were invented to disguise men's thoughts. Yes, that's just what they said. You weren't saying a little prayer, Mike. What I saw on your face when I said the girl had been killed was plain relief. Now, why was that?"

Mike looked at him, eyes wide with fear. He backed away, saying in a cracked voice, "I didn't do anything, honest, sir."

"You afraid of me, boy?"

"No, sir."

"How come I saw such a look on your face just now?"

"Before, I was afraid they might think it was me, but once she was killed—well, they couldn't then, could they?" He had blurted all this out. Now finished, he remained standing there with his mouth open, as if surprised at himself.

"Killed Billy Penrose?" Mike looked away, nodding. He blinked rapidly, swallowing again. "Why would they think that, Mike?" Mike shrugged. "I don't think it," Dade said gently.

Mike turned quickly toward him, relief flooding through his face. "He come out on the deck late at night when I was asleep and he . . . he tried to interfere with me, sir."

"He tried to interfere with you, you say?" Dade's eyes were points of light.

Mike nodded emphatically. "Yes, sir. I knew it was him as soon as it started happening, even before I saw who it was. See, he'd been watching me, the whole time. You know that look when you see it. Well, when he come on deck and started in, I told him to lay off. Then I had to give him a shove. I didn't push him all that hard, sir, just enough to let him know I wasn't having any. I didn't hurt him, honest."

"I'm sure you didn't, Mike."

"Then in the morning, when I heard, I thought, Oh, sweet Jesus, they're going to think I did it, maybe find my fingerprints on his chest or something, and I didn't, I swear before God."

"I understand. Now, think carefully: do you know what time this was?"

"I was asleep. Let's see . . ."

"You happen to look at your watch afterward?"

"I don't have a watch, sir."

"You go right back to sleep?"

"No." He thought. "There were voices. Some people were talking. Very low. Oh, and the moon was up, just a sliver of moon. That tells me. Sometime after eleven."

"He go away right after that?"

"Yes, sir."

"No further conversation with him?"

"No."

"I mean—now, don't take this the wrong way, Mike—he didn't, say, offer you money not to say anything to his girl friend?"

"That girl as was killed?" Mike looked at Dade with surprise, then grinned broadly. "His girl friend? Bloody unlikely, I'd say!"

"I don't mean to be talking to you in these familiar terms, but there are some men who like both boys and girls."

"I just said that because—" Mike broke off, reddening.

Dade shot him a quick look. "Because what?"

"It's nothing, sir. Really."

"You let me be the judge of that."

"I don't want to lose my place, sir."

"I'll see you don't."

"It's all very well for you to say, sir, begging your pardon, but in this particular line of work, you open your mouth about some things as goes on and you're out on your ass, I beg your pardon, sir."

"Don't you trust me, boy?"

Mike took a deep breath. "You know where her cabin was, the young lady as got herself killed today?"

"Forward."

Mike nodded vigorously. "Right under the deck where I been sleeping. Well, I hear things on trips when I sleep out there—not that I muck about eavesdropping, I don't want you to go getting any wrong ideas about me, begging your pardon—"

"No, indeed not."

"—but it's quiet at night, still as a tomb, and sound travels up through the ventilator. Where I sleep, which is right near the vent, I can hear things—not that I want to hear them—sometimes they just keep me awake, like last night."

196

"What did you hear?"

"Voices."

"Saying what?"

"Couldn't make it out. Just voices. That girl's and somebody else's. Very low. Whispering."

"Was the somebody else a man or a woman?"

"A man. And they were . . . you know."

"Lovemaking?"

"I guess. Then it kind of changed."

"How?"

Mike thought about this and then said, "Like they were going to part brass-rags. Almost an argument, I think. That's sort of what it turned into. All that whispering, like mice scratching. I started hearing it just after he waked me up. That's how come I know it wasn't him."

Dade said, "Mike, you've been very helpful." They started back toward the bus. "Now, you set your mind at rest about all of this. I don't want you to worry."

"Thank you, sir." Mike heaved a sigh of relief.

Slowly, they walked back to the bus and climbed on board. Dade paused, looking around for a moment at the faces of the others. After that, he made his way to his place beside Ellen and sat down slowly, sighing and clasping his hands over his belly.

Ellen turned and gave him a kiss on the cheek. Putting an arm around her, he whispered into her ear what Mike had told him. She gasped. Looking at him with round eyes, she whispered back, "That's why she wasn't with Billy when he was murdered! There was someone else! And there has been all along!" He nodded, silent.

39

In another twenty minutes Joliet and Lebrun had returned, followed shortly by Marbeau. Ned headed the bus down to the lower entrance to the park grounds of the reservoir, bumping along slowly through the dense fog. At the entrance to the park grounds, a motorcycle escort awaited them. As they left the damp environs of the reservoir the fog began to lift, and by the time they had reached the highway the weather was clear. Dusk had fallen now. They traveled rapidly down the highway toward Castelnaudary. It took them half an hour to reach the town and another half hour to reach the barge. During the whole time, there was complete silence.

The area around the towpath where the barge was now moored had been cordoned off, and beyond the police lines they could see crowds of reporters and photographers and mobile TV units. As Ned and Mike began helping everyone off the bus, banks of quartz lights went on, and the whole barge was brilliantly illuminated, like the walls of a castle in a *son et lumière*. At the same time a chorus of questions was shouted down at them in half a dozen languages from the dark huddled ranks on the road above them, questions no one really expected to be heard or even answered, but rather, a desperate effort to attract their collective attention, to tempt at least one of them (as indeed Dan had been tempted by the photographer swinging in his wicker basket from under the balloon) into making some newsworthy gesture or response, something in which a clever reporter could find himself a headline or a provocative question, perhaps, and on that, construct a story of speculations. The barge had already been nicknamed "The Death Ship," and more than one reporter had noted that its name, *La Veuve*—The Widow—was the soubriquet of the dreaded guillotine. Evidently, word of Cissy's fate had not yet reached them, for one piercing tenor voice rose above the babble, crying out to the others, "Look! Look! There are only five of them! Where is the girl?"

As Maggie quickly got on board, the others following, they were barraged by shouted questions about Cissy's absence, questions that quickly merged into a chant: "Where is the girl? Where is the girl? *Where is the girl?*"

On the foredeck, Maggie's knees suddenly buckled. Dan grabbed her around the waist, supporting her. She broke down then, sobbing hysterically.

Leo asked in a wondering tone, giving her a smile as brief as a tic, "Is it something I said?" Reacting to this with a shuddering intake of breath, Maggie suddenly lunged at Leo, her long-nailed fingers crisped like claws. Seizing her wrists, Leo said, "Oh, no, you don't!"

She screamed. Dan pushed her aside, swung at Leo and hit him squarely in the mouth. His lip began to bleed. Olivia slapped Dan's face with all her strength. The crowd of reporters above roared their approval, like bloodthirsty spectators at a Roman arena. Even at that distance, they could hear the metallic clicking of countless shutters and scattered applause.

George sighed. "Well, it didn't take us long to get back to normal, did it? I'll say one thing about our family: we're resilient." He turned and gave a big Irish grin. Then, single file, they made their way down the steps and into the saloon.

Hurrying up to Dade, Marbeau said, "They have found the weapon. It was a knife taken from the kitchen and then returned there and was only identified by traces of human blood discovered during a microscopic examination of all the knives in the chef's possession. Our murderer has a sense of humor. Instead of throwing the weapon overboard, the murderer cleaned it and returned it after using it!"

As they entered the large lamplit cabin, Ned and Mike hurried from window to window, hastily pulling the shades to block out the glare from the banks of lights above. It was seven-thirty and Jean-Claude was waiting dinner. He bowed, shaking hands with himself with his beefy hands. The table was set with snowy linen, crystal and silver.

Blotting at his cut lip, Leo glanced at the table and then said to Jean-Claude, at the same time picking up a plate and set of silver and handing them to him, "Just eight for dinner tonight, Jean-Claude." Maggie, her hands to her ears, as if she could not bear to hear any more from him, swept by him and down the stairs, Dan striding after her. George collected a drink at the bar, then, carrying it, went on downstairs behind Leo and Olivia. The constables had now boarded, and on instructions from Marbeau, the two of them had carried collapsible chairs down to the hall, where they now sat. Marbeau stood at one of the windows, peering out from behind the drawn shade.

Dade sat down heavily, elbows on his knees, and ran his fingers through his thick mat of white hair. Ellen went to him and began rubbing his shoulders. Eyes closed, he leaned his head against her.

"I have a present for you," she said. Taking her pen out of her purse, she said, "Guess what excites compassion and at the same time is contemptible?" He looked up at her quickly. She reached in his pocket, took out his notebook and wrote in it: Pitiful.

"Ten!" he exclaimed.

Just then a constable came into the saloon from the deck and went toward Marbeau, a hand touching his cap. Taking an envelope from his pocket, he handed it to the inspector.

Marbeau glanced at it, dismissing the constable with a nod. Catching Dade's eye, Marbeau made a slight motion of his head at the envelope. Coming over to Dade and Ellen, Marbeau showed him the envelope. It was a cable. Marbeau said, "It arrived this afternoon, when we were away." Through the cellophane window of the envelope, Dade could read the name of the addressee: "Cicely Schuyler, care of the *Péniche la Veuve* on the Canal du Midi, en route to Carcassonne." Marbeau's brown glass eye glinted in the lamplight as he nodded at the envelope. Still seated at the table, Dade took it from him and gave him an inquiring look. Marbeau nodded and Dade opened it. The message read: "Urgent you repeat change of instructions in writing with live signature. Shirley Moffat, Escrow Officer, Beverly Hills Title and Escrow Company." Dade studied the cable for a long moment.

"What is it?" Marbeau asked. Slowly, Dade translated. Marbeau frowned, puzzled. "What is a live signature?"

"Notarized."

"Instructions," Marbeau echoed. "If she sent them unsigned instructions, clearly she must have sent them by cable."

Dade pointed at the date and time on the cable. "This was sent by them at twelve minutes after ten A.M. their time the day before yesterday, Thursday." Punching a thick finger at the cable in his hand, Dade said, "My guess is, this must have been sent immediately on receipt of a cable from *here*. Now, a cable normally takes about twenty-four hours to arrive. This cable of theirs took about a day and a half to get here, but sending a cable to a barge on the Ascension Day weekend would almost certainly take longer. Backing up, that means the latest the cable from *here* could have been sent to Beverly Hills was just before five P.M. Wednesday, since the post offices here close then. So it had to have been sent before boarding."

"And before Mrs. Mulvaney was killed." Marbeau looked at him steadily.

"Has to have been," Dade said. He looked off into the distance, lips pursed, eyes narrowed. Then he said slowly, ticking points off on his fingers, "There is something in escrow. An attempt was made to change the instructions by cable. The escrow company sent a cable back and used the word 'urgent.' Those facts, taken together, suggest that this escrow is about to close, in which case, Cissy'd have to have the escrow instructions with her. Wait a minute—!"

Dade got to his feet so suddenly that he jostled the table and knocked over a glass. He said, "That's what it was!" Marbeau looked at him blankly. Dade said impatiently, "That's what Kate wanted! That's what she had to have that very night. That's what Billy went to Aigues-Mortes to get from Cissy. That's what he took from Kate's cabin right after her murder. That's what he burned. And since Aigues-Mortes is where Kate told me the reliquary was, my guess is, those escrow instructions must have told Kate when and where the reliquary was to be handed over!"

"Of course!" Trying to control his excitement, Marbeau said, "But it is very simple for us, my friend! Since these instructions were issued by the escrow company in Beverly Hills, call and have them repeat the instructions on the telephone!"

Dade shook his head. "They won't tell me. Bound by the same rules of confidentiality as attorneys and priests. Have to get a court order." He started toward the door. "Let's go find us a phone."

40

An hour later Dade put down the telephone in the police station in Bram and sighed, rubbing his eyes. He had reached Judge Benjamin Katz at home in Beverly Hills, gotten a court order, waited while it was hand-carried to the home of Shirley Moffat of the Beverly Hills Title and Escrow Company a few blocks away and then placed a call to her. The conversation was brief. Marbeau looked at Dade attentively.

"Well, I found out what's in escrow in the United States. Uncut emeralds. Five million dollars' worth. All in Cissy's name." Marbeau whistled. "To be traded for something held in escrow by the Crédit Lyonnais in Aigues-Mortes. I think that clinches it. But we still can't prove it. Escrow's to close Monday after sight inspection and approval by both parties. Cissy made sight inspection and gave her approval Tuesday. Now we know what she was doing in Aigues-Mortes. Other party's already given approval in the States. Name is Jacques Dubois. Mean anything to you?" Marbeau shook his head. Dade went on: "Sounds about as convincing as John Smith would back home. My guess is it's made up.

"Shirley Moffat told me, by the way, that that cable they got said to *terminate* escrow. It was sent Wednesday, *after* Cissy gave sight approval. That's what threw them. But there was no way to cancel escrow without that live signature. That's why it was so urgent that they get one. Since they didn't, escrow closes day after tomorrow, as planned."

Marbeau said, "Clearly, once Mrs. Mulvaney found out what was going on, the Schuyler woman sent a cable asking that escrow be terminated so that Mrs. Mulvaney would not be able to get her hands on the reliquary."

"But unless we can break that escrow, we have no proof." Dade scribbled the name of the bank in Aigues-Mortes and an escrow number on a scrap of paper and handed it to him. "We'll need a court order."

Marbeau consulted a directory, found the number he wanted and telephoned a Judge LeNôtre in Toulouse, calling him away from dinner and rapidly explaining what he wanted. The judge was reluctant. Dade could hear the slow, reasonable speech of a nasal voice coming out of the receiver in the inspector's hand, which he held slightly away from his ear for Dade's benefit. Mouth full, LeNôtre spoke of the sanctity of property rights, pointing out that no connection had been shown to exist between the private belongings of an individual held in trust by a bank in Aigues-Mortes and the death by misadventure of the young American lady.

"But she was murdered!" Marbeau exclaimed. "I have no doubt of it!"

"Not until the inquest has been held and the coroner rules," the judge said. "Until that time, she is only deceased." Politely, the judge terminated the conversation, breaking off the connection.

Marbeau put down the phone, stunned. "He has refused!"

"Call Paris."

"And go over LeNôtre's head? It would give offense!" Dade pulled his little notebook out of his pocket and, riffling through it, picked up the telephone. Marbeau said uneasily, "Whom are you calling?"

"Saint-Cloud. In Dinard."

Marbeau blew out his cheeks and lifted his eyebrows.

Saint-Cloud came on the phone, saying, "My dear Cooley, what a frightful affair!" The resonant voice was full of sympathy. Yes, he had read all about the case in the newspapers, yes, Paris was greatly concerned, yes, of course he stood ready to offer whatever help he could. Dade explained what he needed. Saint-Cloud's tone was hesitant. He said that he would do what he could but to get another judge to overrule LeNôtre was a delicate matter.

"I know that," Dade said.

"Tell Inspector Marbeau that if I am successful, he will hear from me. And give Ellen my love."

Dade had no sooner put down the phone than it rang again. It was a transatlantic call for Dade from Motke in Winnipeg. "Arnie?" he said.

Motke's speech was soft, as usual, his voice placed like a whisper at the front of his mouth, so that there was no resonance in his tone and Dade had to strain to hear what he said. "Manitoba," said Motke. "Wildcatters. Big scandal. It just broke. Got up here to find the news all over town. Office is empty. Nobody there. Nothing in it but rented furniture. This dead woman . . ."

"Kate Mulvaney?"

"That's the one. She invested in Manitoba. Every well came in dry. Then, when she was just about to quit, she hears Manitoba sank a new well and struck oil the first time out. Up here in Canada. Virgin field. Stuff pouring out of the ground. She came up and saw it all for herself. They capped the well, sank a few more and then made a deal to tie right into the Alaska pipeline. Instead of investing more money in Manitoba, she bought the lease for this gusher from Manitoba a few weeks ago. Paid millions."

"How many millions?"

"Like five."

Dade whistled. "That's my lucky number," he said. "You say they capped the well?"

"Waiting for decontrol and a rise in prices. That's what they told her. Fact is, they capped the well to keep her from finding out that there was no oil. The oil she saw when she made her trip up here was all stuff being recirculated—out of the well, through the pipes, into the storage tank and then—this is the part she didn't know— back into another storage tank they'd sunk in the ground under the derrick. Whole thing was a scam."

"Who handled the company?"

"A blind trust held by an attorney in a bank who didn't know beans about anything except that the principal traveled a lot and wanted him to handle things. Custodian's all he was. Phony papers, phony statements of earnings, phony everything. I wouldn't have been able to find out as much as I did except that some dumb clerk kept making copies of everything they did and sending them off to the attorney, who just kept putting them in the file. Then, Manitoba failed. Whatever money Manitoba had is gone. Company's bust."

"How many principals?"

"Just the one. Cicely Schuyler."

"Okay."

"That do it?"

"For now." There was a click at the other end of the line. Dade put down the phone, then clasped his hands, rapping the knuckle of a forefinger against his strong teeth. He looked up to see Marbeau's eyes fastened on him. "Here's what happened," Dade said, telling him.

The inspector looked at him sharply. Dade stomped toward the door, Marbeau following him. They rode back to the barge in silence. The saloon was empty. They went down the companionway. The two constables were sitting in chairs at either end of the hall. "Carcassonne by midday," Marbeau said.

Dade nodded, still silent. They shook hands formally. Then Dade made his way down to the end of the corridor and nodded at the constable with the jutting jaw who had gotten to his feet and saluted him. Dade went into his cabin, shutting the door firmly behind him.

Ellen was sitting up in bed, her volume of Apicius propped on her middle, glasses perched on her nose. Her eyes were closed and she was breathing evenly. Quietly, Dade got undressed, put her book aside, removed her glasses, turned out the light and lay down with a deep sigh. He turned on his side. A hand closed hard on his arm. "Don't you dare go to sleep without telling me!" she whispered.

"In the morning."

"Now. The way things are going, there may not be a morning."

He murmured to her what he had found out about the escrow and about Manitoba. She let out little whispered explosions of surprise, then said, "Two people scheme to defraud a third. The victim finds out about it and threatens to put them in prison. She is murdered, then they are. Logic tells us that there must have been someone else involved—and that someone else must be our murderer! Dade?"

"Um." He flung an arm over her. "Make sure I get up first thing."

"All right." She sighed. Then she said, exasperated, "Oh, I wish I could put all this in a book without being sued. Maybe if I changed how the victims are murdered. I could poison them. That ostrich recipe! Yes, that's it! An epicurean barge trip with ancient Roman cuisine and the title . . . let me see . . . the title of the book is— *Murder Most Fowl!*"

Dade sat up so suddenly, he banged his head hard on the sloping ceiling and let out a cry of pain.

"Oh, my dear!" Ellen said, putting her arms around him, "I know just how that feels! Did you hurt yourself badly?"

"Don't sound so gleeful." Then, swinging his legs over the edge of the bunk, he held his head in his hands and stared off into space.

"What's the matter?"

"I think that's it!"

"What?"

"Something you said." He lay down again, hands behind his head.

"What? What on earth did I say?"

"Yes, logic does tell us. How true that is."

"Give me a hint."

"How's Apicius?" he asked, taking her book from the bedside table where he had put it. "Still on ostrich?"

"No, I'm on elephant."

"Good grief!"

"And if you don't tell me what I said, I'll open the book and read you the recipe for broiled feet. Not to mention trunk."

"Here, poor old Gibbon went to all that trouble trying to figure out why Rome fell, and a fistful of those damned recipes is all the explanation anyone needs."

"Dade—!" She started beating her fists on his chest.

"You know everything I know."

"Except what I said."

"Honey, you made me promise—"

"Dade—"

"Besides, that blow on the head stunned me. I must rest now." He closed his eyes and folded his hands across his belly.

41

In the morning they were awakened by the sound of knocking on successive doors in the passageway and Mike's voice calling out, "Seven o'clock. Breakfast in half an hour, under way for Carcassonne promptly at eight."

Ellen sat up in the cramped berth, yawning, pulled back the curtain and peered through the porthole at the overcast sky. "It's going to rain."

"Good." Dade turned over, pulling the covers up over his ear.

Ellen listened for something and then said, "Somebody beat us to the showers. We'll have to take sponge baths in the sink. You first." A snore answered her. "Dade?"

"He's just stepped out."

"Dade—"

"If you'd care to leave your name—"

"Dade, you said you wanted to be up first thing."

He rolled over on his left side, leaning on his elbow and putting a heavy arm across Ellen's waist. He said in a somnolent voice, "Some people say there's a kind of territory of the mind one visits between waking and sleeping where things otherwise inaccessible can be encountered. What is your opinion?" His breathing grew slow and regular. His eyes closed.

"My opinion is that you're looking for an excuse for not getting up." He began to snore. Bending over him, she whispered, "Dade? What is it I said last night?"

He opened one eye and said, "You made me promise."

"Oh, you!" It was stuffy in the cabin and she leaned across the bunk to open the porthole. It had begun to rain heavily. The air was full of the fresh smell of the fields.

Dade got up, stretching and yawning. Stripping off his pajamas, he soaped himself, allowing Ellen to scrub his broad back. After they were dressed, Ellen put their nightclothes and toilet articles in the suitcase she had already packed.

Then she said, "How wonderful that I was able to help you figure everything out, dear, even if I don't know quite how." When he took a quick, impatient breath and opened his mouth to speak, she held up a hand and said to him, "No, don't tell me. I wouldn't dream of spoiling your fun."

"You listen here, Ellen—!"

"My only wish is that all this happened in . . . let me see, what language don't you know a single word in? Aha! Chinese. I wish that all this had happened on a junk on the Yangtze—"

"Ellen—"

"All those smiling people marching up and down and waving flags and beating drums and you not able to understand one blasted word!" She saw that Dade was frowning. "What is it?"

"If we can't break that escrow, the damn thing could go to the grave with Cissy and our murderer might just get off scot free."

They went upstairs to breakfast. Now there were separate tables once again. Olivia and Leo sat at one, having café au lait and croissants. They did not look up. George was having the same thing at the bar, where he sat on a stool, his back to the room. Dade and Ellen sat down at another table and Kitty came over to them with a tray of hot rolls, sweet butter, Bar-le-Duc jelly and steaming pitchers of hot milk and coffee. Maggie entered, followed by Dan. Marbeau, who had finished breakfast, started out of the saloon. Dade caught his eye. Marbeau answered Dade's inquiring look with a slight shake of his head, then went below.

Maggie glanced around the cabin. "Are we all here?"

"Don't be ghoulish," said Leo.

Underfoot, they could feel the faint throb of the engines as the barge moved slowly away from the bank.

Ignoring Leo, Maggie greeted Olivia, asking whether she planned to change before disembarking and ruminating about whether she herself should appear in the lilac wool jersey pants suit she was wearing, since she was in mourning, and lamenting the fact that she had nothing in black. Olivia did not answer her. Maggie said to her, "Is something wrong?" When Olivia still did not say anything, Maggie said to her back, "I asked you a question. Is something wrong? Why won't you answer me?"

Olivia's spoon clattered in her saucer. Turning in her chair, she looked up at Maggie, returning her stare, and said, "I don't like conversation before breakfast."

"Really? I didn't know that."

"You've known it for over twenty years."

"Well, I know you're neurotic but I can't be expected to remember every single one of your numerous symptoms."

Olivia sprang to her feet and said, "How can you be so unfeeling?"

"I'm not unfeeling!" Maggie cried out, wounded.

"Then why do you keep talking all the time?"

"Maybe that's how I keep up my spirits!" Maggie's lower lip trembled. Tears flooded the violet eyes. "I'm fifty years old! My sister was murdered! I feel bad! Worse, because I never liked her! My nephew was murdered! My sister-in-law was murdered! I'm afraid! I never played Saint Joan, like you. I play comedy! I don't have any repertory of emotion for any of this! I can't stand any more!" Maggie burst into tears.

Olivia rushed toward her, embracing her, stroking Maggie's hair and murmuring words of comfort. "I'm sorry!" she said. "It's just that it's all such a nightmare!"

Maggie wailed, "I mustn't cry!"

"It's all right!" Olivia answered her, blinking back tears.

"No, it isn't! My mascara is running and I don't want my picture taken that way!"

George swung around on his stool at the bar, applauding, and saying at the same time, "Upstaged again! You can't beat her, Olivia. She's an absolute master. That's how she stays on top!" Dan glowered at George, who grinned and then, gesturing at him, said, "Get a load of the hothead!" Sliding off his stool, George lumbered over to Dan and stood hulking over him, fists on his hips. "Why don't you pick on someone your own size?" he said. Dan began massaging the knuckles of his right hand.

"Oh, *please*—!" Maggie said. Dan put an arm around her.

George said, "Maggie can take care of herself. She doesn't need your protection."

"You mean, the way she didn't need yours?" Dan asked. George flushed.

Olivia, putting a rounded arm on Maggie's shoulders, turned her head toward George and, raising her voice, said, "This is no time for us to be quarreling. We're all in this together. Don't forget that, George."

"All in it with a murderer," Dan said softly. Olivia looked at him as if he had just used foul language in her presence. "Well, one of us is. Don't forget that either," he added.

For the next four hours, the barge continued its slow passage down the green canal in a light rain, with Ned and Mike at one point having to lift off the big pilot's wheel and substitute a smaller one so the barge could pass under a very low stone bridge, the two of them meanwhile crouching on their knees. The character of the houses they passed had changed. Now they had a Spanish look, with little wrought-iron balconies and walled gardens planted with bougainvillea.

Dade and Ellen returned to their cabin, climbing topside when there was a break in the weather and they could go out on deck for fresh air and watch the ever-changing view. The others remained in the saloon, playing poker endlessly, the two constables sitting in a corner.

Marbeau kept to his cabin, filling out reports he confessed he had no heart to make. Two or three times he came topside and looked at the slowly unfolding view as the barge moved through the rippling waters, then looked at his watch and then again at Dade, sighing and shaking his head.

At noon Jean-Claude served them a farewell luncheon: ragoût of rabbit, presenting them at the same time with a young Châteauneuf-du-Pape, made, he said, with grapes brought to the region almost a thousand years before by the Crusaders. Dade drank his wine with pleasure, but pushed his plate away.

"Eat your rabbit," Ellen said to him, putting the plate back in front of him.

"I don't fancy rabbit," he said, pushing it away for the second time.

Ellen said brightly, "Rabbits originated in Africa. Pliny writes that from there they were brought to Spain and got to be so numerous in the town of Tarragona and dug so many tunnels that twenty-five or thirty houses tumbled down. And the moral of that is, it is your duty to eat all the rabbit you can." He scowled at her.

As they were finishing coffee Marbeau came up the stairs into the saloon and the constables rose. Marbeau gave a brief, formal nod, glancing around to include everyone, and then Joliet and Lebrun walked over to the door leading onto the deck and took up their stations there, facing the room, hands behind their backs. The barge bumped against the bank. They could see Mike jumping ashore, throwing a thick rope over a stanchion. Conspicuous on the cordoned-off towpath were police cars waiting to escort the bus and its suspect occupants to meet the French prosecutor at Carcassonne. Now they all looked around at the waiting bus, at the inspector, at Joliet and Lebrun, at one another.

"The tumbrel waits," Olivia said in a theatrical voice.

Hearing the word "tumbrel," the inspector said, "You must tell the lady we no longer have the guillotine in France."

"The guillotine!" Maggie exclaimed, reacting to the word. A hand to her throat, she looked at Marbeau transfixed.

George said, speaking slowly in a soft voice, putting his hands flat on the table in front of him, "It was done like this. The date of the execution was kept a secret from the condemned man. At ten minutes of four in the morning on the appointed day, the warders removed their shoes and crept down the hallway to his cell. Then they threw open the door and seized him as he lay asleep on his cot, gagging him so that he could not yell out." The sheer size of the man added weight to his words and made them seem somehow more ominous. Maggie began whimpering.

George went on in the same tone: "Then the prison governor appeared and spoke the words, 'You must be very, very brave.' The condemned man was taken down a darkened hallway—"

"Stop him!" Olivia shouted suddenly.

"—where a portable altar had been set up so a priest could give him the Last Sacrament." Maggie, at this point, put her fingers in her ears and began singing "America, the Beautiful" at the top of her lungs, trying to drown him out. "Finally," George went on in the same monotone, "bound hand and foot, the condemned man was dragged to the guillotine, his body lashed to a board, which was then tipped down so that his head could be placed in the lunette."

Maggie was still singing at the top of her lungs, fingers in her ears. Olivia had abruptly turned to Leo, embracing him, hiding her head under his arm. Dan clenched his hands and said to George, "By God, you really are asking for it!"

George went on: "Then the knife falls. They say the head remains alive for as long as several minutes, eyes still able to move, the features contorted in agony."

Maggie had evidently been able to hear him, for she began to scream at that point. Olivia had turned white. She tried to take a step and then grew faint. There was an outcry.

Just then, a constable jumped on board and ran up to Marbeau, saluting and handing him an envelope. Marbeau opened it, read the brief message inside and then, smiling broadly, took Dade aside and whispered to him, "Monsieur le Comte de Saint-Cloud has obtained the court order and my deputy has arranged for armed guards to pick up whatever the bank in Aigues-Mortes holds in trust and deliver it to us in Carcassonne. Now we have everything we need, Mr. Dead Cooley!"

All of them boarded the bus at noon. Almost as soon as they began driving away from the canal, the storm broke. If they had expected to see Carcassonne in the distance, they were disappointed. In the downpour, almost nothing was visible except the rain itself, long needles of it caught in Ned's headlights, in the taillights and the flashing blue and red turret of the police car preceding them, and in the amber dazzle of the police car's headlights behind them.

When they reached the lower city they drove down an avenue lined with acacias, crossed the town and started up the hill toward the ancient fortress, rain still streaming down the windows, nothing visible anywhere. Then a sudden bolt of lightning almost directly ahead of them split open the sky and illuminated the whole of Carcassonne, the immense oval of crenellated double walls and towers sitting on the summit of a hill like a Gothic crown. This was followed by a thunderclap, not only deafening but immense, reminding Dade that sound could have scope as well as volume, a sound that seemed to stretch away on all sides, reverberating through the whole of the valley below. A fresh cloudburst followed. Quite suddenly it ended.

Now, as they bumped slowly across the drawbridge, Carcassonne became visible again, the Porte Narbonnaise, a giant's gate flanked with thick, high towers open before them. The police car ahead of them made its way up the steep, narrow, cobbled street lined with little souvenir shops and cafés, turret lights flashing.

They were expected. As they slowly followed the police car escorting them, they could see people on both sides of the tiny, medieval street crowded in doorways, drawing back so as not to be brushed by the bus, all of them staring up at the faces of the Americans, the expressions of the bystanders fixed, almost menacing, as if well aware that these crimes they had all read about, crimes committed by a stranger, a foreigner, threatened them, endangered the peace and commerce of their lives.

At the top of the road the squad car led them around a little square, then turned into an even narrower road, hardly more than an alley, and climbed up it into the square at the summit, before them, the Basilica of St.-Nazaire, and, to their right, built into the walls, the ancient Hôtel de la Cité, where they were to stay while being questioned by Monsieur Sartie. The bus stopped there.

They heard Marbeau give orders to Ned and Mike to remain there with the bus until Monsieur Sartie arrived and decided whether they were free to go. Four constables got out of the two police cars that had escorted them and stood waiting as the group got off the bus. Everywhere there were people in doorways, faces at windows, eyes fixed on the emerging passengers.

Ellen collected her knitting and her guidebook and put them in her string bag, hooking it over her left arm along with her purse, and got off after the others, catching her heel on the last step and losing her balance, Mike grabbing her by the arm before she could fall. She dropped her purse, which opened as it hit the cobblestones, scattering her belongings all over the street. Mike and the constables scrambled to gather her things as Dade bounded down the steps to come to her aid, Marbeau, Joliet and Lebrun following him.

Dade took Ellen's arm. "Are you all right?"

"I'm just fine." Mike collected her belongings from the others and brought them to her in his cupped hands, like an offering, welcoming her to the city. She held her purse open and he emptied his hands into it. "Thank you," she said to him.

Dade said to her, "You're not just fine."

"I am."

"Then why are you standing on one leg like a crane?"

"I twisted my ankle a bit. It's nothing, really." She leaned on Dade's arm, resting for a moment. To get everyone away from the stares of the curious and from the reporters with cameras and notepads held back by the town's police behind barricades, Marbeau made a sign to the constables, and the others were all shepherded hastily through the heavy door of the hotel and out of sight. Ellen was rummaging through her purse. She looked up at Dade and said, "My Florentine pillbox. The one Susannah gave me." She cast her eyes on the cobblestones, searching the street. "It's round. It must have rolled away."

Dade looked around. Not finding it, he hunkered down and peered under the bus. "I see it," he said. He edged toward it.

"Dade, don't. You'll get all dirty."

He stretched an arm under the bus. "I think I can just—no, I can't." He lay down flat on the wet cobblestones and eased himself a few inches under the bus, arm outstretched.

"Dade, let someone else!"

Mike started to run toward him. Dade waved him away. "Got it." Then he lay still.

"Dade? What is it?" He lay where he was, motionless, for a few seconds, and then crawled back out from under the bus and got to his feet, brushed himself off and handed her the chased gold pillbox. "Thank you." She opened it, glanced inside, closed it again and put it back in her purse. "Thank goodness it didn't open."

"Look." He held out his other hand. In it was something that looked like crumpled brown paper. "Found it stuffed up in the wheel well."

"What is it?"

He opened it, smoothing out the wrinkles in the paper and showing her the name of a restaurant printed on it: BRASSERIE LANGUEDOC. "A doggie bag. Kate's, that's my guess." He stared at her, his big eyes full of light.

"But what on earth was it doing under the bus?"

"Having finished off Kate, person finished off her supper." Ellen shuddered. "That's why Mike never saw the murderer get back on board. The murderer never did. Spent the night on the towpath, under the bus. Come on." He took her arm, steering her toward the hotel.

43

Joliet was waiting for them. He conducted them down a wide corridor carpeted with Oriental rugs and faced with diamond-paned windows looking out on the square, and then left into the main sitting room, with windows overlooking a wide terrace built into the outer fortress walls. To the right, where two constables stood guard, green glass doors led into a banquet room with tapestried chairs and a fireplace with a pink marble chimney piece.

Marbeau came toward them, his flipperlike arms slapping his sides. "Monsieur Sartie has not yet arrived. It is most disconcerting."

"When is he expected?" asked Dade.

"I have sent word inquiring." He gestured at the others gathered in the room. "I could send them to their rooms to wait, of course, but I would have to keep all of them under surveillance."

"While you wait to hear from Monsieur Sartie, may I have a few moments with them?"

Relief showed in Marbeau's face. "Please do."

Dade hesitated for a moment, glancing around at the expressionless faces of the five others huddled together in a semicircle in a mullioned bay. As Dade's eyes rested on them, their expressions hardened. He put his large hands on the small of his back and took a few steps toward them. He cleared his throat.

"The Public Prosecutor, that's Monsieur Sartie, he's due to meet us here soon." He glanced around at them, gesturing at the chairs and sofas. "Why don't you people make yourselves comfortable while I put on a little dog-and-pony show. I'm going to tell you what I'm going to be telling him."

At first they only continued to stare at him as before. Then the five of them seated themselves on the down-filled tapestried cushions of the sofas and armchairs in the bay. Ellen sat down on a little velvet sofa facing them, Marbeau beside her.

Then, while all of them looked at him, curious, Dade pursed his lips, turned away and paced up and down in front of them all, collecting his thoughts, the thick eyebrows alternately arching and frowning, as if in response to some inner dialogue he now held with himself. They all sat attentive and motionless, like a small audience at the run-through of a new play.

Now, apparently satisfied with his private calculations, Dade stopped his pacing, took up a stance in front of the group and said, "In order to understand the motive for these murders, it's necessary to know something about a firm called Manitoba. It was a scam invented by Billy to rip off Kate." He repeated to them what Motke had told him. They looked at him, dumbfounded.

"Now, here's what set everything in motion. When Kate saw that gusher, she did something nobody could have predicted. She said, 'I don't want to invest any more money in Manitoba. I'll buy the lease. How much?' Words to that effect. Billy, caught off-guard, says, 'Manitoba wants five million,' and Kate, she says, 'Sold.' She writes Manitoba a check for that amount. And now Billy, he has himself a big problem: he has five million—for the time being—Kate has nothing but great expectations, and when she finds out that she's been ripped off, if she can ever tie Billy to Manitoba, it means prison.

"Time to cut and run. But money like that you can't just move around. Money leaves tracks. Money like that, as we all know, has to be laundered. What happened next? Well, one week Manitoba had five million dollars in the kitty. The next week, Manitoba was bust. And little Cissy had five million dollars' worth of uncut precious gems. Emeralds."

A shocked murmur ran through the group. Dan said suddenly, "I don't want my sister talked about that way, do you understand? She's not here to defend herself and you haven't given us any proof at all of her involvement!"

"Bear with me. Please," Dade said. "All right." Dade nodded again, lips pursed, the big eyes slitted. "Why precious gems? Well, if you try to leave the country—and Billy and Cissy were damn well going to have to leave the country after pulling a stunt like this—if you try to leave the country with more than five thousand dollars, the government, they want to know all about it. Precious stones are another matter, my friends. You can take out a bushel basket of them and, so long as they're not set, no questions asked.

"But Cissy didn't try to take them out of the country. Instead, these uncut emeralds I'm talking about ended up in escrow in the United States, to be traded for something Cissy was to pick up over here. And whoever ended up with the emeralds could move them around the way you can never move money—take them right out of the country—for example, leaving no trace behind.

"Nice and neat, isn't it? No way of proving the precious gems ever represented Manitoba's assets. Oh, we can guess. We can guess all we like. But, in law, we don't *know*. All we know for certain is that Cissy, as the *sole and legal owner* of those gems, put them in escrow. All clear so far?"

He paused, still looking at them, meanwhile walking over to the table, poured a glass of water and drank it off, still watching their faces over the rim of the glass. They looked back at him, amazed. Dade put down the glass and crossed back toward them. He took a deep breath, then went on.

"Beginning of the week, you all flew to Paris together to begin this trip. Kate went down to Montalban with Billy and, at that point, demanded that he hand over the escrow papers, which shows that she knew what was going on. She needed to know where delivery was to be made and when, because she wanted the contents of that escrow. And Billy damn well had to give her what she wanted if he and Cissy hoped to stay out of prison."

Dade plunged his hands into his trouser pockets and looked up at the coffered gilt ceiling, meanwhile putting his lower teeth against his upper lip and sucking air audibly. "And now, here you all were on the barge." Dade walked up and down again for several moments in silence, as if listening to another inner dialogue, alternately nodding his head and shaking it. Then he turned back to the group and said, "That's the background for the night Kate was murdered, the night eight of you left a restaurant in Narouze to walk back to the barge." He broke off, hearing something.

From the town came the far-off sound of a klaxon. They all heard it, and as it came nearer, all of them turned slightly in the direction of the sound and sat motionless, intent. The sound grew rapidly louder. Then, when it seemed almost as if whatever it was had breached the bastionlike walls of the hotel and some engine of destruction now hurtled toward them like a juggernaut, the sound broke off.

Now they could hear the tramp of boots on the cobblestones of the square, raised voices, someone calling out orders, heavy doors opening and slamming and, moments later, muffled footsteps coming down the corridor.

Joliet crossed swiftly to the doors and opened them. A police lieutenant, helmeted and booted, a package under his arm, strode into the room, glanced quickly around, caught sight of Marbeau and saluted him with a rigid, white-gloved hand. Marbeau returned his salute. The lieutenant then turned and snapped out an order. Four constables, all wearing side arms, marched into the room and stood at ease just inside the doors, which Joliet now closed.

The lieutenant said formally to Marbeau, "Sir, I have here a package brought from escrow at the Crédit Lyonnais at Aigues-Mortes"—reaching a hand into his tunic, he pulled out a stiff, folded parchment document, which he opened, revealing a red wax seal at the bottom—"which, by order of the People, I am instructed to deliver here to you."

"To whom is it consigned?" Marbeau asked.

"At the close of escrow, at five tomorrow, it is to be delivered to a woman named Cicely Schuyler."

"Deceased," Marbeau replied. "Since it's evidence in a capital case, we have been authorized to open it." He took the package from the lieutenant. Turning to Dade, he said, "And since Cicely Schuyler was an American, will you act as her agent?" He handed Dade the package.

"With your kind permission." He put the package on the heavy, carved table, took out his gold penknife and rapidly cut the string and the gummed paper sealing the box, yanked open the flaps, emptied out handfuls of styrofoam pellets protecting the contents, then lifted out a small box, not more than eight inches long. He cut the box open carefully, took out some cotton wadding and, with everyone's attention riveted on what he was doing, lifted out first a little box containing a jeweler's loupe; then, from beneath more cotton wadding, he carefully lifted out a cross some five inches high.

It was made of ivory, crazed and yellowed with age. The slender cross had been delicately carved with an early Gothic restraint that was almost severe. At the center of the cross was a ruby. It was a huge stone shaped like a cushion, a blood-red rectangle with rounded corners, asymmetrically faceted so that one could view the glowing interior of the stone. Carefully Dade unfastened the crude gold finding in which the ruby was set and hinged it back, exposing the deep pavilion of the jewel. Now, with the blood-red ruby swung out from the cross, a little square of beaten gold set into the ivory was exposed. It had a groove in its center. And, in the groove was the relic, the Thorn.

Dade held it high up for them all to see. "The Remords reliquary," he said. They all began talking at once.

"Christ," George said. "Oh, Christ."

Dan said, incredulous, "That belongs to my *sister?*"

Olivia, enthralled, let out a little moan and said, "Oh, my *God!*"

Leo took out his wallet and said, "We'll take it."

Maggie got to her feet suddenly, looking around at the others. "Wait a minute," she said. "From what Dade said, it didn't belong to Cissy, it belonged to *Kate*. And if it's hers, it's *ours!* I mean, we're just as much his descendants as she was!" She turned to Leo. "And when I think of those awful things I said about the poor bishop—!"

"Sit down, Maggie," Leo said.

"Didn't you hear me?" she asked him.

"Just sit down." Leo took a quick breath. Maggie slowly sank back into her seat.

Dade looked toward Ellen. She sat very still, hands clasped, her eyes fixed on the reliquary. She caught her breath. Then, as if feeling the weight of his glance, turned toward him, met his eyes and shook her head in wonder.

He handed the reliquary to Marbeau. Holding it in both hands, Marbeau stared down at the Thorn in amazement, then crossed himself.

Dade said, "Now, let's find out if what we've got here is the real thing." Marbeau handed it back to him.

Holding the cross up to the lamplight so that it shone through the gem, Dade screwed the loupe into one eye and studied the ruby. One glance was enough. He took the loupe from his eye and gave it to Marbeau, then handing him the cross. As Marbeau put the loupe to his good eye, inspecting the jewel, Dade said, "See that bit of cross-hatching? That's what gemologists call 'a patch of silk.' That's the clincher."

Dade took out his notebook and read the lines he had copied out from the book Ellen had shown him. "'When such a stone grows in the earth, it will enclose octahedral-shaped crystals and what they call silk, an inclusion of rectile needles . . .' See them there? See how they intersect and form little nests? Well, no spinel looks like that and no artificially grown ruby can ever exhibit such a formation." Dade asked Joliet to turn out the lights in the room. Then, after the long velvet drapes were drawn and the room was dark, Dade took a pencil flashlight from his pocket, held it up behind the huge gem, and switched on the light.

The stone vanished. In its place, in the darkness, they saw only a pulsing red glow. It twinkled and trembled, giving the illusion of growing larger, flashing as it sent out spars of light the color of pigeon's blood, the glowing jewel ineluctable, ever-changing, at one moment solid, the next melting, seeming somehow to burn in the air before them like a magic fire, a captive star. There was a collective sigh, as when the Host is elevated.

At a word from Dade, Joliet switched the lights back on. Again Dade held up the reliquary cross, showing them the gem. Dade said, "It's cut in a way no ruby would ever be cut today. See, they didn't know much about cutting precious stones back in the thirteenth century. They didn't know how to unlock the beauty of a jewel by making it brilliant and giving it scintillation. All they did was polish away the rough spots and the pits and cavities."

He looked around at the ring of faces, eyes fastened on the fiery ruby in his hand, and said, "That's a ruby, all right. That's a pigeon's blood ruby, with just a hint of purple, like an aftertaste. Largest ruby I've ever seen in my life and my guess is, it's the largest in the world.

"I'm sure you're all curious about its value. Well, the going rate for a flawless ruby today is very likely in excess of a hundred thousand dollars a carat. Multiply that by thirty-five—which this is reputed to be—and you get three and a half million dollars, which is all it would be worth if it were cut up. But when there's only one this big in the world, its value is priceless. At the time it was stolen in Aigues-Mortes back in 1970, it was thought to be worth ten million dollars. Rich private collectors who buy stolen goods of this sort generally pay half their value—that's the going rate—which is what Billy and Cissy were going to pay in uncut emeralds. Worth every cent of it and far more, especially when it's a French national treasure."

Dade turned to the lieutenant who had delivered the escrow package and said, "The escrow instructions indicate that the package was to be delivered to a Miss Cicely Schuyler. As we have told you, Miss Schuyler is deceased. Do the instructions name a beneficiary?"

The lieutenant opened the folder he still carried under his arm, scanned the first page and then answered, "In that event, the escrow instructions specify that it is to be delivered to a Mr. Billy Penrose, who is her named beneficiary—"

"Also deceased," Marbeau said shortly.

The lieutenant nodded, expressionless, and went on, "—together with his co-beneficiary . . ."

When the lieutenant hesitated over the pronunciation, Marbeau said sharply, "Whose name is—?"

"Mr. George Mulvaney."

45

George got suddenly to his feet, his ordinarily ruddy complexion now changed to a leaden pallor. He took a step or two backward, almost stumbling over his own feet, at the same time looking toward Dade and saying in an unsteady voice, "I don't know what this is all about."

"Don't you?" Dade asked.

"No," said George. He looked around at all of them, his pallor now replaced by an angry flush. "There's nothing to connect me with Manitoba!"

"Doesn't have to be. Case against you runs like this, George: Three people are about to get their hands on a priceless reliquary. Stolen property. A woman they bilked says, Give it to me or I'll have you all sent to prison. Then she's murdered and, after that, so are two of them. The third man stands in line to get it. That's you, George. You, who would have had this reliquary in your sole and secret possession as of tomorrow if we hadn't found out about the escrow. I call that motive, George. It's enough to hang you."

Dade broke off, staring down at the cross he still held in his hands. Then he looked up, meeting Marbeau's eyes, and stepping toward him, offered it to him. Marbeau took the cross from him, thanking him.

Holding the reliquary cupped in both hands, Marbeau said formally, "I hereby seize the Remords reliquary in the name of the People of France, as a national treasure." He turned to the lieutenant. "Call the Crédit Lyonnais and let them know." The lieutenant saluted smartly and left the room. Marbeau began reciting a set speech in rapid French to George, meanwhile nodding at Joliet, who quickly stepped forward with another constable, seizing George's arms.

Dade said to George, "He's arresting you for the murder of your wife, of Billy Penrose, and of Cicely Schuyler."

"You *bastard!*" yelled Dan suddenly. "You dirty bastard!" He lunged at George, shoving at him with all his strength and knocking George and the two constables off balance. Joliet released George and grabbed Dan's arms, restraining him. Dan backed away, trembling. Maggie seized his arm.

George, slowly struggling in the grasp of the constables, like someone writhing in the grip of a nightmare, said hoarsely to Dade, "I didn't kill any of them! Tell them I deny it!" George's knees buckled. At a sign from Marbeau, the constables let him sit down. He sank back in a chair. Then, gripping the armrests, he stared up at Dade, his mouth open, his eyes wide and staring.

Dade went on, speaking slowly, hammering home each point. "We found out that Billy wasn't Cissy's lover. *But he pretended to be.* Why? To justify her continued presence in your circle while the two of them were busy skinning Kate? That wasn't necessary. Cissy worked for Billy, that was justification enough. Only reason he could possibly have for pretending to everybody that he and Cissy were engaged and about to be married was to cover up. See, Billy, he wasn't the lover. He was the beard." He broke off, looking around at all of them. They stared back up at him, open-mouthed. "Now that I've told you, you all see it, don't you?" He nodded to himself. "You see it, all right. Well, now, let's just ask ourselves: why in the dickens would two people like Billy and Cissy—both of them risking their necks and a long prison sentence—ever take time out to play a game like that unless the man they were covering for *was in it with them?* That man *is you*, George, that man is *you.*"

"It isn't true," George said. "None of it is true."

Dade said, "I'm going to make another guess, George. Kate, she found out you were carrying on with someone—again. She suspected Olivia. That's why she withdrew her backing from Leo's play." He looked directly at Olivia. She looked away. Leo watched her, motionless as a lizard. Dade went on: "See, when Kate told Billy she'd found out and demanded those escrow documents to protect herself, all she seemed to know about was Billy and Cissy. She never mentioned *you.* But somehow, by the time she had boarded the barge, she knew you were in it with them—that the other woman in your life wasn't Olivia at all—that it was Cissy." Dade's gaze rested on the shaken George, who looked back at Dade, the whites of his eyes showing in fear.

Dade said softly, "But how did she find out? That's the question." Suddenly, Dade wheeled on Olivia and said, "Maybe *you* knew." She looked around, as if for a means of escape. He pressed her. "You, Livvy, the one who collects secrets. Everybody's. Maybe you had found out about George and Cissy—you wouldn't have had to know anything else. All you needed was to see them together once where they shouldn't have been—and maybe *that's* what you went down to Sarlat to tell her in revenge." Olivia looked at George, twisting her hands. Dade said quietly, "And *that's* what I heard in her voice when she telephoned me. That's what devastated her."

Turning back to George, Dade said, "When you got to the barge, Billy and Cissy must have told you Kate had found out about the reliquary. From what they said, it was clear that she knew about Billy and Cissy. What you didn't know was whether she knew about you. Kate, she kept you beside her until late that first night and then all the next day, playing acey-deucy. She wasn't playing acey-deucy, George, she was playing *you*. She was keeping you from going near the others. Obviously you had to make plans. You were in trouble.

"The first chance you had to meet with Cissy was that night in Narouze after dinner. That's why you sneaked out the back door— to go looking for her. But Kate, she was waiting for that, waiting to catch the two of you red-handed, wasn't she? And did she catch you? My guess is that she did. Cissy would have run off. There you were in the dark with Kate. She held all the cards. She was the one who stood between you and everything you wanted. You killed her then."

"No," said George hoarsely.

Dade nodded to himself. "You killed her but you kept your head. You knew that since you were her sole heir, this had to look like an accident or else suspicion would certainly fall on you. You tried to make it look that way. And you would have succeeded except that Billy came by. You had to hide, and that delayed you long enough so that a coroner's report would show that she was dead before her body was put in the water."

George's eyes darted around the room. "I didn't kill her," he said, moistening his lips. He began breathing heavily.

"The next morning," Dade said to him, "when her body was

found, the three of you were suddenly off the hook. But who killed her? Cissy and Billy at first suspected each other—then *you*."

"But . . . but why would I kill *them*?" There was an edge of hysteria in George's voice now. His eyes moved restlessly around the ring of faces watching him. "Why?"

"Because they didn't bargain for murder," Dade said quietly. "Billy knew he was innocent, so that meant, in his mind, it was you or Cissy or both of you. Billy had lied. Billy had no alibi. Billy was right there at the scene of the murder with a witness to prove it. Billy had motive and opportunity and knew he was about to be arrested for murdering Kate. What did he do, George, threaten to tell the truth about Manitoba to the police to save himself?"

"No!"

"You had to kill him, George, didn't you? And, as soon as you had, Cissy knew that the murderer wasn't Billy but you, and she was afraid. You thought she'd understand that you'd done it so you both could be together, but she didn't understand, her reaction was just like Billy's. She wanted to save herself. She ran away, trying to find you in the fog to tell you they were about to arrest *her*. She must have been terrified. You had no choice. You had to kill her, too."

"I didn't do it." The big Irish face sagged. The eyes were the eyes of a drowned man.

"Didn't you? The clinching proof is, you keep lying about everything. If you were innocent, you'd be desperate to lay out the truth, tell us what your own role was, tell us about Manitoba, tell us what we're going to find out anyway. The guilty lie." Dade's eyes bored into him.

George said finally, his voice low and strained, "Kate wanted that reliquary. Spent a couple of years searching for it, putting out word that she'd buy it secretly, knowing it was stolen, so she could donate it to the cathedral at Sarlat in exchange for having herself buried there, right next to Remords. It was an obsession. Then somebody tried to get in touch with her, somebody who said he knew where she could get hold of it, and succeeded in getting hold of *me*. That was just after she bought the oil lease from Manitoba and we had to get all that money out of the country. It was a natural, it was a godsend. The seller wanted to be paid in uncut gems and in the States. I pretended to be acting for Kate and said she'd buy it. Billy set up the escrow in Cissy's name. Christ only knows how Kate found out."

A constable appeared in the doorway at that moment, eyes searching the room. Seeing him, Joliet jumped up and hurried over to him. Dade turned, watching him. Joliet crossed quickly back to Marbeau and said, "Monsieur Sartie sends his apologies. A pressing matter delayed him in Toulouse. We are assured he will be here within the hour."

Marbeau said to Dade, "Please continue."

Dade said to George, "Go on."

George said, "It wasn't planned. Not at first. We fell in love. Billy saw it. He offered to cover for us. He said he had a plan—a way we could all get away from Kate and Cissy and I could be together and none of us would ever have to worry about money again! I swear that's the truth! It was all his idea! But I didn't kill her! You've got to believe me!"

"Do I?" Dade said. "Do I, George?" There was a silence.

Marbeau said to Dade, "Tell the others they will be escorted to their rooms to wait for Monsieur Sartie. It is just a formality. As soon as he comes I am quite sure all of them will be free to leave." Dade translated Marbeau's instructions.

"Wait a minute—!" George yelled.

Olivia said, her voice rising with almost a note of panic in it, "I have to have some air! I can't bear being cooped up any longer!"

Dade had a brief exchange with Marbeau and then said to them, "You will now be escorted to your rooms. However, under French law, you may not be deprived of the consolation of your religion, so those of you in need of solace will be allowed to visit the cathedral next door."

The others continued to stare at George, eyes wide, fixed, unable to speak. Gripping the arms of his chair, George looked from one to the other of their faces, incredulous, then, his own Irish face darkening with rage, he lunged out of his chair, rushing at them, bellowing like a bull, yelling out as once before, "One of you, one of you! Oh, Christ, God, one of *you!*" They drew back from him, afraid. Joliet seized him.

Marbeau spoke in an undertone to the lieutenant, who gave orders to the four constables who had accompanied him there, and together they escorted Maggie, Dan, Olivia and Leo from the room.

At the door Leo halted in his tracks and, turning around, opened his mouth to say something, then abruptly turned away and left the room. The door closed.

George said to Dade with a pleading look, "You don't understand! I didn't kill her! I didn't kill anybody!"

"I know that, George," Dade said.

"You what?" George looked at him, at first not understanding. Then he said, "Wait a minute! You knew? And you put me through all this? Why?"

"You're the Judas goat." Dade looked up. Marbeau had stepped away from them and was conferring with Joliet. Starting toward the door, Dade said to Ellen, "Get Marbeau to our room without anyone seeing you. I'll meet you there in two minutes."

46

In the main corridor Dade stopped at the desk of the concierge and consulted the guest register briefly. Then, going out the front door of the hotel, Dade looked around and saw the same crowds still penned behind the barricades. Catching sight of Mike lounging by the bus, Dade beckoned to him. Mike came toward him. Dade took his arm and hurried him through the door of the hotel, down a side corridor and then up a back stairway to the third floor. As Dade, still gripping Mike by the arm, strode quickly down the broad hallway, Mike tried to pull free, saying, "Here, what's this all about?"

"You'll find out soon enough." Dade stopped in front of the door of the suite assigned to him and Ellen, opened it and half pushed Mike into the room, quickly closing the door behind them. Mike looked up and saw Ellen standing there, Marbeau beside her. Mike looked at Dade, alarmed. Dade said, "Inspector Marbeau, you remember Mike Crane, our deckhand. Mike is also a very fine actor."

"You got no right—!" Mike, with his powerful strength, wrenched his arm free and the girlish face looked up at Dade's, fear in the eyes. "I told you what I know! What more do you want?"

Dade said, "Mike, we're going to give you an audition. Now, come over here and sit down for a minute." He pointed at a chair. Mike went slowly over and sat down in it. He was trembling. Dade went to the chair opposite and sat down there. A table separated them. Dade pulled a sheet of hotel stationery from the desk folder, picked up a pen and carefully printed a few sentences on it in block letters. Then, throwing down the pen, he shoved the paper over toward Mike, saying, "Myself, I think you have quite a career ahead of you and I'm going to help you."

Not looking at the paper, Mike began, "I mean it when I say I told you everything—"

"No matter what roles you play in your life," Dade went on, "you're never going to read lines more important than these. You're only going to get to read them once. We have to believe them. You understand me, Mike?"

Their eyes met. Mike picked up the sheet of stationery and read through the words silently. A subtle change came over his face. The muscles under the skin tightened. When he looked up, the expression on the girlish face had hardened.

Dade picked up the phone and said to the hotel operator, "Room two-four-seven, please." When the phone was answered, he handed the receiver to Mike.

Mike said into the phone, "This is Mike. I'm the guy who sleeps on deck, remember? You got what you wanted. Now, let's talk about what I want. I'll wait for you in that church next door. In the confessional. Ten minutes." Dade took the phone from Mike and banged down the receiver. Mike looked at Dade steadily. "Okay?" he asked.

Dade gripped his shoulder and grinned at him. "You're going to go a long way, sonny. Go downstairs and then walk across the square and over to the cathedral. Walk to the far end of it and then enter by the front door. I want you to take your time. Once you're inside, come to the back and wait in the sacristy." Mike left the room. At Dade's request Marbeau made a quick telephone call.

Ellen said, "What can I do to help?"

"Be with me." Marbeau looked bewildered. Dade said to him, "I'll tell you about it on the way. What we're going to need is to talk to the operator in Toulouse who sent that cable to the escrow company in Beverly Hills." He hurried both of them out of the room.

Minutes later Dade, Ellen and Marbeau were let through the back door of the cathedral into the sacristy. The door into the cathedral was open a crack. While they waited, Marbeau picked up the phone in the sacristy and called Toulouse. A short time later they saw one of the big padded doors leading from the vestibule into the cathedral swing slowly open. Mike appeared. He walked quickly across the rear of the cathedral, then up a side aisle, past the carved confessional and into the sacristy. Dade opened the door for him, slipping out just after he entered and hurrying along the wall toward the confessional.

Entering the priest's box, Dade closed the door and sat on the narrow bench, pulling the purple velvet curtain across the grille connecting his booth with the penitent's box. He could see nothing. After his eyes became accustomed to the darkness, he became aware of faint light coming through a crack between the edge of the door and the jamb of his box. He put his eye to it. All he could make out was a line of pews stretching away toward the outer side of the nave. He sat motionless, watching and waiting.

A thin, white-haired woman in the black alpaca smock of a shopkeeper crossed his field of vision, genuflected and made her way into the pew he could see. She knelt there, making a spire of her long, slender hands, head bent in medieval resignation. An aged man wearing a long, bulky overcoat, a gray scarf around his neck and a beret on his head, shuffled into view, genuflected, hanging onto the pews on either side of him for support, then took a place beside the old woman, fell to his knees, pulling off his beret and, still clutching it, buried his face in his hands. Another old woman, bent with the weight of years and walking slowly, leaning on a cane, made her way up the aisle past Dade's narrow field of vision toward the altar. The elderly always came, at the close of day, at the close of life, as if this vast hushed place, the only light the jeweled glow of robed figures in stained glass and the flickering of the distant votive candles, were the hallowed antechamber of the hereafter.

Dade waited, watched. The man in the bulky overcoat hoisted himself painfully to his feet and made his way out of the pew, the white-haired woman slowly following him. The cathedral was perfectly still. Dade imagined that he could hear the ticking of the hunting watch in his pocket, counting out the minutes. He wanted to move, to stretch. He had a cramp in his leg. He told himself that he must not move. He concentrated on the sound of ticking, pretending to himself that if he truly listened, he would indeed be able to hear the tick of his watch, deep in his vest pocket. Was there any sound so faint as a watch's ticking?

Then footsteps, light, quick, and suddenly someone he recognized crossed his field of vision: Olivia.

She stopped opposite the confessional and stood quite still, her eyes uplifted, as if tracing out the design of something high above them (the balustrade of the gallery? the stone arches rising to form the nave?), reminding him of how she had appeared when he had caught sight of her alone, weeping in the ruined cloister of St.-Papoul.

Then she shifted her gaze, and Dade found himself looking directly into her eyes, almost as if she had discovered him hiding there. The focus of her eyes shifted. Her glance swept over the confessional. No, of course, it was an illusion, she couldn't see him. Biting her lips, she took a step toward the confessional. At that moment, Dade caught sight of Leo as he came up to her. Seeing him, she started.

"What's the matter?" he said.

"You startled me."

"I've been looking for you."

"Have you?" asked Olivia.

"I think we should do something about getting George a lawyer."

"Can't Dade?"

"You mean, having gone to all this trouble to put him in jail, Dade is now going to make a similar effort to get him out?"

"Oh, *I* don't know!"

"What's the matter?"

"Nothing."

"Maggie's looking for you," he said.

"Me? Why?"

"To talk about this." He was trying to keep the impatience out of his voice and not succeeding.

"I'll talk to her later."

"Now. Don't you think you owe George that much? Considering all you two haven't been to one another?"

"Go to hell!"

"I already have. I was hoping you'd join me."

"Poor Leo! I am so sorry for you."

"That makes two of us."

"You can't help it, can you?"

"All right, I was mistaken." She eyed him. "About George," he added.

"I can't save us both." She strode away.

He stared after her, then followed her, half running, calling her name. Now, Dade could not see them any longer. He heard her say, "I'd like to be alone now, if you don't mind."

"Livvy—"

"Later," she said. The quality of her voice changed slightly, so that Dade had the odd impression that she was addressing not Leo but him, as she added, "We'll have to talk later." He heard her footsteps retreating, then Leo's.

The minutes ticked by in Dade's head. After a little while, on the other side of the cathedral, Dade recognized Dan's figure crossing his line of sight, hands behind his back, eyes on the high roof of the nave. In the dim recess of a shrine, Dan paused, looking up at the statue of a saint, then walked on, out of Dade's view.

Minutes later, walking soundlessly in crepe-soled flat shoes, Maggie suddenly appeared, making what seemed almost like an entrance onto the little stage of Dade's narrow view. She walked by him and out of sight. Silence. Neither Maggie nor Dan was visible now.

After a few moments Maggie crossed in front of him again, hesitating close to the confessional, looking around as if searching for someone. Her eyes looked in Dade's direction. She stood still, head on one side, as if listening for an answer to an unspoken question. Then, turning, she vanished from view.

For a long time no one else appeared. To Dade, sitting motionless, cramped, in the dark, scarcely daring to breathe, it seemed at that point too late. Too much time had gone by. Then the bells of the cathedral began to peal. He counted. It was three o'clock. The reverberations of the bells slowly died away. At the same time he became aware that someone had entered the confessional, now sat opposite him behind the velvet curtain. A long moment passed.

Then, a whispered voice asked, "All right, what do you want?" When there was no sound except Dade's soft breathing, which he now allowed to become audible, the whispered voice said again, "I said, what do you want?"

Dade pulled aside the curtain then and saw a familiar face: Dan's. Dade said, "To hear your confession."

47

Dan leaped to his feet, a look of utter astonishment on his face, and banged open the door, starting out of the confessional, then looking up to see Marbeau and Joliet waiting. Dan said, his eyes blazing, "What the Christ is going on now?" Joliet manacled him.

Marbeau met Dade's eyes. He smiled and nodded. Marbeau and Joliet led Dan through the sacristy toward the rear door, Dade and Ellen following. Mike was standing there, a scared look on his face, his mouth open. Dan caught sight of him and his face hardened. Joliet marched Dan out the back door and into the square.

The crowds still waited behind the barricades. At the sight of Dan being led manacled out of the cathedral by a constable, there was a roar of excitement. Above, windows were thrown open. Now they were watched by a huge audience. The mob pressed forward, making it seem to grow in size, as constables struggled to hold back the crowd. On all sides, cameras were trained on them. The crowd began to yell out insults at Dan. Someone threw a bottle. It smashed on the cobblestones. Suddenly the crowd grew ugly. Rocks and sticks were hurled in Dan's direction as Joliet hurried him away from the crowd toward the hotel's entrance. Marbeau strode after them, followed by Dade and Ellen.

They all went quickly into the lobby of the hotel. Marbeau went to the desk, picked up a telephone and asked to be connected to the préfecture. Maggie, Leo and Olivia were at the hotel desk. They looked around, dumbfounded at the sight of Dan in handcuffs. Maggie ran toward him with a scream, the others following her. Just then George came down the staircase, stopping in his tracks at the sight of Dan in Joliet's custody. Seeing George, Leo wheeled around and said to Dade, "What is all this? You told us George—"

"We played us a little game. Dan here lost."

"Are you telling us . . . ?" Leo began.

"Dan's your boy," Dade said. "Three times over." Behind him, Dade could hear Marbeau on the phone sending for a police van.

Maggie said in a frightened voice, an unreal smile on her lips, "Dan? Dan?"

"He's crazy," Dan said, the lines of strain white in the deeply tanned face. "What the hell motive would *I* have?"

"You're Cissy's heir," Dade said. George, hearing that, strode up to them, standing in front of Dan, eyes fixed on him, his face pale with anger.

Maggie said, "Cissy's *heir?* But Cissy never had any money at all!" There was a note of desperation in her voice, as if she felt that Dan's innocence hung from the single thread of her faith in him.

"Cissy left five million in emeralds," Dade said evenly. "Dan knew that. He knew everything, including the fact that he couldn't just kill Cissy because then everything she had would have gone to Billy and George. No, this was a far more complex plan than that— and its very complexity afforded protection, by concealing his motive. Worthy of one of his own thrillers, wouldn't you say? Well, Billy Blue Hill! Why shouldn't it be? He wrote the whole scenario himself, now, didn't you, Dan?"

Dan, struggling in Joliet's grasp, yelled out to Dade, "By God, you'd better hope he hangs onto me because if I get loose—"

"You want to fight?" Dade said to him, suddenly angry, "you want to fight? For Kate's sake, I'll fight. I'll fight with you till hell freezes over and then skate with you on the ice afterward!" Then, controlling himself, he said, "*You* told Kate about Manitoba to set your whole plan in motion. Then you had to kill her. When I showed up, that knocked you catty-wampus. You weren't sure how much she'd told me on the phone. And you had to know. So you played it rough and crude. That was your cover, wasn't it? Because certain questions can be asked in the heat of anger which, if asked in a reasonable way, might arouse suspicion. Once you felt safe, you went ahead and killed Billy and then your own sister and framed George."

"You!" George said to Dan suddenly, clenching his big fists. "You!"

"Don't listen to him," Dan said to George. His eyes were unnaturally bright.

"You found out, didn't you?" George shouted. Dan looked at him, expressionless. Turning to Dade, George said, sucking air, his breathing uneven, "That company we both invested in didn't go under! Billy set that whole thing up to get Dan's money! Sure, it was bought out for ten cents on the dollar but what he didn't know is, it was bought out by *Manitoba!* That's where Billy got the seed money for the whole operation! It was all Billy." He turned back to Dan, realization flooding through his florid face. "You son of a bitch, you found out! And that's when you started spying on us! You found out, all right! You found out everything! And that's how Kate found out!"

"'I told you so,'" Dade said softly. He shot a glance at Ellen.

"It isn't true, is it Dan?" Maggie asked.

"No, of course it isn't," Dan said. "Otherwise, he'd have proof." His eyes were open a fraction too wide. His lips twitched.

"I have," Dade said. Facing Dan, he went on: "Cissy didn't send that cable to the escrow company. You did. Nobody else had any conceivable motive for wanting that escrow to fail. And Cissy herself couldn't have sent that cable. She used to work for a title company, remember? She would never have made the mistake of thinking you could change escrow instructions simply by cable, without a live signature. That's their whole stock in trade. When I heard Ellen here say the magic word 'title,' the whole explanation flashed through my mind and I knew what was going on. That cable was sent so that the escrow company would cable back—which they were bound in law to do—asking for a live signature and alerting us to the fact that there *was* such an escrow. With Cissy dead, we had to look into it. You counted on that, Dan. You knew that when we found out George was the beneficiary, that would nail him, that the French would then seize the reliquary, escrow would fail and you, as Cissy's only living relative, stood to inherit five million dollars' worth of emeralds. Would have, that is, if you'd succeeded in framing George. Now your whole scheme is worth about as much as a four-card flush."

Maggie let out a little cry of fear. Dan said to her, "He has no proof."

She shrank away from him. "What do you mean, he has no proof? It isn't true, is it?"

"Of course it isn't true." He looked at Dade stonily. "That's why he has no proof."

With a glance at Marbeau, Dade said, "There is a witness. The cable signed with Cissy's name was sent from Toulouse. And the woman in the post office there has just told the inspector that she's prepared to identify you."

Maggie gasped. Her hands flew to her face. Straining in Joliet's grasp, Dan's eyes sought hers. She turned away from him. Olivia came forward, embracing her. Dan looked around at all of them. They avoided his eyes. All except Leo, who took a step toward him and said, "I don't want you to give up, Dan. You'll beat this thing. And when you get out, we'll all be waiting for you. I just want you to know that."

Dan flushed an unhealthy red. Then they heard the sound of an approaching klaxon and, through the lobby windows, saw a black police van coming up the steep street toward the hotel. Marbeau nodded at Joliet, who led Dan out the door.

The others had left. As Dade and Ellen had their suitcase put in a cab, she slipped a gloved hand into his and said, "I almost forgot. There was a message for you."

"Oh?"

"From Charles the Second."

"What?"

"When Christopher Wren took him to see St. Paul's Cathedral, you know what he said about it?" She put her face up to his and whispered, "He said it was *awful!*"

Dade's face creased into a broad smile.

"I know you've got your ten, but I thought you'd like a bonus. He also said dreadful and terrible, as a matter of fact—"

"Awful's just fine. A bit on the slangy side but a damn fine addition." Pulling his notebook and gold pencil out of his pocket, he began scribbling.

Marbeau came out of the hotel, hurrying toward them. Seizing Dade's hand in both of his, he cried, "My dear friend, Dead Cooley, I am in your debt! I am forever in your debt!" Then, grasping Ellen's hand, he bent over it and kissed it. Moments later he had bounded into his waiting squad car and was driven away.

Dade and Ellen got into their cab and the driver set out, winding his way down the narrow alleys and streets of the ancient town toward the Porte Narbonnaise. The cobblestone street there was so narrow that two cars could not pass abreast, so a stop signal had been installed. Traffic alternated from one direction to the other. As their cab reached the light, it turned from green to red. The driver swore under his breath. They waited.

Dade said, "He's in for a promotion, Marbeau is."

Then a black limousine with a flashing turret light came up the street, swinging around them at the entrance to the square to get by. Dade turned, seeing the single passenger in the rear of the chauffeur-driven limousine, a black-suited man with a sunburned face and a self-important expression.

"Scratch that," he said.

Their cab drove on. Ellen said, "Dan must have told Kate about Manitoba when they were in Paris, isn't that so?"

"Only chance he had. Told her everything except George's involvement."

"One can see why. She might have fallen apart, as she did in Sarlat, canceled the trip, and Dan's whole plan would have blown up in his face."

"Score one for you."

"All right, Bright-eyes, what was she doing alone on the towpath at ten o'clock at night?"

"Dan called all the shots. He would have arranged it."

"You're evading my question."

"No, I'm not. I don't know, of course, but I can make a guess."

"Go ahead."

"In Dan's place, I would have shown her a copy of the cable sent to the escrow company in Cissy's name and told Kate they were double-crossing her, canceling escrow; that they were going to cut and run and a car was picking them up sometime after ten that night, after everybody was in bed asleep. That's how I would have done it."

"Oh."

"Near as I can figure, he almost got caught twice. Billy interrupted him, and by the time the coast was clear so's he could dump Kate's body in the lock, he was trapped by the bus returning, and of course, Mike sleeping on deck. That forced him to spend the night on the towpath, so in the morning, after Mike left to get the breakfast rolls, I figure Dan began jumping up and down making noise, doing his Air Force exercises, then climbed back on board."

"But he took a terrible risk. Suppose Maggie had gone looking for him for some reason?"

"Oh, she wouldn't have. Myself, I think he drugged her. At least, in his position that's what I'd have done." She looked at him quickly. "What's the matter?" he asked.

"Dade, you do love me, don't you?" He gave her a startled look. Grinning at him, she held up her right hand.

48

Dan's trial began in Paris in November. Dade was summoned as a witness. On the flight over, he was preoccupied. He could see the French courtroom in the Palais de Justice in his mind's eye, the curious spectators crowded behind a wooden balustrade at the rear of the courtroom, the mostly empty rows of benches before them reserved for witnesses; at the far end, on a dais, the three scarlet-robed justices, flanked by the ten members of the jury, could hear the angry voice of the Advocate General interrupting, the person who represented neither prosecution nor defense but the People of France, there to insure against legal error. He thought of Dan.

Dade and Ellen arrived at De Gaulle around four in the afternoon. It was a crisp autumn day, and after leaving their bags at the

Relais Poulenc, they went out for a walk up the Boulevard-St.-Germain as far as St.-Germain-des-Prés and then sat down at a sidewalk table at the Deux Magots. Dade was in the midst of ordering when Ellen grabbed his arm and said, "Look!"

He turned. Maggie was sitting a few tables away from them. She wore a full-length sable coat, her usual hat and scarf, as well as dark glasses, and as she spoke with animation to her escort, she sparkled and glittered, the emerald earrings she wore dangling from their pendants, the emeralds in the choker around her wimple-like scarf, the emeralds in the bracelet around her wrist and in the rings on her gloved hands flashing and winking at them in the late light.

Her escort slumped in his chair. He wore velvet trousers and a cashmere sweater, a large, soft cap pulled down over his eyes. She turned, catching sight of Dade and Ellen at that moment, let out a cry that caused everyone in the café to look at her, and stretched out both hands toward them. Dade and Ellen rose, going toward her.

She made a feint of embracing each of them, then put a hand on the thigh of her escort, who had gotten to his feet, saying, "You remember Mike?" Mike pulled off his cap, exposing his curly red hair. The gold earring had now been replaced by a tiny emerald. Maggie said to him, "Don't do that, dear. It makes me think of a monkey with an organ grinder. Just touch the brim, there's a darling."

Mike blushed beet-red, pulling his cap back on and seating them. Maggie leaned toward Ellen and whispered, "I've never seen anyone blush like that in my life! And it's not just his face!"

A waiter brought the Cinzano Dade had ordered. Dade said, "I hope all this isn't proving too much for you, Maggie."

She gave him a roguish smile, then touching his cheek with a gloved forefinger, at the same time emitting little poufs of expensive scent, and said to him, suddenly serious, slipping out of the sleeves of her sable coat and turning her pencil-thin body toward him, "It isn't easy but I do my best. Really, I should be in black but I feel I must do something to keep up Dan's spirits."

Ellen leaned forward and said, "I was just admiring your jewels."

Turning her wrist and touching the emerald bracelet, Maggie said, "I will say this much for Cissy: she had taste. They're Dan's by rights, or will be if he's found innocent. Meanwhile, the court appointed me receiver. Of course, if he's found guilty, I inherit, as his wife, since one can't profit from a crime, but we just mustn't let ourselves even *think* of such a thing!"

Ellen said, "I'd be afraid to wear them in the street."

"Oh, so would I!" Maggie said, the violet eyes wide. "These are just the babies. The big ones are all in the vault."

Ellen sipped her drink. Clearing his throat, Dade asked, "And how is Dan holding up?"

Maggie shrugged. "How does one answer that? He's got religion."

"Oh?" asked Ellen.

Maggie nodded emphatically, twinkling and flashing. "Saint-Cloud says it will help his defense but it has simply ruined his conversation." Flinging up her hands, she cried, "Dan says he's committed the unforgivable sin, whatever that is."

"It's a sin against the Holy Ghost," Dade answered.

"Which is what?" She looked at him.

"They don't make it clear, but if you die in the arms of the Church and wake up in Hell, it's what you've committed." Maggie pursed her rouged lips at him and rounded her eyes in mock surprise. Then she looked at her watch, exclaiming at the time. Stretching out a hand, she squeezed Ellen's wrist, saying, "I'm late for a fitting. Look, won't you come by for drinks at around seven?"

She took a card out of her purse and handed it to Ellen. "It's an old seventeenth-century ruin and you have to ride in a claustrophobic cage up two floors, but it has its good points." Rising, she held out her hand to Dade. Mike got to his feet. Taking his arm, she said to them, "He was simply wonderful in the picture. A small part—I insisted they write it in for him—but wait till you see him!" Maggie hurried away, taking tiny steps, clinging to Mike's brawny arm.

Ellen picked up her glass, tipped her head back and swallowed her drink at one gulp. Dade stared at her. "I've never seen you do that before," he said.

"Well, from now on, you're going to see a lot more!"

"What's that supposed to mean?"

"Never mind." Putting her elbow on the table, she leaned her chin on her fist and said, "Tell you what. Let's get tanked up, go over there and smash all the furniture."

"Ellen, what on earth's got into you?"

"That woman, Dade, is the limit. She is the limit!"

At seven o'clock they took a cab to the address Maggie had given them. It was on the oldest square in Paris, the Place des Vosges. Beneath an arcade, doors opened onto a cobblestone courtyard. To their right was a narrow stone doorway with a plaque on it identifying the building as a national monument. Getting into an elevator that was so small Dade had to hold himself in to make room for Ellen, he pressed the button and they rode slowly up the well of a circular stone stairway, coming to rest at the second floor.

Maggie let them in, thanking them for coming. She had put aside her emeralds and now wore only a mohair caftan that matched her eyes. She was alone. She showed them into a sitting room furnished with Louis Quinze furniture and led them to the windows, gesturing at the view. Lights were on in the surrounding houses, there were still people strolling behind the wrought-iron railings of the little park in the center of the square and the tables in the cafés below were crowded. "What will you drink?" she asked. "I'm having a kir."

"The same," said Ellen.

Maggie looked at Dade. "Fine," he said. Ellen and Dade seated themselves on down cushions. There was a moment of silence as Maggie fixed drinks at the bar. Then they heard the machinery of the elevator. It bumped to a stop just outside the door.

"Excuse me," Maggie said. She went to the door, opened it and exclaimed with pleasure as Mike pushed in Saint-Cloud's wheelchair. Dade and Ellen got to their feet. They shook hands, greeting each other. After a few moments, Saint-Cloud excused himself, nodding at Mike, who wheeled him out of the room, closing the door.

They sipped their drinks. Maggie said, "I saw George yesterday. He's here to testify, of course. They're still trying to indict him for bilking Kate. He said they lack something."

"Evidence," Dade said. "He admitted it in France but denied it in the United States. Said he hadn't been warned of his rights. Without his confession, the government is helpless."

Maggie smiled at him. "Isn't that a shame?" She smoothed her hair. "And, of course, my dear brother—well—you've heard about his new play?"

"We're dying to see it," said Ellen.

"When I'm next in New York," Maggie said, "he's promised me tickets. If he can get them." She made a face. "They say it's all Livvy. The way he hovers over her—the next thing you know, he'll be having her delivered to and from the theater in a Brink's truck."

In a few minutes Mike wheeled Saint-Cloud back into the room. He had changed into a velvet smoking jacket. Maggie mixed him a drink, handing it to him and giving him a peck on the cheek. He saluted them. Ellen asked after him. Maggie said, "He suffers so. Don't you, darling?"

"But I am prepared for it!" Saint-Cloud exclaimed. Looking at Ellen, he said, "Remember what I told you, my dear? I am always prepared!" A crippled hand smoothed back the strands of iron-gray hair. "When I am in pain," he said, "I remind myself that no matter how bad things get, there are always two wonderful moments of the day: lunch and dinner." He looked at Maggie. "Three," he said.

A maid in a starched uniform entered with a tray of hot hors d'oeuvres. Taking Dade's drink from his hand, Maggie said to the maid, "He doesn't want this. I've just remembered he drinks bourbon. I can't find any on the bar but there's some in the library."

"*Oui, madame la comtesse,*" said the maid.

"Not yet," Maggie said. Ellen choked on her drink. Dade patted her on the back. Maggie smiled around at all of them.

When they were once again in the street, striding toward the hotel, Ellen clinging to Dade's arm, she put her face up to his and said, "Say it to me."

"Say what?"

She punched him hard. "You know what I want to hear! Just once. Please."

He stared at her. "I don't have any idea what you want me to say."

"*Dade—!*"

"Really, *madame la comtesse . . .*"

She squealed with delight, pounding his arm with her fist. "I can't stand it!" she said. "I simply can't *stand* it!"

They had dinner by the fire, the chef roasting chickens on the

N28

hearth. Dade sipped a 1970 Château Margaux the sommelier had poured out for him and nodded. As the sommelier filled their glasses, Ellen said suddenly, "Will you do something for me?"

"Do what?"

"Defend him yourself."

"Me?"

"You can get him off. You know you can."

"Ellen!"

She put a hand on his arm, looking at him intently with her lidded, dark blue eyes. "And just think what that would mean to Maggie!"

He shook his head slowly and said wonderingly, "Ellen, I never knew you had it in you."

"Neither did I, until she brought it out!"

"I'd better get you out of this place."

She took a long swallow from her wineglass, then slapped the table with the flat of her hand and said, "All right, that's *it*!"

"What?"

"Let's go home and drive the Baja, what do you say?"

He grinned at her. They clinked glasses.

About the Author

GENE THOMPSON, a native of San Francisco, graduated from the University of California at Berkeley, after which he worked and studied in Europe for some years. He and his wife, also a writer, now live with their four children in a village in a national forest high in the San Jacinto mountains of California.